Posh Pup
and Other Puppy Stories

D0795313

Other Jenny Dale titles

The Snow Puppy and
Other Christmas Stories

Jenny Dale's Puppy Tales
Crumble and Custard and
Other Puppy Tales

Jenny Dale's Kitten Tales
Felix the Fluffy Kitten and
Other Kitten Stories

And coming soon
Charlie the Champion Pony and
Other Pony Tales

Posh Pup

and Other Puppy Stories

Jenny Dale

Illustrated by Mick Reid

A Working Partners Book

MACMILLAN CHILDREN'S BOOKS

Special thanks to Karen King,
Lorna Read and Narinder Dhami

'Teacher's Pet' and 'Tug of Love' first published 1997,
and 'Posh Pup' first published 1999, in three separate
volumes by Macmillan Children's Books

This bind-up edition published 2018 by Macmillan Children's Books
an imprint of Pan Macmillan
20 New Wharf Road, London N1 9RR
Associated companies throughout the world
www.panmacmillan.com

Created by Working Partners Limited
London WC2B 6XF

ISBN 978-1-5098-7128-5

1 3 5 7 9 8 6 4 2

A CIP catalogue record for this book is available from the British Library.

Typeset by Nigel Hazle
Printed and bound by CPI Group (UK) Ltd, Croydon CR0 4YY

Contents

1

The black and white Border collie stood very still, his ears pricked and his expression alert as he gazed down the track.

"What is it, Sam?" asked Neil Parker excitedly. He crouched down and put his head close to Sam's, straining into the sun to see exactly what it was that had caught his dog's attention. As far as he could make out, the wide track ahead was empty. It was a popular route for people walking their dogs at weekends, but today Neil had thought they had it to themselves.

"I can't see anything either," said his younger sister Emily, standing behind them both. She held a hand up to her face and squinted into the bright light. "Perhaps he's imagining things, or . . ."

"Wait! There. Look!" Neil pointed down the long track. A woman on a bicycle had just come into view, cycling towards them. Then, from far off, they heard the sound of a dog barking. A large and energetic Dalmatian suddenly appeared, obviously chasing the bicycle.

"Sam's brilliant, aren't you, Sam?" said Emily, ruffling the sleek coat behind his head. "I bet he could teach a few of the dogs in Dad's obedience classes a thing or two."

"Not half," agreed Neil, proudly. "And some of the ones we have boarding!"

Bob and Carole Parker, Neil and Emily's parents, ran King Street Kennels – a boarding kennels and rescue centre, in the grounds of their house a couple of miles outside the nearby town of Compton. Dogs had been part of their family life for as long as Neil could remember – and he was crazy about them. It was his dream to work full time with dogs himself when he was old enough.

The spotted Dalmatian was barking loudly as it bounded along the road towards them. The cyclist looked nervously over her shoulder, and her bicycle wobbled dangerously as the gap between her and the dog narrowed. Behind them, a man was running after them both, shouting desperately, "Dotty! Come here, girl!"

The Dalmatian completely ignored him. She caught up with the cyclist, leaping about alongside her, looking very pleased with herself.

Sam fidgeted with excitement and looked eager to join in the fun.

"No, Sam!" said Neil, firmly. "Stay!"

Sam immediately obeyed, sitting quietly close to Neil's left leg.

"Dotty! Stop! Will you come here!" the man shouted over and over again. But Dotty continued to gallop alongside the woman on the bicycle, barking excitedly and snapping at the wheels.

Neil could see that the woman was extremely nervous. He recognized her now as Mrs Smedley from the newsagent's in Compton.

"It's OK, Mrs Smedley!" he called to her. "Dalmatians are really friendly and playful! If you stop, she'll probably stop as well."

"I hope you're right," called Mrs Smedley. She came to a halt beside Neil, looking anxiously down at the dog. The Dalmatian stopped too, her big pink tongue hanging out, tail wagging and a look of anticipation on her face.

"Dotty! Come here!" The man had reached them at last. Looking quite red in the face, and panting, he grabbed the lead hanging from his dog's collar. The Dalmatian immediately jumped up at him, covering his jacket with dirty pawprints. Staggering, the man lost his balance and fell backwards into a muddy puddle, his legs spread-eagled in front of him.

"Oh, no!" they all cried. But dismay turned to smothered laughter as the daft Dalmatian began to lick the man's face enthusiastically. Even Mrs Smedley smiled as the man squirmed in the mud, trying to fend off the dog's sloppy kisses.

"No, Dotty! Dotty, down!" he spluttered. At last he managed to push the dog away and get to his feet. Dotty promptly shook herself, sending specks of mud flying all over her owner's face and clothes.

It was the last straw. Brushing himself down as best he could, the man glared furiously at Neil and Emily, who were still grinning. Then he finally managed to attach the lead to the dog's collar and pulled her sharply towards him.

"I'm sorry if she frightened you," he said to Mrs Smedley. "I'm afraid Dotty can be rather playful. But she really wouldn't hurt anyone."

"I can see that," Mrs Smedley smiled. "I hope you're all right, though."

"Yes, thank you," he replied stiffly. He turned to go and jerked at the lead again. "Come on, trouble!"

"What a fantastic dog!" Emily remarked as the man marched off with the Dalmatian.

"Yeah. Shame it's so out of hand, though," Neil replied. "Some people just have no idea how to train dogs."

Neil must have said it louder than he realized

because the man turned around and glared at him again. He opened his mouth as if to say something, but before he could get a word out Dotty had raced off again, dragging her exhausted owner with her.

"Oh dear, the poor man!" chuckled Mrs Smedley. "I'm afraid that dog is a bit too much of a handful for him."

"Yeah, it certainly looks like it," Neil agreed. "Although my dad always says there's no such thing as a problem dog, Mrs Smedley, only a problem owner!"

"I expect he feels dreadful, really," said Emily, always sympathetic towards people.

They all stood and watched until Dotty and her owner disappeared from view. Mrs Smedley put her feet on the pedals of her bicycle and pushed off.

"Well, I'd better be on my way. See you both soon," she called over her shoulder.

Sam barked at Neil. He was eager to continue their morning walk after all the excitement.

"C'mon then, Sam. Another ten minutes, then we'll turn back."

Sam sped away, eagerly darting about and sniffing at every familiar tree and bush, but always alert for commands from Neil.

As they approached the rear of the kennels, the sound of dogs barking reached them clearly. They had to leave the track and cross a large, grassy meadow before jumping over the fence at the back of the kennels.

"What a racket!" said Emily. Luckily, the Parkers' house and kennels were set well away from the main road, where their nearest neighbours lived. King Street Kennels was always noisy, though: it showed just how popular they were. Some boarders came from up to twenty miles away.

Neil glanced at his watch. It had just gone nine o'clock. "Feeding time!" he said, breaking into a run. "We can help out if we're quick. C'mon!"

Neil gave Sam a quick rubdown with a thick towel kept outside the back door and topped up his drinking bowl with fresh water. As Sam retired to his favourite spot in the back garden underneath a leafy privet hedge, Neil and Emily headed across the courtyard and towards the first kennel block, where Carole Parker was busy preparing food for the boarding dogs.

"Where's Dad and Squirt?" asked Neil, using his favourite nickname for his five-year- old sister.

"Your father and *Sarah*," his mother replied, arching an eyebrow at him, "have gone into Compton to see Uncle Jack." She looked up from the clipboard on the feeding table where she was measuring some dried food into a dog bowl, ready to mix with water. "I think he said he was going to get that video from Steve, too. He knew you were after it." She pushed a stray lock of her short black hair out of her eyes and took a tin from the shelf above the table. She was a strikingly tall woman, dressed in brown cords and loose sweatshirt.

"Great." Neil was always borrowing things from his cousin, Steve Tansley. He usually spent all of his own pocket money on books and magazines about dogs. "Can we help?"

"Yes, indeed. Why don't you go and join Kate in Block Two? Thanks, Neil," said his mother, placing another dog bowl on the table and checking her clipboard again. She emptied the tin of dog food into it and mixed it with some dried biscuit mix. The dogs were all kept to the diet they were fed at home which often meant mixing lots of different meals. "Emily, you and I can finish off here."

Neil crossed the courtyard to Kennel Block Two. The door was open, so he walked in and looked around for Kate McGuire, their kennel maid. Both kennel blocks consisted of two rows of ten pens either side, with individual sleeping quarters in each, and a central aisle.

The large inside pens were light and airy, and heating pipes set in tunnels in the concrete floor kept the kennels cosy in the winter. A lever on the outside of the pen controlled the door that gave the dogs access to the large wire mesh runs outside. Each pen generally had a personal touch, as owners insisted on bringing their pet's own basket or blanket from home and some favourite toys.

Neil soon found Kate with Buttons, an adorable little black and white, rough-coated mongrel. Buttons had two comical black ears perched on top of her head, and bright, friendly eyes. Her owners, Mr and Mrs Timms, lived just outside Compton. They had brought her to the kennels the day before and were now on their way to America for a three-week holiday.

Kate's long blonde hair was up in a ponytail, and she wore her usual baggy sweatshirt and leggings. "Poor Buttons. She's pining terribly," she told Neil. "Won't touch her food at all."

Buttons was lying listlessly with her head on her paws. Sad eyes gazed down at the ground.

"She's lost her sparkle since yesterday, hasn't she?" Neil said thoughtfully. "Come on, girl, cheer up!" He went over and stroked her gently. "You'll be fine here."

Buttons closed her eyes and sighed deeply.

"I'll leave the food down for a while. She'll probably eat it later," Kate decided.

Neil closed the pen behind them, gazing anxiously at the sad little dog. Sometimes dogs did pine for their owners at first, but they usually settled down once they got used to the routine of the kennels and to the love and attention that the Parkers and Kate gave them.

In the pen next to Buttons was Jed, a huge fawn-coloured Great Dane with a gentle nature and an enormous appetite. The large bowl of food Kate put down for him disappeared in seconds.

Then came Sally, a tricoloured basset hound who was very much at home at King Street Kennels. She'd visited plenty of times, as her owners often had to go abroad. As soon as Neil opened her pen, Sally rolled over on to her back with her legs in the air, eager to have her tummy tickled. Neil remembered how Sally had pined when she first came to the kennels a few years ago. He felt sure Buttons would soon be just as much at home.

Kate fed the last of the dogs. Ruff was a golden retriever who was due to go home the following day. He'd attached himself to Kate straight away and sulked if anyone else fed him.

"Well, that's me done until Monday," she said, closing the pen door. "You're back at school then, aren't you, Neil?"

"Yeah, worst luck!" Neil grimaced. He'd really enjoyed spending so much time at the kennels during the long summer holidays. "We've got a new teacher and I'm dreading it!"

"Oh, it's always like that to start with," said

Kate, sympathetically. "Don't worry, I'm sure you'll be fine."

Neil hoped so. Mrs Oakham, who had been his teacher until she left last term, had always encouraged his interest in dogs. It was probably too much to hope that her replacement would be as understanding.

2

"Come on, Neil. We'll be late!" Emily shouted towards the kennels from the back door of the house. She always liked to get to school in time to chat to her friends before going in to class. The first day of term was especially important.

"OK, I'm coming!"

Neil was crouching beside Buttons, stroking her head. She had pined for the rest of the weekend, refusing most of her food and moping in her basket. She hadn't even ventured into her outside run.

"I'll be back soon," he whispered as he stood up. With one last glance at the sad little dog he firmly closed the pen door after him and ran across the courtyard to the house.

"Hurry up!" called their mother. She was waiting outside on the driveway in their green

Range Rover. Neil could see Emily and Sarah already on the back seat behind.

Usually Neil would cycle the couple of miles to school with Chris Wilson, his best friend, who lived a little further along the main road. Although they were the same age and were both short, with dark brown spiky hair, they had some very different interests.

Today, however, Neil had wanted to spend time with Buttons – even if it meant arriving at school with his sisters.

*

"Well, I hope you all like your new classes," said Mrs Parker as she pulled up alongside the entrance to Meadowbank School.

"I just hope my new teacher's as good as Mrs Oakham," said Neil, opening the door and jumping out.

Mrs Parker gave Sarah a quick kiss and waved to Neil and Emily. "Bye. I'll see you all later this afternoon."

"Hey! The Puppy Patrol's arrived!" quipped a familiar voice as they walked through the school gates.

Neil turned and smiled at Hasheem, the class joker. He was used to his friends and other people in the town referring to them as the "Puppy Patrol". The name had stuck because they were seen around Compton so often in their Range Rover with its King Street Kennels logo.

"Hi, Hasheem. What's new?" he asked.

"Nothing much. Except our new teacher is friendly, easy-going and doesn't believe in homework . . ." Hasheem grinned.

"Really?" said Neil, falling for Hasheem's serious tone.

"In your dreams!" laughed Hasheem.

Neil punched his arm playfully.

When they walked into the classroom their new teacher was already there, writing on the board. He had his back to the class but something about him struck Neil as familiar. When the teacher turned around, Neil gasped in dismay. It was the owner of the Dalmatian they had met on Saturday!

The teacher's gaze fell on Neil and his face coloured slightly. Obviously, he remembered Neil, too.

"Be seated, please," the teacher commanded briskly. "And no talking!"

He looked at Neil coldly, as if his remarks were solely for Neil's benefit.

Just my luck! Neil thought bitterly as he walked to his desk. *Of all the people in the world, our new teacher has to be him!*

Once they had all taken their seats, they could see the words MR HAMLEY written in block capitals on the blackboard.

"Good morning, everyone. As you can see, my name is Mr Hamley," he said. "In a minute

I'll ask you all to introduce yourselves. But first I want to make one thing crystal clear: you are here to learn, and I am here to teach you. I will not tolerate any time-wasting or bad behaviour in my class."

His steely gaze swept over the sea of faces in front of him, then rested on Neil, his eyes narrowing. "Is that understood?"

Something tells me I'm a marked man, Neil thought uncomfortably.

When it was Neil's turn to stand up and introduce himself, Mr Hamley repeated his name as if committing it to memory.

This was just the start to a new term Neil *didn't* need.

Neil felt jittery all morning and was relieved when it was time for break. He couldn't wait to see Chris and give him the news!

Chris ran his fingers through his thick hair and whistled. "Wow, that's really tough luck! But maybe he'll loosen up after a couple of days."

"I hope so," sighed Neil. "But I'm not going to hold my breath. You should have seen him looking at me. I'm definitely not his favourite pupil right now!"

The rest of the class weren't too impressed, either.

"Man, it's just our luck to get landed with a monster without a sense of humour," said Hasheem. "I thought I was done for!"

Mr Hamley had asked if anyone knew where the United Nations sat and Hasheem's reply, "On chairs, sir!", had resulted in a withering look and a threat of extra homework.

"If he smiled he'd crack his face!" said one of the others.

"And he's really got it in for you, hasn't he?" Hasheem asked, turning to Neil. "What have you done to rattle his cage?"

So the other kids *had* noticed. Neil shrugged his shoulders. He thought it best not to mention the episode with the Dalmatian. "Maybe he just doesn't like my face!" he replied, trying to laugh. If Mr Hamley knew Neil had told the rest of the class about Saturday, he'd be even more annoyed. Neil just hoped his new teacher would forget all about it sooner rather than later.

But Mr Hamley's mood didn't improve. He frowned all day and his manner was very abrupt. Especially with Neil. Neil breathed a sigh of relief when the bell rang for the end of school.

Thankfully, Neil shrugged on his jacket and walked out of the school building. He could see the Range Rover parked across the road opposite, and hurried over.

His father was in the driver's seat this time. Bob Parker was a very large man and had short brown hair not unlike Neil's. He was wearing one of his green jumpers that had the King Street Kennels logo across his chest. Sarah and Emily were already sitting in the back, grumbling at Sam who was climbing all over them, trying to reach Neil.

Neil made a huge fuss of the collie.

"Hi! How's Buttons, Dad?" Neil asked as he fastened his seat belt. "Is she any better?"

"No, she's not too bright," replied his father, slipping the car into gear. "But it's still early days. It's the first time she's been away from home, so she's bound to be unsettled. I'm sure she'll pick up in a day or two."

"And guess what, Neil," Emily said. "There's a new dog at the rescue centre!"

"Is there, Dad? What breed is it? Where did you find it?"

"Hang on, one question at a time," Bob Parker smiled. "Yes, we have got another dog. Someone found him wandering around in the woods. No collar, a bit skinny, obviously hungry and very frightened."

"Just like Sam," said Emily. "Remember?"

Neil had been seven when the poor, weak puppy was found abandoned and brought to the rescue centre. It didn't take much to persuade his parents to break their own rule and to keep Sam as the family pet, either.

The rescue centre had ten pens for strays but only two were occupied at the moment – by Diamond, a beautiful Afghan hound whose owners had got tired of grooming her, and Max, a black and tan mongrel who had almost certainly been dumped – perhaps when his owners went on holiday – without a collar to identify him.

"If people don't want their pets, why don't they find them another home instead of abandoning them?"

"It makes me angry too, Neil," his father told him quietly. "But that's why your mum and I started the rescue centre in the first place. It's good to be able to help these dogs and find them a new home if we can."

"Can we go and see the dog when we get back, Daddy?" Sarah piped up.

"Yes, but don't go in the pen, love," Mr Parker replied. "He's very nervous and jumpy. He needs some rest and quiet and time to settle down. OK?"

He turned the car into their gravel driveway and pulled up. The three children piled out and hurried over to the rescue centre, a small block set aside from the main kennels.

Their mother was there, filling in a form with details about the new dog. It was important to note the stray's description and where and when it was found, in case the owner turned up to claim it.

"I suppose you've come to see the new arrival?" she asked, smiling at them.

"Can we?" Neil asked.

"Of course. But remember he's been living rough for a while so he doesn't look too good. And he's very nervous, so don't alarm him."

She led them to the end pen where a thin, sandy-coloured mongrel was lying in the corner. It stood, hackles raised as they approached, and growled.

"Poor thing," said Emily softly. "He's all skin and bones!"

"Not for long," her mother reassured her. "He's so wary of us, though, I'd guess he's been treated badly at some time."

The dog looked neglected and frightened.

"It's all right, boy, we won't hurt you," said Neil gently, crouching down outside the pen, but the dog backed into the furthest corner of the enclosure and snarled at him.

The pens in the rescue centre were pretty much the same as the ones in the boarding kennel blocks, but a bit smaller, and with basic plastic dog baskets for ease of cleaning. Like the others, there was an outside run as well.

The centre was mostly maintained with the

help of money from the local county council and the occasional coffee morning or other fund-raising events put on by friends.

The Parkers would nurse mistreated or sick dogs back to full health and then try to find them new, more responsible owners.

"What shall we call him?" asked Sarah.

"How about Growler?" suggested Emily.

Neil shook his head. "He won't always be a growler, Em," he said. "Let's call him Sandy."

"Sandy it is, then," said their mother, writing it down on her form. "Leave him to settle, now. You three go and get changed. You'll find some snacks in the kitchen."

"Well, how was your first day back at school?" Carole Parker asked as they all sat around the large wooden kitchen table waiting for Bob to serve the dinner. It was his turn to cook the meal tonight.

"Ace!" said Emily. "Mrs Rowntree's made me Rabbit Monitor."

"Rabbit Monitor?" asked her dad. "Does that mean you have to keep counting them?"

There was laughter round the table.

"No, silly! I have to look after them with Angie Smith. You know, feed them and stuff."

"And I suppose it means you have to bring them home in the holidays?" said her mother, with a wry look at her husband.

"Well, I don't know. We haven't got any yet."

More laughter, even louder. Emily flushed, but had to grin as well.

"There's no need to laugh. Mrs Rowntree says we can get a couple later in the term, when we start learning about them."

"I got two stars for my picture!" said Sarah, then beamed with pleasure at everyone's congratulations. She loved drawing and painting.

"How about you, Neil?" his father asked, placing a bowl of hot spaghetti on the table in front of him.

Neil's smile faded. "Don't ask," he said. "Our new teacher, Mr Hamley, is really strict. He's got no sense of humour, and he's *already* got it in for me."

His parents exchanged worried glances.

"Why? What's happened?" asked his mother with concern.

Neil described the incident with Mr Hamley and Dotty the Dalmatian on Saturday. "I didn't mean him to hear what I said about people who don't know how to train their dogs," he explained. "But he did hear it and I suppose it upset him."

Bob Parker looked thoughtful. "The poor man's probably feeling very embarrassed. And worried, maybe, that you won't respect him or that he'll be laughed at if you tell the rest of the class about him. Not the best way for a new teacher to start off, is it?"

Neil nodded. Dad could always make him see things from another person's point of view and that wasn't always easy to accept.

"So what should I do now?" Neil asked. "How can I convince him I'm not out to cause trouble?"

"Work hard and try to forget what happened last Saturday," advised Carole Parker. "This will soon blow over. When he's settled in a bit more and got to know you, I'm sure you'll both get on fine."

Neil hoped his parents were right.

3

The next morning Sarah came rushing downstairs looking excited.

"I've done it!" she announced triumphantly. "I've taught Fudge to sit."

Fudge was her pet hamster. Sarah knew he was the cleverest hamster in the world, and was always trying to train him to do tricks. Even the fact that hamsters like to sleep a lot during the day didn't deter her. As soon as Fudge poked his head out of his house for a quick drink or nibble at his food, Sarah seized him for another training session before he could go to sleep again.

"Get real, Sarah, you can't teach a hamster to do anything," Emily told her, rolling her eyes in mock exasperation.

"Yes, you can!" Sarah replied. "I told Fudge to sit and he did. So there!"

Neil looked up from his breakfast cereal and grinned at his sisters. It was no use telling Sarah that Fudge only sat because he wanted to. She'd never believe it.

"That's very good, Sarah," smiled Bob Parker. "Keep at it and you'll soon be able to take Fudge out without a lead!"

"Oh, but . . ." Sarah suddenly frowned as she realized her dad was teasing her. The others laughed loudly.

"Oh, you!" she said and stomped out again.

The doorbell rang.

"That'll be Chris," said Neil.

He grabbed a piece of toast off the table and picked up his school bag on the way out. "See y'later."

"Neil! Your hair!" his mother called after him.

Neil grunted and smoothed his hand over his spiky hair which always seemed to be a mess. He gave a quick goodbye fuss to Sam and grabbed his bike.

Chris was waiting in the drive for him. "What kept you?" he asked. "I thought you weren't coming for a minute!"

"I wish I wasn't," Neil told him. "I don't fancy another day with Hamley. I wish I was in your class."

"Maybe he'll be in a better mood today," Chris said as they set off.

Somehow Neil doubted that.

The two boys cycled through the school gates and over to the bicycle sheds. They locked up their bikes and went over to join a group of friends before the start of lessons.

"Hope you're ready for another fun-filled day with Smiler," Hasheem said to Neil.

Neil chuckled. "Just don't make any more wisecracks," he warned him.

"Who? Me?" replied Hasheem with wide-eyed innocence. "Would I ever?"

To Neil's relief, their teacher seemed in a slightly better mood today.

"This morning I want you all to write about yourselves," Mr Hamley told the class. "Tell me about your families, your hobbies, what you want to do when you leave school. Anything you like. That way I'll get to know you all better."

There was the usual clatter of desk lids, sighs and rustling of notebooks, but eventually the room was silent apart from the occasional cough or sneeze and the creak of chair legs.

Neil set about describing King Street Kennels, and his experience with Sam and the other dogs. The words flowed. This was his passion, after all. He was always at his best when he was writing or talking about what he loved most. When the bell went for break, he looked up dazed. Where had the time gone? He felt quite pleased with his work and just hoped Mr Hamley would like it too!

That afternoon when Neil got home, he saw Emily playing their version of football with Sam in the courtyard behind the house. Immediately, Sam lost all interest in the game and ran over to greet Neil joyfully.

"Hello, Sam!" Neil bent down to fuss the dog roughly and playfully. Sam almost seemed to laugh with pleasure. He pushed his head at Neil and pretended to chew his hand.

"Want a game?" Emily asked.

"Sure," he nodded. "But Chris'll be here soon.

Let's wait for him, then we can go over to the field."

Chris arrived a few minutes later and they set off with Sam, a well-chewed ball and some jumpers for goalposts. Once in the field behind the kennels, they divided into two teams – Neil and Sam against Chris and Emily – and kicked off.

"The ball, Sam! Tackle the ball!" Neil shouted as the Border collie ran after Chris, who was dribbling the ball towards the goal. Sam caught up with Chris, pounced on the ball and nosed it

away towards Neil. Neil booted it towards goal but it just fell short.

"Goal, Sam!" he called as Emily raced over to defend. Sam cut in front of her and charged between the two jumpers, pushing the ball ahead of him.

"*Goal! Yeah!* Way to go, Sam!" yelled Neil, jumping up and punching the air in triumph.

Sam barked and ran round excitedly.

"We need a new rule," said Chris, gasping for breath. "No touching the ball with your nose allowed!"

"I don't reckon there's much that dog can't do!" laughed Mr Parker, who had been watching them. He leaned his arms on the top rail of the fence.

Sam was now dancing around Neil, barking for the game to go on. Neil bent down to fuss him, then turned to his father. "He's really great, isn't he?"

"Well, he should be – you've been training him since he was a puppy," Chris reminded him.

Bob Parker stroked his chin thoughtfully. "You know, I've heard they're going to include a special Agility event at the county show this year. It's at the end of this month. Why don't you enter Sam? It would be good experience for him – and you!"

"What's agility?" asked Emily.

"It's a kind of obstacle course which dogs have to run round against the clock," explained Bob.

"Wow! Sam would be great at that. Go for it!" said Chris.

Neil looked at them both, wondering, then down at Sam who was looking up at him, tongue lolling.

"How about that, Sam?" asked Neil, fondling Sam's ears. Sam barked with enthusiasm. He could tell by Neil's voice that something exciting was in the air. "You could probably do something like that with your eyes shut, couldn't you?" Sam's tail wagged furiously.

The county show was held on the showground near Compton every year. It was a huge event and attracted crowds of people.

"I'd bet on him, anyway," said Chris.

"Hey, that's an idea. Why don't we get people to sponsor him to complete the course?" suggested

Neil. "We could raise some money for the rescue centre."

"No, let's send the money to the RSPCA for a change," suggested Emily. "They help all animals, all over the country." She was a member of several animal support societies and was always looking at ways to raise funds for them. "We could do that, couldn't we, Dad?" she asked.

"I don't see why not. We'd have to arrange it properly of course and get some official sponsor forms from the RSPCA." He nodded approvingly. "But yes, I think it's a very good idea. I'll look out the details of the show. There are rules for these things, and you probably have to register early."

"And I'll be the first sponsor," offered Chris.

Back at the kennels, they found Kate just finishing in Block Two.

"How's Buttons, Kate?" asked Mr Parker.

Kate looked a bit worried. "Still very low, Bob. And she's hardly touched her food again."

"We'll get Mike to look at her when he calls tomorrow, just to be on the safe side," said Mr Parker. Mike Turner was their local vet from nearby Padsham. He came to check on the dogs twice a week, or when there was any emergency.

"How about Sandy?" asked Neil. "Is he any friendlier, Kate?"

"Not really. He still won't let me get near him," Kate replied.

"We'll go and take a look at him," said Bob. He turned to Neil and the others. "But remember, don't come in the pen unless I tell you to."

"OK. Are you coming, Em?"

"No way! That dog scares me," she confessed. "Anyway, I want to see Mum about sponsoring Sam for the show."

"I'm off as well," said Chris. "See you tomorrow, Neil. Bye, everyone."

Emily took Sam with her while Neil and his father headed over to the rescue centre.

Sandy was lying in his basket. As soon as he saw them approaching, he jumped out and crouched in a corner, growling softly and quivering.

Mr Parker spoke gently to him as he opened the pen. He walked slowly over to the dog.

Sandy bared his teeth and snarled louder. He looked ready to attack. Neil watched anxiously outside the cage, keeping very still so as not to alarm him. He knew his father was very good with dogs, but this one looked really fierce and unapproachable. Almost like a wild animal.

Still talking, Bob Parker stood very still and slowly took a couple of small dog treats out of his pocket. He placed them on the floor between him and Sandy.

"There now, good boy," he said quietly, and slowly backed out of the pen.

"I was a bit worried there for a moment," Neil admitted as his father shut the kennel door. "Do you think he would have gone for you?"

"If he felt threatened. That's why you mustn't go in the pen yet. This dog has been very badly treated by someone and it's going to take him quite a time to trust anyone again."

Neil looked anxiously at Sandy.

Even Sam had never been this bad.

Chris phoned after dinner to say that his mum and dad had offered to sponsor Sam in the county show, too.

"That's brilliant," said Emily when she heard.

Mrs Parker had been delighted at the whole idea and had readily agreed to write to the RSPCA for sponsor forms. "Why don't you ask Mrs Smedley if you can leave a sponsor form in the newsagent's?" she suggested over the top of her newspaper. "I'm sure a lot of people in the town would sign up too."

"Hey, we could call him the Puppy Patrol dog," said Emily. "That'd be cool! Brilliant publicity for the kennels too."

"Sponsor the Puppy Patrol dog – yeah, I like it." Neil nodded.

"It's not fair. I want to enter Fudge in the show too," Sarah pouted.

"There's a cleverest pet competition, Sarah," her father told her. "You can enter Fudge in that."

Sarah's face lit up. "Oh, good! In that case, I'll have to go and start on his training as soon as he wakes up!" she said, seriously. "I should be able to get him to beg as well as sit, in time for the show."

There were snorts and chokes from the others as they tried to suppress their laughter, but Sarah ignored them and left the room.

"Poor Fudge – he won't get a minute's peace now!" laughed Carole Parker.

"Maybe I'd better start a training schedule for Sam too," said Neil.

"I can help, if you like," offered Emily. "We want to make sure Sam does well against all the other dogs!"

"Well, there's one dog you won't have to worry about," his mother told him. "And that's your teacher's Dalmatian. From what you say, he won't be entering her for any obedience competitions!"

"You're right," said Neil, suddenly chilled by the memory of that awful encounter. "That would take a real miracle!"

4

Neil was so excited about the coming show that he found it difficult to concentrate on his schoolwork the next day. Reluctantly, he tore his thoughts away from his daydream of Sam being presented with the trophy for first prize and started doing the work his class had been set.

He had felt Mr Hamley's eyes on him a few times that morning and it made him nervous. Was Smiler still angry with him?

Then, just as he was leaving the classroom for lunch, Mr Hamley called out to him. "I'd like a word with you, please, Neil."

"Uh-oh. There may be trouble ahead!" sang Hasheem softly as Neil turned back.

Neil walked over to his teacher's desk, trying not to look nervous.

"Yes, sir?"

Neil could see Mr Hamley was reading his essay about King Street Kennels. He bit his lip. Was it awful?

"I found your essay very interesting, Neil."

Relief flooded through Neil. He wasn't in trouble, after all. He relaxed slightly and discovered he'd been clutching the strap of his school bag in a death grip without realizing it.

"Especially this bit about your father's obedience classes," Mr Hamley continued. He gave Neil an awkward smile. "As you know, I have a rather unruly Dalmatian. My wife and I have been trying to train Dotty for some time, but without much success. In fact, we've almost given up hope. So I wondered if your father would help us train Dotty."

Neil grinned hugely. He could hardly believe his ears.

"Of course he would, sir! Do you want me to ask him tonight?" he asked eagerly.

Mr Hamley smiled. He didn't look half so fierce when he relaxed a bit, Neil thought. His eyes sort of twinkled.

"Thank you, but I think it would be better if

I telephoned your father myself," he replied. "Can you give me the number and I'll get in touch with him tonight."

Neil left the classroom walking on air. This was better than he dared hope. His dad would teach Dotty to be obedient in no time! Then perhaps Mr Hamley would forget about their first encounter.

Chris was waiting for him outside school, looking worried.

"Hasheem said Mr Hamley kept you behind," he said. "What's the problem?"

Neil shook his head and told Chris about his conversation with their teacher.

"Wow! Your dad's going to train that crazy dog?" Chris raised his eyebrows in surprise. "That'll be something!"

Neil found his father in the kennel office when he got home from school and told him to expect a call from Mr Hamley.

"I'm looking forward to meeting this Dalmatian," said Mr Parker. "She seems quite a challenge."

"She is! Mr Hamley said he's been trying to train her for ages."

He bent down to greet Sam, who had nudged open the office door to come and find him. "And I'd better start practising with you, hadn't I, Sam? The county show's only a few weeks off."

Sam wagged his tail eagerly. If Neil was excited, then Sam was, too!

"I've been reading about Agility courses in my dog books," said Neil to his father. "Can we use some things from the store to make an obstacle course in the field?"

"Help yourself. But make sure there's nothing Sam can hurt himself on. That reminds me – I haven't found those application forms yet. We must get you both registered."

"OK. Come on, Sam." Neil ran across to the store between the two kennel blocks with Sam bounding beside him.

"Hey, Em!" he shouted, seeing his sister in the garden. "D'you want to help me make an Agility course for Sam?"

"Sure." Emily ran over to join him. "Loads of people were interested in it at school today. He's sure to get plenty of sponsors. He'll raise stacks of money for the RSPCA if he completes the course."

"You'll do better than that, won't you, boy?"

Sam wagged his tail and barked.

"See!" laughed Neil. "He agrees!"

Inside the store they found some small steps, a few planks of wood, an empty food barrel with both lids removed, and an old tyre. Armed with these and some bricks to help build the jumps, they soon made a makeshift course in the nearby field. Then Neil took Sam through his paces.

Sam looked a bit puzzled at first, but Neil ran around the course with him as he would on the big

day itself, showing him what to do, and the dog made a fantastic effort to obey. Crawling through the barrel caused some hilarious moments, but to Sam it was all a wonderful game.

"Well done, Sam." Emily clapped as the Border collie ran along the simple see-saw they had made with a plank and two bricks. This was probably the worst item on the course, since Sam had to make it tilt once he got to the centre and not jump off too soon.

Neil rewarded him with a favourite treat, and Sam looked ready to do it all again.

"No, Sam. That'll do for today," Neil said. His dad had always told him to finish a training session when a dog had been successful at something, so you could praise him. That way he'd be happy to work with you again.

Neil glanced at his watch. It was five thirty. Mr Hamley had probably phoned by now. He and Emily hurried over to the office to find out.

Mr Parker was talking on the telephone.

"We'll see you at seven thirty then," he was saying.

Neil sat in his mother's swivel chair at her

desk, while his dad finished the conversation. He couldn't resist spinning around just once.

"Was that Mr Hamley?" asked Neil eagerly, as soon as his father had replaced the handset. "Is he bringing Dotty tonight?"

"Yes, and I think it's going to be an interesting challenge," Mr Parker said. "Apparently, Mrs Hamley is expecting a baby so they've been trying to get their Dalmatian trained before the baby arrives. Dotty is very high-spirited and they've already had to take her away from three schools in disgrace."

"From what I saw of her on Saturday I'm not surprised," said Neil. "But *you* can sort her out, can't you, Dad? You can work miracles with any dog!"

His father laughed at Neil's faith in him. "Thanks for the vote of confidence, but training is just as much for the owner, you know. It's important that the dog knows who's boss. Dogs are pack animals, Neil. They have to look on their owners as the pack leader, or they won't obey them."

Well, Dotty certainly didn't look on Mr

Hamley as her boss, Neil thought. Still, Dad would soon sort that out.

Suddenly an awful thought struck him. What if Dotty never improved? Would he and Mr Hamley be back at square one?

"Can I stay and watch the obedience class tonight?" he asked eagerly.

"I've got a better idea," his father said. "I'd be glad if you'd help me out. There are two long-haired dachshunds coming tonight – Candy and Honey – and I could do with an extra handler for one of them. But if that Dalmatian plays up, don't laugh, OK? You don't want to upset Mr Hamley again, do you?"

"I won't," Neil promised. He was delighted his dad had asked him to help. "Can I go and see Buttons and Sandy now?"

"Dinner first. Then you can do the rounds with me before the lesson starts."

After dinner, Neil and his father went to check on the dogs. It was a warm night, still light, and the dogs were all out in their runs. All except Buttons. She was still lying in her basket.

"Well, at least she's drunk the glucose water the vet gave her this morning," Bob said. "He gave her a vitamin shot, too. That should pick her up a bit."

Over in the rescue centre, Sandy growled at their approach and once again backed into the far corner, watching them warily.

"He's still scared," said Neil.

"Yes. And it will probably take him a while to realize he's safe here." Mr Parker turned to Neil. "So promise me – no going in the pen for now, OK?"

"I promise, Dad. But can I give him something?" Neil always kept a couple of doggy treats in his pocket for Sam. "I'll put it through the wire."

Mr Parker nodded. "Go on, then."

Neil pushed the food through the wire mesh. It landed on the floor just in front of the ragged animal.

"Here you are, Sandy." Neil spoke very gently to him. "Come on, boy. Don't be scared."

Sandy growled softly, his eyes fixed on the treat in front of him.

"Let's move back," suggested Mr Parker. "Then he might take it."

Sandy eyed them warily as they backed away, then trotted over and, still watching them, snapped up the biscuit.

"Good boy!" Neil encouraged him warmly, but Sandy had already scuttled back into the corner.

"Let's leave him now," said Mr Parker. "I'll look in on him again later."

"Hey, it's nearly time for the obedience lesson to start," said Neil, checking his watch.

"I know. Everything's just about ready." Mr Parker usually held his classes in a large converted barn set to one side of their property.

As they walked back they heard the office bell ring. Mr Parker opened the gate at the side of the house. It was Mr Hamley, holding his Dalmatian on a lead.

"Hello, sir!" Neil smiled, reaching down to stroke the dog. "Hello, Dotty!"

Up close, she really was a beautiful animal and in the peak of health. Neil guessed that she was probably about eighteen months old. Her gleaming white coat was peppered with black spots. Black, silky ears framed her elegant face.

"Dotty looks a smashing dog," said Mr Parker. "You obviously care for her very well indeed." He squatted down and Dotty received his gentle stroking with interest and a wagging tail.

"Thank you. She has her moments though. I just hope she doesn't misbehave tonight." Mr Hamley still looked tense.

"If she does, she won't be on her own," said Mr Parker. "My nephew, Steve, is bringing his Labrador, Ricky, and we can always rely on him to disobey orders!"

Mr Hamley's face relaxed a little. "Sounds like they'll be a good pair, then."

They were interrupted by loud barking as the other dogs began to arrive and greet each other enthusiastically.

Head of the bunch was Ricky, who had cast an eager eye at Dotty and decided he liked what he saw. He was barking and pulling at his lead, trying to drag Neil's thirteen-year-old cousin, Steve, over to his new friend.

"No, Ricky! Heel!" Steve was shouting, to no

effect. The golden Labrador was a short but solid, powerful dog. Slightly built Steve was no match for him.

"Ricky! Sit!" Mr Parker commanded, loudly and firmly. The golden Labrador immediately sat down and looked at him, ears raised, listening for the next command.

"I don't know how you do it, Uncle Bob," said Steve, shaking his head and out of breath. "He never does that for me."

"Well, I hope you have the same success with Dotty," remarked Mr Hamley, greatly impressed by the simple demonstration.

"Let's go and find out," said Mr Parker.

5

Six boisterous young dogs and their owners packed into the barn. Ricky and Dotty both managed to tangle their leads in their efforts to play and make friends.

Mr Hamley looked embarrassed, but Steve was laughing. He was used to Ricky's antics. Catching Neil's eye, he raised his eyebrows in mock despair as he bent down to untangle the two dogs.

Neil grinned. He loved these sessions. Most of the dogs were fairly unruly at first but gradually, as the lessons progressed under his dad's expert coaching, they all became much better behaved. It was a bonus if his dad gave him a dog to handle as well.

"Hello, everyone. Thank you all for coming," Mr Parker said in a loud, friendly voice. "I hope you enjoy the lesson. Training your dog should be fun as well as rewarding." He smiled as he looked around the barn at the assortment of dogs and their owners. "I believe that a well-trained dog is a happy dog, and a pleasure to its owner. If you follow instructions and practise the work we do here, there's no reason why your dog shouldn't be well behaved."

Ricky barked loudly and Mr Parker grinned at him.

"Yes, even you, Ricky!"

There was a ripple of laughter as Ricky barked again, as if in agreement.

"Now, there's one thing I'm going to draw to your attention before we start." He held up a crumpled plastic bag. "The dog owner's most important equipment after the voice and the lead!"

Neil smiled – he'd heard this speech before – and noticed that some of the owners were looking baffled while others seemed to know what was coming.

"Never go out for a walk with your dog without one of these in your pocket to clean up after him! It's not only the law now, but it's also responsible consideration for the environment and other people – and for your dog, who can't clean up after himself even if he wanted to!"

More laughter. Point made.

"Right, let's start off by getting your dogs to walk to heel," continued Mr Parker. He demonstrated how they should hold their leads correctly. "I'd like you all to walk your dogs around the barn now, please. If you'd like to go first, Steve?" He nodded at his nephew.

Steve started walking with Ricky bounding alongside him. Behind them was Bella the Gordon setter, pulling ahead eagerly. Then Candy, one of the long-haired Dachshunds, who was busily sniffing the ground and darting suddenly off the track in all directions.

Neil followed with Honey, her litter-sister. She was much quieter than Candy and trotted sweetly alongside Neil, gazing up at him with button-black eyes as if making sure she was doing everything properly. Behind them came Scamp, a bouncy Old English sheepdog puppy with a nature true to his name, and finally Lady, a lovable

little Yorkshire terrier, owned by Mrs Swinton, a neighbour of Steve's.

But where was Dotty? Neil looked around, puzzled. Then he saw her, stretched out on the floor of the barn, refusing to budge. Mr Hamley was pulling ineffectually at her lead and calling her quietly, trying to make her stand, but Dotty was completely ignoring him. Neil smothered a grin. Trust Dotty!

Mr Parker strolled casually over to them.

"Dotty! Get up, girl!" Mr Hamley whispered, his face red with embarrassment. "Come on, get up!"

"Having a bit of trouble, Paul?" asked Mr Parker.

"Er, she doesn't seem to want to join in."

"Pull her up sharply with the lead and tell her firmly to stand."

Mr Hamley tugged gently on Dotty's lead. "Come on, Dotty, stand!" he hissed.

Neil could see the other dog owners glancing sympathetically at Mr Hamley, and he knew how awful his teacher must feel with all the attention.

But Dotty wouldn't move.

"Now, you must show her you mean it," Mr Parker told Mr Hamley. "Your voice is very important. Try imagining you are back in the classroom! A dog will only obey you if you speak with authority. Pull her lead again and tell her firmly and loudly to stand. It won't hurt her, and it will give her the jolt she needs to get her to pay attention to you."

Mr Hamley tried again. "Dotty, *stand*!" His voice echoed round the barn and Neil winced. This was the Hamley he knew back at school!

Dotty stared at him in surprise and got to her feet.

"That's it! Good!" Bob said to him. Mr Hamley flushed with pleasure and relief.

"And always praise your dog every time she

does the right thing," Mr Parker instructed the whole group. "Let's see you making a big fuss of your dogs now."

While everyone stooped to pat and fuss their dogs, Mr Hamley led Dotty over to join the others on their circuit round the barn. "Good girl, Dotty," he said to her. "Good girl!"

For a while Dotty trotted quite happily alongside Mr Hamley. While she wasn't actually walking to heel, she wasn't way in front of him either so Neil felt she was making progress.

"Now, we're going to get your dogs to sit," said Mr Parker. "And when they do, give them lots of praise again."

Steve groaned and Neil smiled. Getting Ricky to sit was always a problem.

"Sit, Ricky!" Steve ordered firmly, pressing his free hand down on Ricky's rump.

Ricky wagged his tail and stayed standing.

"Sit!" Steve said, holding his hand out flat and moving it in a downwards motion to try and show the Labrador what he meant.

Ricky immediately lay on the floor, his head on his front paws, and sighed.

Beside them, Mr Hamley was having the same trouble with Dotty.

Dotty lay on the floor waiting to be tickled. Poor Mr Hamley looked around desperately.

"Don't worry, she'll pick it up," Mr Parker told him. "It might help if you show her more clearly what you want her to do. Here, let me show you."

Bob took Dotty's lead and made her stand beside him. "Sit, Dotty!" he said. He pressed her rump down firmly while pulling back on her lead. "Sit!"

Dotty sat.

"Good girl," Bob told her, giving her a titbit from his pocket.

Dotty gobbled it down and sniffed around for more.

"Just keep at it patiently," he told Mr Hamley, "and always try to reward her, either with a titbit or by making a big fuss of her. After a while she'll sit on command and you can just reward her every now and again."

They practised the sitting command once more. Honey was so obliging that Neil was able to relax. It gave him a chance to watch the others, and he was especially pleased to see Mr Hamley finally get Dotty to sit. Was she responding at last?

"Now, let's try the 'stay and recall'," Mr Parker said, arranging the class in a long line. "I want you to tell your dogs to sit, then back away from them a few paces to the extent of their leads and call them to you with a tug on the lead." He waited while everyone complained about being asked to do the impossible. "When they obey, give them lots of praise and fuss."

Honey didn't like Neil backing away from her. She tried at first to keep up with him, so he had to concentrate on making her sit and stay. Finally she got it right and he was able to look up and watch Dotty's progress.

Mr Hamley did his best. As soon as he started to move back, though, Dotty got up and followed him.

"No, Dotty! *Stay!*" Mr Hamley pleaded.

Dotty finally stayed. She watched her owner curiously, her head tilted on one side as he walked back a few paces, the lead at its full length.

"Come, Dotty!" shouted Mr Hamley, tugging her lead. "Come!"

Dotty immediately bounded over to him, jumped up and started licking his face.

"Down, Dotty!" Mr Hamley whispered, trying to push her down. The dog just continued licking his face. Mr Hamley tottered, trying to keep his balance as the young dog pressed her paws against him.

Mr Parker came up behind and pushed Dotty down sharply. "*Down, Dotty!*" he commanded sternly.

Dotty sat down suddenly.

"Good girl," said Bob, patting her. Dotty pushed her nose into his pocket, thinking she might have another treat.

"No, Dotty, that's greedy!" Mr Hamley scolded her.

"That's OK," laughed Bob. "At least it shows you she's a quick learner when she wants to be!"

Steve turned to Neil. "She's even worse than Ricky," he marvelled, a hint of admiration in his voice. "Mr Hamley's your teacher, isn't he? Lucky you – he looks really soft!"

"Only with his dog," Neil whispered. "In school he can be a real nightmare."

As the lesson continued, Neil looked over at Dotty from time to time but he saw little sign of improvement. She pulled at her lead, barking and trying to chase the other dogs. He felt sorry for Mr Hamley trying to control her. The teacher was probably very relieved when Mr Parker announced a final circuit of the barn, walking their dogs to heel.

"Well, she got off to a bit of a bad start, but that's only to be expected at first," Bob Parker told Mr Hamley at the close of the session. "Young dogs like Dotty can be very high-spirited – it's a bit like having a teenager around the house. But a couple more lessons and you'll see a big difference in her. And you might find it easier to control her if you use a choke chain. They're very good for preventing big strong dogs like Dotty from pulling ahead too much – but you must see that you put it on correctly."

Mr Hamley nodded. "Thanks. I'll see about one tomorrow. Anything that helps me control Dotty is worth a try!"

Mr Parker was addressing everyone now. "I want you all to practise the walking-to-heel and sit commands with your dogs. Just a few minutes a day will do. And remember that praise!"

"Bob's a marvellous trainer," Neil heard Mrs Swinton say to Mr Hamley. "He worked wonders with my sister's dog you know, and she was awful – really disobedient and aggressive. But within a couple of months Bob had totally transformed her. It was wonderful."

Dotty was standing up now, pulling impatiently at her lead, eager to go.

"Wait a minute, Dotty!" said Mr Hamley. Dotty barked loudly and looked over at the door. Then she tore off, catching her owner off guard and tugging the lead out of his hand.

"Oh, no! Dotty! Come back!" he shouted, giving chase as the Dalmatian bolted from the barn.

Other dogs barked and tried to follow. They wanted to join in the fun, too. The noise was deafening as the owners struggled to hang on to their animals.

Neil quickly gave Honey back to her owner

and joined his father as he went after Dotty. They were just in time to see the Dalmatian disappearing towards the Parkers' back garden with Mr Hamley chasing after her. Suddenly she stopped in the middle of the lawn. To relieve herself.

"Maybe we can catch her now!" laughed Mr Parker, watching the dog squatting on his newly mown grass.

Neil grinned. Dotty was such a character!

"Dotty! You naughty girl!" Mr Hamley roared, running over to her. "Come here!" As he lunged for the lead, Dotty promptly turned and ran between his legs. He lost his balance and fell just a bit too close to the mess Dotty had deposited on the grass. Neil thought this was perhaps not the time to remind him of the poop-scoop rule.

A gale of laughter from the direction of the barn told Neil that the other dog owners had come outside to see what was happening. Now they stood enjoying the joke, thanking their lucky stars that Dotty wasn't their dog.

Dotty, meanwhile, was heading towards the boarding kennels. Neil looked at his father. His lips twitching, Mr Parker turned and caught Neil's eye. "Whatever you do, don't laugh," he whispered, his own eyes twinkling. "The poor man feels wretched enough already."

Neil understood.

"I'll get her, sir," he called to Mr Hamley, who was staring in dismay at his dirty jacket.

Neil soon found Dotty, standing outside the pen of Jed, the Great Dane. The two dogs were showing great interest in each other, so Neil sneaked up behind Dotty and quickly grabbed her lead.

Instantly she tried to pull away.

"Oh no you don't!" Neil told her, holding the lead firmly.

"Well done, Neil!" said his father, coming up beside him.

Mr Hamley was trailing behind, looking weary and flustered. His normally immaculate dark hair was rumpled and his cheeks flushed. He'd taken his jacket off and was carrying it over his arm. Once he saw Dotty was caught, he strode over.

"Thank you," he said stiffly. "I'll take her

now." He almost snatched Dotty's lead out of Neil's hand and walked away.

"I'll see you all next week," Mr Parker said loudly for the benefit of Mr Hamley's departing back. "And remember there's also a class on Sunday morning at ten thirty if you'd like to come along."

"I don't think we'll be coming again," said Mr Hamley, turning back briefly. "It's obvious that Dotty is untrainable and I don't intend to be a further source of amusement for anyone."

"But, sir . . ." Neil began.

"Come on, Dotty!" he ordered, tugging her lead.

Neil watched them go with a sinking heart.

6

"Do you think Mr Hamley meant it about not bringing Dotty again?" Neil asked his father as they ate breakfast the next morning.

Mr Parker chewed his toast thoughtfully.

"I think he was more embarrassed than anything else," he replied. "Maybe he'll change his mind when he's calmed down a bit."

Neil hoped so. He finished his breakfast and grabbed a few doggy treats before hurrying over to see Sandy. He was sure he knew how to get Sandy to trust him. He wanted to try, anyway.

The other two rescue dogs started barking excitedly as Neil opened the door of the centre and stepped inside. He stopped to say a quick hello to them both as he passed.

As usual, Sandy retreated to the far wall when Neil approached.

"Hey, come on, boy. No one's going to hurt you," Neil said gently. He held up a treat and pushed it through the wire. "Here you are."

Once Neil moved away from the fence, Sandy came forward and snatched up the food. Then he looked guardedly over at Neil.

"I'll come back and see you later, feller," Neil told him. He knew this was going to be a long process. If he tried to rush it he would make the dog even more nervous.

Neil glanced at his watch. There was just time to see Buttons as well.

The sad little dog showed no improvement, though. She lay in the corner of her kennel and made no effort to come and get the snack he offered.

Neil wished he could stay at home and spend some time with both dogs. Especially today. He was dreading facing Mr Hamley after Dotty's disastrous lesson the previous evening. He was bound to be in a foul mood.

He heard Emily shout as he ran back across the courtyard.

"Neil! Chris is here!"

"Coming!" Neil grabbed his bike and wheeled

it out through the side gate. Chris was waiting for him in the drive.

"So how did the lesson go with Dotty last night?" he asked eagerly.

Neil grimaced and told him all about it. "I'm dreading this morning. I bet my name's mud with Hamley," he said.

Mr Hamley didn't actually say anything to Neil. In fact he wasn't his normal self at all. He was very quiet and preoccupied all day.

"Well, Smiler's in a weird mood, isn't he?" Hasheem said as they walked out of the class-room. "I made two jokes and he didn't even notice. I wonder what's up with him."

Neil shrugged. "Maybe he's got something on his mind." It wasn't hard to guess what.

Mr Hamley must be pretty upset about Dotty's behaviour. But why then couldn't he see that giving up training classes was the worst thing he could do?

To Neil's disappointment, there was no sign of the Dalmatian in Sunday's class.

"Couldn't you phone him and talk him into giving Dotty another chance?" Neil asked his father when the last of the dogs had left. "If you told him lots of dogs behaved worse than Dotty when they first came, he might not feel so bad."

Mr Parker sighed. "You know I can't interfere like that. It's up to Mr Hamley whether he brings his dog to the class or not."

Just then Carole Parker shouted across the courtyard to the barn.

"Bob! Paul Hamley's on the phone!"

"Maybe he's changed his mind after all," said Neil eagerly.

"Maybe," replied his father, striding over to the office.

Neil had just finished tidying up the barn when Mr Parker came back ten minutes later.

"The Hamleys have decided to bring Dotty here for a bit," he told Neil.

"Here?" Neil said, surprised.

"Yes. I got the impression they were both at the end of their tethers with Dotty. Rachel Hamley's baby is due soon and she just can't cope with such a boisterous dog. They want to board Dotty here for the time being."

"Until the baby's born?"

"Until they find another home for her."

"What? But if they kept bringing her to lessons she'd be fine," Neil persisted. Dotty was such a lovely dog. It didn't seem fair that she had to go to another home. It would be terrible for her.

Bob Parker watched his son's face cloud over with concern and disappointment. He understood exactly Neil's sense of frustration. "I could only train Dotty if Mr Hamley was prepared to learn how to handle her, Neil. But he's just too soft with her and a bit nervous. A big dog like that needs firmness and confidence."

Neil nodded, not trusting himself to say anything.

"Well, I'll go and get a pen ready. She'll be arriving later today."

Neil watched his father walk over to the kennel blocks. Poor Dotty! He just hoped that Mr Hamley and his wife would miss her so much they'd come and get her after a day or two.

He couldn't imagine having to give away his dog to some stranger. Supposing it was Sam. No – the thought was too terrible. Whatever happened, he'd make sure he gave the Dalmatian lots of love and attention while she was here.

Mr Hamley arrived with Dotty at three o'clock. Neil and Emily followed their father to the kennels to show Mr Hamley where Dotty would be staying. Neil could see he was very distressed, but trying hard not to show it.

"Now, you . . . you be a good girl, Dotty," he said gently, his voice wavering. He stroked her

head, turning his face away from them while he led her into the pen. "I'll come and see you soon."

He stood up and blew his nose noisily into his handkerchief.

"Sorry – bit of a cold. I'm very grateful to you for taking Dotty at such short notice. I'm not sure how long it will take me to find her a suitable home, so she could be here a while."

"Don't worry, she'll be fine with us," Mr Parker assured him. "I'll use my contacts too, if you like. Dotty's a lovely dog, even if she is a bit unruly. It shouldn't be too difficult to find somebody to take her on."

"Thank you. I'd appreciate that," Mr Hamley told him.

"Maybe you could have Dotty back when Mrs Hamley's had the baby?" Neil said hopefully.

His teacher shook his head sadly. "We wish we could keep Dotty, Neil. Rachel and I think the world of her. But I'm afraid Dotty's just too unmanageable to have in the same house as a newborn baby. It's an impossible situation."

And with one final glance at Dotty, Mr Hamley walked away.

Dotty watched him go, pressing her muzzle to the wire and whining softly.

"Poor Dotty!" Emily said. "And poor Mr Hamley. He seems so sad about leaving her here. Can't we do something, Dad?"

Mr Parker shrugged. "I don't see what. After all, it's their decision. While I think it's a shame for Dotty, they have to think of their baby first. And who knows? Dotty might well be happier with someone who can manage her better."

Neil knew his dad was right but it didn't make him feel any better.

Then he had an idea. There could be a way of changing his teacher's mind. If his father agreed, it was worth a try.

"Couldn't we train Dotty before Mr Hamley finds her somewhere to go?" Neil suggested. "Then he wouldn't need to get rid of her."

His father shook his head. "We can't work with Dotty without Mr Hamley knowing, Neil. It wouldn't be right. She's still his dog."

"But it's Dotty's only chance now," Neil pleaded. "And I'm sure Mr Hamley won't mind. He did want her trained, after all."

"Well . . ." His father hesitated. "I suppose it couldn't hurt . . ."

"Go on, Dad. We can give it a try at least," begged Emily. "Otherwise poor Dotty will be sold. And anyway, she'll still be terrible for her new owners and then they might get rid of her too."

"Point taken. OK, I'll include Dotty in my training classes and see how she gets on," Mr Parker agreed. "And you can give her some extra practice in the evenings. But don't expect it to be easy, will you?"

Neil and Emily both grinned.

It would be tough, they knew, but it would be worth it – for Dotty's sake!

The next day, Emily's sponsor forms came from the RSPCA. Carole Parker helped her fill them in sitting at the kitchen table, while Neil helped Sarah draw a very colourful picture of Sam.

"We'll keep one form in the office," said Carole. "I'm sure some of our regulars will sponsor Sam." Most of the customers who used King Street Kennels usually visited the office at some stage, either to collect their dogs, pay their bill, or arrange for their pets to stay.

"Thanks, Mum. Let's take one to school too, Neil," Emily said. "Some of the kids will sponsor us. And the teachers."

"We could go down to Mrs Smedley's after school and ask her if we can leave one there," said Neil. "Loads of people call in every day."

Bob Parker came in from his morning rounds, looking rather worried.

"How's Dotty?" Neil asked anxiously. He hoped she wasn't pining. He was planning to go and see her, and Sandy and Buttons, before he went to school. His visiting list was getting longer every day, it seemed.

"She's settled down quite well," his father told him. "It's Buttons I'm worried about. She's still not eating very much."

"Maybe Buttons wants something to cuddle up to," suggested Sarah. "Cuddling my teddy always makes me feel better."

"Get real, Squirt," scoffed Emily. "As if Buttons wants a teddy bear!"

"Hang on. Sarah's right. Buttons probably

would like something to comfort her," their father said, thoughtfully. "Not a teddy bear, though. Something belonging to Mr or Mrs Timms that she can lie on in her basket. An item of clothing, perhaps – that sometimes does the trick."

"I've got their neighbours' phone number," said Mrs Parker. "I'll go and give them a ring and see if they've got any suggestions. They might even have a spare key to the house."

When Neil arrived home from school later that day, his mother told him she'd managed to contact Mrs Timms' neighbour.

"He's called Geoff Wilkins, and he sounds really nice," she told them. "He's got an old gardening cardigan that Mrs Timms left there recently when she stopped by for a cup of coffee, and he's bringing it over. He thought Buttons might cheer up if she sees a familiar face, so he's going to give her the cardigan himself."

"Great!" said Neil. "Hope it works."

"So do I. I don't know what else we can do."

Half an hour later, a blue car pulled up in the drive and a tall, broad man with ruddy cheeks got out, holding a green cardigan. Neil ran to open the door, telling Sarah to fetch their mother.

"Hello there! Are you one of the Parker children?" the man asked cheerfully. "Could you tell your mother that Geoff Wilkins is here."

"I'm Neil Parker. Mum'll be out in a minute, Mr Wilkins," Neil said politely.

His mother came out of the side gate.

"Mr Wilkins? How kind of you to come."

"Happy to help," said Mr Wilkins. "Poor old Buttons! Joe and Alice would be very upset if they knew how distressed she was."

He followed Mrs Parker through to where Buttons was lying in her pen, her eyes sad and anxious.

"Oh, dear!" said Mr Wilkins. "Just look at her!"

At the sound of his voice, Buttons pricked her ears and lifted her head.

"Hey, lass, it's me!" Mr Wilkins said as Carole pulled open the pen door. "And just look what I've brought for you!"

He stepped inside and knelt down, the green cardigan draped over his knee.

Buttons ran over and jumped up to him eagerly, licking his face. Then she sniffed at the cardigan. The change in her was remarkable. She nuzzled the cardigan ecstatically, whining and barking.

Geoff walked over to Buttons' basket and arranged the cardigan inside it.

Buttons ran over. She sniffed at the cardigan again, pawed it into place and then lay down on it. The listless look had disappeared from her face.

"Happy now, lass?" he asked, stroking her gently.

"Just look at that!" Mrs Parker smiled. "It seems to have done the trick. Thank you ever so much, Mr Wilkins. Perhaps if we leave her by herself for a while she might even eat her dinner."

They all walked out of the pen and Mrs Parker closed it behind them.

"Would you mind if I popped in to see Buttons again, before Joe and Alice return?" Mr Wilkins asked as they returned to the house. "I'm very fond of her, you know. In fact, I would have taken her in myself if I wasn't out all day at work."

"Please come and visit her any time you like," said Mrs Parker.

"I will then. Thank you!" Mr Wilkins said, waving as he got into his car.

"Well, hopefully that's one problem solved," said Neil's mum as they watched Mr Wilkins drive off.

A quick check on Buttons after dinner showed Neil that the little dog was indeed her old self again. She was running round her exercise pen, tossing and chasing an old rubber bone that her owners had left with her. She ran to the fence, barking, when she saw Neil, and wagged her tail happily.

"Attagirl, Buttons. You've really cheered up now, haven't you?" Neil said, crouching down and poking his fingers through the fence to be licked.

"Sure has!" said his father, behind him. "Eaten all her dinner, too."

"Great!" said Neil. "I'm just going to say goodnight to Dotty."

"Be quick," added his father. "I'll be locking up in five minutes."

The Dalmatian trotted over as Neil approached her pen. She nuzzled his fingers and pawed at the chainlink fence, asking to be let out.

"Oh, Dotty," he said, stroking her head. "I'd love to take you home. But you'll have to be patient. It's not going to be quite so easy getting your problem fixed!"

7

Neil took Dotty through her paces at his father's obedience class on Wednesday, and then gave her extra lessons by himself every night. He took Sam with him to these sessions, to set Dotty an example and help her to socialize sensibly with another dog. To his delight, the two dogs soon became good friends and Dotty enjoyed copying Sam as Neil put them through the basic exercises.

It was tiring work.

It meant patiently repeating and repeating simple commands until Dotty did what he wanted, and always rewarding and praising her when she got it right.

He couldn't overlook his other chores and homework, either.

Emily sometimes kept them company,

admiring Neil's calm determination and Dotty's willingness to please him. Neil never got cross with her.

By Sunday morning Dotty was beginning to show signs of real improvement.

"What do you think, Dad?" Neil asked before lunch that day. He had just demonstrated how Dotty would sit on command and come when he called her.

Mr Parker smiled down at the dog nosing in Neil's pocket, looking for a treat. "She's doing great. And so are you, Neil. Don't tire yourself out, though."

"Don't worry. We're going to train Sam for the show now." Neil grinned as his father rolled his eyes. "Can I take Dotty over too? She learns a lot from watching Sam at work."

"That's fine. Just don't let her run loose, will you?"

"I won't!" Neil clipped a strong lead to her collar. "Come on, Dotty! Let's go!"

Emily was already in the field with Sam, setting out the Agility course as before. She looked up and smiled when she heard Dotty barking and came over to fuss her. Sam joined them, wagging his tail happily at Dotty.

How different the two dogs were, thought Neil. Dotty was taller and sleeker than Sam with her smooth, short fur and boisterous, playful personality. Sam was an older dog, steady and reliable, with a long glossy coat. He might have been a little jealous at first of all the attention Dotty was getting from Neil, but he had soon got over it.

Neil handed Dotty's lead to his sister. "Here, you hang on to her while I put Sam through his paces."

Emily led the Dalmatian away and they sat together in the grass to watch as Sam ran around the course, jumping over the hurdles, through a tyre, weaving in and out of posts and running up and down planks. He particularly loved the tunnel, barking excitedly as he ran through. He seemed to know exactly what to do and completed the makeshift course in no time.

"Terrific!" Emily clapped her hands enthusiastically. "Well done, Sam!"

Dotty barked and stood up, looking eagerly at the course.

"I think Dotty wants to have a go," called Emily. "Shall we let her?"

Neil looked at the Dalmatian struggling to come across and join him.

"OK, give her a go, but keep her on the lead, Em," Neil agreed. "Let's see what she can do!"

As soon as they reached the first jump, Dotty sailed over it in one graceful leap.

"Wow! Look at that!" exclaimed Emily, running hard to keep up. "Dotty's a natural!"

Neil watched as the Dalmatian raced through the course. She had to run around some of the obstacles because Emily had her lead in a firm

grip, but she cleared every jump. Sam stood watching her, barking his approval.

"Neil, I've got a brilliant idea!" Emily said excitedly.

Neil groaned. Emily's brilliant ideas often meant trouble. "I don't think I want to hear this, do I?"

"Yes, you do. Listen. Why don't we train Dotty and enter her in the show as well as Sam?"

"Why?"

"If she does well," his sister continued, "Mr and Mrs Hamley will be able to see how well trained she is, and they'll be so proud, they're bound to want to keep her. What do you think?"

Neil shook his head. "We can't do that! Dotty would never be good enough in time. The show is next week."

"She would if we worked with her every night. And it might be Dotty's only chance to go back home," Emily pointed out.

Neil thought about it. It wouldn't be too difficult for him to enter two dogs for the competition – he and Emily could share the extra registration fee – and he remembered only too well Dotty's sad face and pitiful whining when Mr Hamley had walked away after his visit yesterday. If there was a chance of helping her go back home again he had to take it.

"OK," he decided. "But we'll have to ask Dad. He may not agree."

"There's only one way to find out. Let's take the dogs back and ask him."

They found their father in his office, frowning over some papers. He listened as Neil and Emily eagerly outlined their plan. Then he shook his head.

"Sorry, kids, it's a nice idea, but it wouldn't work," he said. "Dotty isn't our dog. We would need to get Mr Hamley's permission before entering her in a show. And what if she runs off? She'd be the responsibility of King Street Kennels and it wouldn't look very good for us if she behaved badly."

"I'll train her to manage it," Neil insisted. "I can do it."

"I know you'll try, Neil. You've worked wonders with Sam. But Dotty's different. She's not a young puppy like Sam was – she's much harder to train. It's too risky. Sorry, but I have to say no."

"But, Dad . . ."

"I'm sorry, Neil. Come on, take Dotty back to her pen, please. She could probably do with a drink of water and a rest now."

Neil and Emily turned away, disappointed.

"Well, I guess that's it," said Emily as they walked away. "Dad sounded pretty serious."

"Never mind, we'll still keep working with you, Dotty," Neil said, stroking her. "We'll show your owners what you can do, eh?"

"If they don't sell her first," Emily reminded him. "I don't think they'll have any trouble selling such a beautiful Dalmatian. Do you think Mr Hamley's advertised her yet?"

Neil hadn't thought of that. Emily was right. Dotty would be a prize catch for the right kind of owner. "I think he'd tell Dad if he had. Besides, people would have to come to the kennels to see her, wouldn't they?"

"Oh, yes. I hadn't thought of that." Emily nodded. "C'mon, I'll take Sam back while you see to Dotty."

After Neil had settled Dotty in her kennel he hurried over to the rescue centre to look in on Sandy.

Neil had been taking him a biscuit every day and to his delight the dog had started to respond. He no longer growled when he saw Neil, although he still watched warily from the corner of the pen and wouldn't touch anything Neil left until he had moved well back.

Today, Sandy was lying in his basket. He sat up and silently watched Neil approach, but made no other attempt to move.

"Hello, Sandy," Neil said softly, pleased with Sandy's response. If he could just get him to trust people again, there might be a chance of finding him a good home.

After school the next day, Neil and Emily cycled down into Compton to the newsagent's to see how many sponsors had signed their form. It had been displayed for over a week now and they were hoping for a good response.

"Hi, Neil, Emily," said Tom cheerily as they walked in. Tom was Mrs Smedley's son and a student at college. He helped out at the newsagent's whenever he could. "What can I get for you?"

"We wondered if anyone had signed our sponsor form," Neil told him.

"I'll say they have. Just look at this!" Tom grinned and showed them the form. It was almost full. "Bring another form down and I bet we'll get that filled up too before the show."

"Actually," Emily said with a straight face, pulling a sponsor form from her pocket and flattening it out on the counter, "I just happen to have one on me."

Tom laughed aloud and Neil smiled. Trust Emily to come prepared!

They called for Chris on the way home. He answered his front door wearing very muddy football kit which had once been black and white.

Neil looked him up and down with a raised eyebrow.

"You up for a training session with Sam, then?" he asked his friend. "You look as if Dotty's been walking all over you!"

"Funny!" Chris replied drily. "Let me get

changed first. I've just got back from football practice."

"I'd never have guessed!"

Half an hour later they were all in the field with Sam. As usual, the clever dog completed the Agility course with flying colours, still enjoying it all hugely despite the number of times he had been through it.

"Wow! Look at him go!" Chris yelled, whooping with delight.

"Way to go, Sam!" Neil said, making a big fuss of him.

"I bet he's the fastest dog in the show!" said Chris. "And the cleverest!"

"'Course he is, aren't you, Sam?" said Emily. Sam barked his agreement and they all laughed.

"How's Dotty's training coming on?" asked Chris.

"She sits and comes on command now," Neil told him proudly. "Let's take Sam back and I'll show you."

Dotty was in her outside run. She came bounding in when she saw Chris and Neil enter the pen.

She barked excitedly, raced over to them and went to jump up at them.

"No, Dotty. Sit!" Neil told her firmly.

Dotty sat obediently, but quivered with excitement and wagged her tail furiously. It was hard for Neil not to laugh, she looked so comical.

Chris was not so restrained. "She'll fall over in a minute!" he laughed.

"Good girl," Neil said, fussing her. "Now, stay!"

Dotty sat still, not moving a muscle, but watching Neil intently as he backed away from her – alert for his next signal.

"Come, Dotty! Here, girl!"

Dotty charged over to sit at his feet, waiting to be praised.

Chris looked really impressed. "I can hardly believe she's the same dog," he said. "Old Smiler's going to be surprised."

Neil told his friend how he and Emily had wanted to put Dotty in the show as well as Sam. "Dad said we can't. He's worried Dotty might run off or something."

"That's a real shame," said Chris. "Any chance he might change his mind?

"Not a hope," Neil told him. "When Dad says no, he means it."

After Chris had gone, Neil made his regular trip to see Sandy. To his surprise, Sandy jumped out of his basket and ran over to the fence, barking and wagging his tail. Neil was delighted.

"Sandy! Hey there, feller! You look pleased to see me."

Sandy cocked his head expectantly at Neil.

"So, you want a treat?" Neil asked, reaching in his pocket.

"Hold on, let's go into the pen to give him that. I'd like to see how he reacts."

Neil turned around to see his father standing by him.

"Dad! I didn't know you were here."

"I was cleaning out one of the other pens when I heard you come in," said Mr Parker. He opened Sandy's pen. "Now make sure you go in quietly and slowly," he told Neil.

Sandy backed away a little and watched them warily as Neil stepped inside.

"Come on, Sandy. Good boy." Neil held

out a biscuit and put it on the floor by his feet.

Sandy hesitated for a moment before running over and snatching it up. He came over to Neil and nudged his hand.

"Want some more, do you?" Neil laughed softly, reaching out to stroke Sandy's head.

Sandy flinched and stiffened for a moment, then started to lick Neil's hand.

"Look, Dad. He trusts me!" Neil said, overjoyed. "He isn't growling any more."

"So I see," said Mr Parker. "You've done a

good job, Neil. He's nowhere near as receptive to Kate. And you know how good she is with the dogs."

As they left the centre, Neil told his father how he'd been to see Sandy every day, giving him treats and gradually building up his trust. "I just wanted him to know that not everyone is going to ill-treat him," he said.

"And you've succeeded," his father said. "Well done! I thought Sandy was settling down a bit, but I didn't realize it was thanks so much to your efforts. I had a call this morning from someone looking for a new dog but I didn't think Sandy would be right for them. A family over in Padsham. They have a son your age. I'm thinking now that maybe I can help them after all."

"Sandy might have a new home?" Neil was pleased that this was one story that was going to have a quick, happy ending. "Brilliant!"

"You've certainly got your dad's way with dogs, Neil," said Carole Parker that evening as they prepared to eat their meal.

"I know," Emily agreed. "He can get them to

do anything. I bet he could train Dotty to do the Agility course in no time." She cast a sly glance at her father who had just entered the kitchen with a printed leaflet in his hand.

"What's this? You're putting Dotty in the show?" her mother asked.

Bob Parker took his time before answering.

"Is there some problem, Bob?" asked Carole, suspecting something was amiss.

"I've found the entry form at last for the show," he replied heavily, looking apologetically across at Neil.

"What's the matter, Dad?" asked Neil, a feeling of dread creeping over him.

"Well, the last date for registration forms and fees is the day after tomorrow. That's all right – I know the secretary of the show and I can drop it round to his house. The problem is, all dogs have to be registered with the Kennel Club before they can enter."

He waited for his news to sink in.

"Kennel Club?" asked Neil, not understanding. "But Sam's a rescue dog, not a pedigree."

"It doesn't matter. He has to have a Kennel

Club name and a number before he can enter an Agility contest. It's the rule, Neil."

"Does that mean he'll never be able to compete?" Emily asked.

"No. We can get him registered. But it will take time, and we don't have long enough before this county show. He'll have to wait until the next one. I'm sorry, son."

"Poor Sam," said Sarah. "Will Fudge have to have a number, too?"

"No, dear," her mother reassured her quietly. "Fudge is going to be in a different competition."

Neil stared miserably at the kitchen table, not really listening. All his hopes were squashed. All Sam's training for nothing.

"I suppose we'll have to cancel the sponsorship and everything," said Emily.

An atmosphere of gloom settled over them all.

"Well, maybe not," said Mr Parker slowly. "I've been thinking about your idea of putting Dotty in for the Agility competition, Emily, and I reckon it might be possible after all."

"Dad, that's brilliant!" Emily squealed.

Neil looked across at his father, wondering.

"Your idea got me thinking, so I took the liberty of asking Paul Hamley to send over copies of her registration forms and pedigree. It did occur to me that she might not be old enough to compete." He turned to the others to explain. "Dogs have to be at least eighteen months old to take part in Agility competitions – the course is too demanding for younger dogs. Anyway, it turns out Dotty is just eighteen months old and she *is* registered with the Kennel Club, so she qualifies on both counts."

"Yeah! Magic!" yelled Emily, who had always thought her idea was brilliant.

"But what about the Hamleys, Dad?" Neil asked. He couldn't believe the problem could be solved so simply.

"Well, they did take some convincing, I admit," replied his father, "but Paul has given his permission on the understanding that King Street Kennels takes full responsibility for the whole thing – and pays the fee, of course!"

They all laughed. But Neil didn't know what to think. He was desperately disappointed about

Sam being disqualified, but this new development meant that Dotty might get a chance of being reunited with the Hamleys. And Neil would still get to take part in his first Agility competition – something he had really been looking forward to.

"You've worked wonders with Sandy, Neil," Mr Parker said. "I'm impressed."

Neil went slightly red.

"I think you deserve a chance to work with Dotty. And I think it's just the kind of character reference Dotty needs, too, if the Hamleys are to give her a second chance."

"You mean it, Dad?" Neil asked. "We can really enter Dotty in the show?"

Their father nodded. "On condition that her training continues under my supervision and according to my instructions. OK?"

"OK, Dad," Neil promised. Getting Dotty trained was too important to mess up. He was going to do everything properly and show Mr and Mrs Hamley just what an obedient dog Dotty could be. "So where's this entry form?"

8

Neil's first task as soon as he and Emily arrived home from school the next day was to fill in Sam's registration form for the Kennel Club. He had to think of three names for him, so that the Kennel Club could choose one not already in use. Although Emily begged him, he refused to let her see what he had put.

The second task was to start Dotty's training. Sam and Emily came along as well.

Dotty watched, barking encouragement as Sam ran round the course first.

"She's dead keen! Look!" Emily said.

Neil called Sam over and commanded him to lie down. Then he took Dotty to the starting point and released her.

As soon as she was off her lead, the Dalmatian ignored the jumps and sprinted across the field, bounding playfully in the long grass and barking at Sam. Emily put up a hand to show Sam he was to stay.

Neil felt a stab of fear as he saw Dotty running around so wildly. He called her back.

She did not respond the first time, but at the second command she obediently trotted over to him.

"Good girl!" he praised her with considerable relief. He took her back to the start of the course.

"Go, Dotty! Go!" he shouted.

He ran alongside her, getting her to stop at every obstacle so he could show her what to do. Dotty had no trouble with the jumps but was confused by the planks – the "dog walk" as they were called – and kept jumping off them. Neil made sure they finished the course with a jump so he could praise her lavishly.

Emily, however, looked anxious. For the first time she was having doubts about what they were doing. "Do you think you'll get her trained in time? The show's on Saturday."

"I think so. If I work with her every night this week, she should pick it up. She's got to."

"I just hope Mr Hamley doesn't come to visit while we're practising," Emily said as she took Dotty back to her pen. "She'd forget what she was doing."

"He usually comes after dinner, Em. So if we keep working with Dotty straight after school, we should be OK."

"How's Dotty?" asked Carole Parker on Thursday evening, as she worked at the computer. Neil and Emily were in the office, helping their mother file paperwork. Sarah was building a paper clip mountain.

"We had to get Sam to go along the dog walk three times first," said Neil, "and I went along it myself before Dotty got the hang of what to do. I'm just glad I didn't have to show her how to jump through the tyre!"

"She kept jumping off too soon," Emily explained.

"Huh! Climbing isn't hard. Fudge can do that," Sarah piped up. "He climbs up his ladder and he goes in and out of his tubes. He'd come first in any Agility course."

"I'm sure he would, Sarah," said Carole. "But training Dotty is a bit special. It sounds to me as if you are both doing extremely well." She smiled over at them. "Keep it up, kids."

Neil and Emily grinned. A little encouragement helped a lot.

"But what if the Hamleys don't come to the show?" Emily asked suddenly. "What do we do then?"

"They'll be there," her mother assured her. She hit a button on the computer keyboard. The nearby printer buzzed into life and began to churn out a copy of her document. "Rachel Hamley told me she wants to watch a friend in one of the horse-riding events."

"So they're bound to come and watch the Agility competition, aren't they?" said Neil. "Especially after Mr Hamley's sponsored our entry."

"He has?" said Mrs Parker, wide-eyed with surprise.

"I just hope Dotty doesn't let us down," said Emily.

"So do I," said Neil. He didn't want to

think how angry his teacher would be if Dotty misbehaved and their whole plan backfired.

Chris called round after dinner for a game of football.

"Let's get Dotty to join in too," said Neil. "She's been working really hard. I'm sure she'd enjoy a bit of fun."

Dotty wasn't sure what to do at first, but she ran around enthusiastically, trying to get the ball and tangling herself in everyone's legs. It was a trick Sam soon learned too. He took fiendish delight in tripping them up. No one was spared.

Tired of being outsmarted by dogs, Chris cheated by picking up the ball and running with it towards the goal.

"Sam!" Neil shouted. "Tackle the ball!"

The Border collie ran like a rocket in front of Chris, making him trip and drop the ball.

Chris tried to call "Foul!" but was laughing too hard.

Sam stole the ball away from him, started to push it over to Neil, who was yelling encouragement, but lost it to Emily, who kicked it away. The ball went shooting over the field towards Dotty, with Sam in hot pursuit.

Both dogs raced after the ball. Dotty had a longer stride than Sam, though, and reached it first. Determined not to let Sam steal it, she picked it up in her mouth and ran back triumphantly with it to Neil, dropping it at his feet.

Then she wagged her tail, looking very pleased with herself, as if to say, "How about a reward?"

Emily, Chris and Neil collapsed in the grass, laughing and gasping.

"Well, that's one way of getting the ball!" Neil said when he could speak at last.

"I don't think Dotty is cut out for football, somehow!" laughed Chris, still trying to get his breath back. "She doesn't appreciate the finer points of the rules, does she, Sam?"

"Look who's talking!" scoffed Neil, and the game degenerated into a wrestling match, involving them all.

"Do you think she's ready, Neil?" asked Emily on Friday evening. They'd set off with Dotty for her last training lesson in the field.

"Well, we won't be able to tell until the real thing," Neil told her. "She's been doing well on our home-made course, but who knows what she'll do with all those people watching and a different course to follow."

Emily watched anxiously as Neil took Dotty round the course once more. The Dalmatian seemed to have no trouble now with any of the obstacles.

"She's done it! She's done it!" Emily clapped excitedly as Dotty completed her first clear round in excellent time.

"Good girl, Dotty! I knew you could do it."

Neil beamed with pleasure as he hugged the Dalmatian.

Dotty licked him happily.

He looked up to see his dad and Kate standing at the gate, watching.

"What do you think, Dad?" Neil called over to his father.

"Terrific. Both of you! All of you!"

Neil and Emily grinned. Sam wagged his tail.

"I'll just take her through it one more time," said Neil.

To his immense relief and satisfaction, Dotty completed another clear round, to enthusiastic applause from her small audience.

"She's so good. Any chance she might win?" Emily asked.

"It depends a lot on what it's like tomorrow and the other competitors. I just want her to get round without too many penalties – or being eliminated," Neil told her. "That's what she's sponsored to do and that will show Mr and Mrs Hamley that she can be really obedient."

Neil and Emily crossed their fingers. The rest was up to Dotty now.

When they returned to the kennels, they found Mr and Mrs Timms had arrived to pick up Buttons. The little dog had settled down really well but she was overjoyed to see her owners again. She bounded over to them, wagging her tail and whimpering with excitement.

"Hello, Buttons! We've really missed you." Alice Timms smiled as the little dog jumped up at her, licking her excitedly and then jumping up at Joe.

"Look how pleased she is to see us!" said Mr Timms as they both fussed their happy little dog.

They were both surprised to see the old cardigan in her basket until Mr Parker explained why it was there.

"We're really grateful to you for looking after her so well," said Mrs Timms.

It was great to see Buttons so happy again. Neil gave her a big goodbye hug before helping Joe and Alice put the little dog and her basket into the back of their car. He was very glad everything had worked out so well.

Looking up as he walked back into the house,

Neil saw his mother watching from the window. He could tell by the expression on her face that something was wrong.

"What's up, Mum?" he asked anxiously as he walked inside.

"Mr Hamley's just phoned," she said. "I'm afraid he's found a new owner for Dotty. It's an old university friend of his who lives in London. He's bringing him to see her on Sunday."

Neil looked at her in dismay. *In London? That's miles away,* he thought. He'd never see Dotty again.

Everything hinged on the show, now. It was the only chance he had to prove to his teacher that Dotty was worth keeping.

9

"Just look at all these people! Where have they all come from?" said Emily, as they walked through the gates into the already crowded showground.

They had come early, so that Neil could report to the Agility ring in order to walk the course with the other competitors before the main crowds arrived.

It was a fine morning, promising to be a good day for the show.

Scores of people were setting up stalls and attractions, or delivering their livestock for judging later in the day. There was even a group of country dancers going through their routine.

"The county show is always popular," said Mr Parker. "It's not just local people who attend. They come from miles around, especially for the horse-riding events."

"I hope Fudge doesn't mind being kept awake," said Sarah, carrying his cage carefully in front of her with both hands.

Now that he was here, Neil was feeling decidedly nervous. Hundreds of butterflies were rising in his stomach.

"I hope we don't meet the Hamleys before our dog event starts," said Neil. "They might upset Dotty."

"Don't worry," his dad reassured him. "I know they're only coming for a short time today. The equestrian event they want to see isn't until late morning. I doubt Rachel will want to walk around too much in her condition."

"I'm glad I'm looking after Sam," said Emily,

glancing at the Border collie walking obediently by her side. "Dotty looks like she's going to run off any minute."

"I'll have to leave Dotty with you, Dad, while I walk the course," Neil pointed out.

"I reckon I can manage that," said his father, smiling.

Dotty was so excited by all the people and noise that she was pulling at her lead, eager to go off and explore.

Neil brought her to heel firmly.

The Dalmatian slowed her pace and walked quietly beside him.

"Good girl!" said Neil.

Mr Parker glanced at his watch. "We'd best get over to the ring."

"I'll take Sarah to enter Fudge in the Cleverest Pet competition," said Mrs Parker. "It's due to start soon in the big marquee."

"Right. We'll join you as soon as we can," her husband said. "Good luck, Sarah!"

"Yeah, good luck, Squirt!" Neil and Emily waved as their mother and sister hurried towards the marquee.

They turned a corner at the end of the display stalls and Neil's heart sank with dismay.

Part of the showground had been fenced off for the Agility course and Neil could see immediately that it was going to be a lot tougher than their homely arrangements of bits and pieces in the field. For a start the colours leapt out. Several items had large yellow squares on them. Contact points, he remembered. They hadn't used them at home. Too late to worry about them now.

The steward of the course was walking towards them.

He checked Dotty's details on his list. In view of Neil's age and Dotty's inexperience he entered them in the Junior category.

This was good in one respect – the course was simpler and they had a longer time limit – but it worked against them in another. The Junior event was open to anyone 12 years old and under, whether they were new to the competition or not.

Neil and Dotty could find themselves competing against a handler and dog with many competitions – and prizes – to their credit already. It was not a comforting thought.

While Emily and his father waited with the dogs, Neil followed the steward into the arena where several other competitors had already assembled.

The steward was brisk, reminding them all of the competition rules as they walked the course; what caused penalty points; what would get their dog eliminated. It was daunting for Neil. After all, up to now the training with Dotty and Sam had been rather like a shared game. This was definitely the real thing.

They began at the first jump – which because of its colour and the shrubs decorating each side seemed much larger than their practice jumps. There were two lyres: one like a 'lollipop' on a pole, and another suspended inside a wooden frame, making it look smaller than it was. Fortunately Dotty would only need to jump through one of them, being a Junior.

There were two tunnels. A rigid one like their empty barrel, but also a long, collapsed one made of bright blue PVC.

Neil viewed it all with growing dismay.

"My Skip just loves these tunnels!" said a strident, confident voice beside him. Neil looked up into the face of an older boy wearing a bright sweatshirt with *Bingley Dog Agility Team* emblazoned across it.

"You've obviously done all this before," Neil said bleakly.

"Oh, yes. Since I was seven. I've trained four dogs so far, but Skip's the most promising. He's already got six silver trophies."

"Which class will you be in?"

"Veterans. We get the worst time handicap, unfortunately," said the boy. "Your first time?"

"Yes."

"Well, the trick is not to agitate your dog just because you're terrified. Let him go. They're not as bothered by all this as we are. Good luck!"

"Thanks," said Neil. At least Dotty didn't have to compete against Skip.

They were just passing the see-saw, with its bright patches of yellow at each end. The steward was reminding them that their dog must touch the yellow contact points or be awarded a five-second penalty.

Then the weave. Dogs must work from right to left.

Here was the dog walk: a long plank up, then a bridge across two piles of bricks and a long ramp down the other side. Contact points at each end. It looked huge.

Neil felt his mouth going dry. How could he have imagined being able to put Dotty through this – or even Sam?

The steward had stopped by a low table with a yellow square at its centre.

"Your dog must jump on to this square and stay in the down position until the judge gives you the sign to carry on. Failure to stay down will result in a penalty . . ."

How long would Dotty have to stay down? She'd never manage it, Neil thought grimly. She just couldn't sit still for long.

The steward was talking again.

". . . and the course time for the Junior class is sixty seconds."

Sixty seconds! Neil groaned to himself. Maybe he should withdraw his entry now and avoid the humiliation of the mess he was going to make of all this.

*

Neil walked the Junior course one more time and then went dispiritedly to find his father and Emily.

"What do you think, Neil?" asked Mr Parker, seeing his son's white, troubled face.

"If I'd known how awful it was going to be, I'd never have started this. I'll never get Dotty round it. Certainly not in the time." He absently patted the dogs, who sensed his worry.

"It does look a bit . . . horrible," Emily admitted, looking over at the arena.

"Now, don't despair before you've even had a go," said his dad. "This is a first time for both of you. You both need the experience. Dotty needs to show what she can do, and you need it to help Sam on his career. That is, if you want to go on with it."

"'Course I do!"

"Well, then, just do your best and let Dotty do hers! The Agility competition doesn't start for another hour," said Mr Parker, "so let's go and see how Sarah's getting on with Fudge."

"Can we have a look round the stalls too?" asked Emily.

Mr Parker nodded. "But after the marquee," he said. "We don't want to miss the pet show."

They were just in time to see Fudge awarded a rosette for second prize. Sarah was delighted. She ran over to them, waving the rosette happily. Carole Parker was behind her, carrying the hamster cage.

"Fudge was really good," Sarah said. "I put a chocolate drop on the roof of his house and he climbed up and got it. Then he went through a tube to get another chocolate drop and he stood up at the bars to beg for more. Everyone thought he was really cute. That parrot only won because it could talk!"

A reporter was trying to take a photo of a lanky youth holding a colourful parrot. Neil laughed as the parrot flapped its wings and yelled at the reporter to "scram".

"I'd like a pet that talks," said Sarah, feeling just a tiny bit jealous of the attention the parrot was getting. "D'you think I could teach Fudge to talk, Mum?"

"I'm afraid not, Sarah." Her mother smiled. "Let's go and put Fudge in the car. He could do with a sleep after all that excitement." She and Sarah walked off towards the car park.

"Well, let's see if Dotty can beat Fudge's success," Mr Parker said to Neil and Emily. "Come on, there's just time for a quick look round the stalls before the big event."

Neil felt too nervous to join them.

"I'll go back with Dotty and watch the early events," he said. "The Junior competition doesn't come until the end." He left Emily, Sam and his father heading for the long rows of stalls and displays.

The Veteran class had already started in the Agility arena. As Neil arrived he saw a German shepherd run into the ring with the boy he had met earlier.

"Please give a warm welcome to John Anderson and Skip!" boomed the loudspeaker.

The crowd applauded noisily.

The boy was right, thought Neil. Skip was a real pro. He shot round the obstacles like a bullet, enjoying every minute. He needed no encouragement to push his nose under the collapsed tunnel and worm his way through to the other side. John yelled at Skip to stay down on the table, but his dog was so excited that he jumped off before the judge gave the signal, which earned him a penalty. His total time was forty-five seconds.

Neil whistled softly in admiration. The course time for Veterans was fifty.

He stayed by the rail with Dotty standing patiently beside him, watching the other experienced competitors take their turns. They weren't all as good as Skip by any means, and as Neil watched, caught up with the exhilaration of seeing dogs working so brilliantly, he could feel his earlier panic easing.

Some of the dogs had a real problem with the tyres. That hole in the centre must look very small to them, Neil figured. Others disliked the see-saw and jumped off the end before it touched the ground, missing the contact point.

In the Novice class, a golden retriever ran around the posts instead of weaving in and out of them. Another dog took two obstacles in the wrong order, so was eliminated.

"Just do your best, Dotty," Neil said softly to

the Dalmatian. She looked up at him and wagged her tail.

The rest of his family joined him at the rail. If they thought his task was impossible, no one mentioned it. Neil suspected that his dad had briefed them all in his absence.

"Oh, look at that dog!" said Sarah, pointing to the rough-coated collie-cross currently running around the course. The animal showed no inclination at all to tackle any of the obstacles properly, but took them at random, inviting his owner to play when she started to get cross and shout at him to come to heel. Despite being eliminated early on, the dog led his owner and the stewards a merry chase before they could catch him.

The crowd was delighted. It was good to have a clown amongst all the serious professionals. Neil couldn't help wondering whether Dotty would behave the same way.

"I haven't seen the Hamleys yet, and it's almost Dotty's turn," said Emily. "What if they don't come?"

"I'm sure they will," said Mr Parker.

But they still hadn't arrived when the Junior event was announced.

Neil couldn't help feeling relieved. Maybe it was best that they didn't see the mess he was going to make of the course. His stomach felt queasy, his palms cold and sticky.

"And now, ladies and gentlemen, we have the Junior event . . ." came the crackly announcement.

This was it. Was Dotty going to behave herself?

The first entry was a black Labrador. He had a clear round in sixty-two seconds.

Neil didn't have time to consider what that might mean.

"And now for Neil Parker from King Street Kennels with his Dalmatian – Dotty, the Puppy Patrol dog!" said the announcer jovially.

"Good luck, Neil!" said Emily as she patted him on the back.

"Come on, Dotty, we're on!" said Neil. As he led the Dalmatian into the ring there was a round of applause. The whistle went and Neil released Dotty's collar.

"Go, Dotty! *Go!*"

*

Over the first jump went the Dalmatian.

"Good girl, Dotty," said Neil, running alongside her.

Up the ramp, along the top. Down the ramp – "Wait, Dotty!" – touch the yellow square. Off to the next.

Into the rigid tunnel – and out.

"Good girl, Dotty!"

Over another jump.

On to the see-saw. Down the other side. Touch the yellow square again.

Weave through the posts. "Careful, careful! Good girl!"

Neil was dimly aware of the crowd shouting encouragement, but he was so absorbed in keeping up with Dotty that his mind could focus on nothing else. Despite his own nerves, he drew some comfort from the fact that Dotty was really enjoying herself. She was obviously loving every minute, showing off what she did best.

She wasn't even fazed by the loudspeakers and their running commentary. How many penalties did she have? Had they followed the right order? Neil couldn't tell. He just wanted to get them both round.

The low table was the last obstacle.

Dotty almost overshot the yellow square, but Neil managed to yell *"Down!"* in time to stop her jumping off the other side. She obediently dropped like a stone and waited for his command to go.

Seconds ticked by. Neil willed the judge to signal before Dotty grew impatient, but just as the hand dropped, fate stepped in and snatched away his victory.

Like some weird nightmare in slow motion, Neil saw Dotty lift up her head towards the crowd. She stood up on the table, as if to get a better view, and before he could say "No!" she was off, galloping away into the crowd of people around the arena.

There were gasps of dismay from the watching crowd.

"Oh dear! Dotty's decided to take off," said the announcer. "What a shame. She was making such good time!"

Neil sprinted after her, calling desperately and deaf to sounds around him.

But Dotty ignored him.

He couldn't believe it. What had got into her?

But Dotty knew exactly what she was doing. Neil heard her barking with delight, and saw her jumping up at a pretty dark-haired lady, obviously expecting a baby very soon, and a man who seemed just as delighted to see Dotty as the dog was to see him.

Mr Hamley and his wife. So that was it. Neil should have known.

"Hello, sir," said Neil, breathing heavily from the chase. "I'm sorry."

Mr Hamley looked up from fussing Dotty and smiled rather ruefully at Neil.

"Hello, Neil. This is my wife, Rachel." Neil shook hands politely with Mrs Hamley. "You don't have to apologize. I had a feeling Dotty might do something like this, which is why we both kept a low profile. Not low enough, I'm afraid."

"But we did see how well she performed before she saw us, Neil," said Rachel, smiling. "She looked as if she was having the time of her life!"

"Yes, I think she was," Neil admitted. "It was me that was scared rigid!"

"I'm not surprised," said Mr Hamley, showing a rare touch of sympathy for Neil. "That course looked horrendous to me. You've done a brilliant job getting her this far."

Hope soared in Neil. Maybe it had all been worthwhile after all. He looked at Mr Hamley with shining eyes.

Dotty sensed something exciting and jumped up at Mr Hamley.

"No, Dotty, down!" he said anxiously.

Mr Hamley's jaw dropped in astonishment

as Dotty promptly lay down at his feet, tongue lolling and tail wagging.

Just at that moment the Parkers arrived.

"You OK, Neil?" asked Mr Parker. "Well, hello, Paul. And this must be Rachel. How do you do?"

Introductions were made, and it was decided that they should all go and get some refreshments before any more serious discussions took place.

Over their cups of tea and coffee, Mr Parker explained everything to the Hamleys, in particular his children's concern that Dotty would have to go away to a strange new home.

"I guessed much of that, Bob," Mr Hamley admitted. "I could tell from the short time I've known Neil that his dogs are the most important things in his life and that he had grown very attached to Dotty. It didn't take much imagination to realize that your son would want to do the very best for her, and try and get Rachel and me to change our minds."

Neil's cheeks burned. Had it been so obvious? Neil stroked Dotty's head and couldn't speak.

He sensed what Mr Hamley was going to say next.

"Rachel and I are delighted Dotty has turned into such a lovely dog, but we can't alter our decision. It does mean, though, that she can go to her new home and we won't be worried all the time that she will be a nuisance. My friend Robert is coming up to collect Dotty tomorrow, so you'll be able to meet him and give him advice on how best to look after her."

Their plan had failed.

10

"Well, I guess that's it," Neil said sadly as the Hamleys left in the direction of the car park. He couldn't remember ever feeling this bad. "Can we go home now, Dad?"

The show was over as far as he and Dotty were concerned. All he wanted was to get back to King Street with her and Sam and make the most of the few hours they had left together. He'd probably never see her again.

Mr Parker nodded and placed his arm reassuringly around Neil's shoulder. "You did your best, Neil. It's not your fault it didn't work out."

Suddenly, someone pushed past, almost knocking them over. Neil struggled to keep his balance and his grip on Dotty's lead. The dogs barked furiously.

"Stop that thief!" a woman screamed from the crowd nearby. "He's got my bag!"

Neil turned round to see a young man sprinting off, a black handbag tucked under his arm. He was running through gaps in the crowds and heading towards one of the exit gates.

"Stop him! Thief!" the woman shouted hysterically.

A couple of men gave chase, but the thief had a good head start. He was going to get away.

Suddenly Neil heard Emily's determined voice behind him.

"Tackle the ball, Sam!" she yelled, sending the collie away from her. "Get the ball!"

Sam took off in pursuit like a streak of lightning.

Emily ran after him, shouting encouragement, and Neil, with his wits restored, followed with Dotty streaking along beside him, barking furiously.

Sam wove through the crowd, ignoring the shouts and yells, barking as he pursued his quarry.

The thief heard Sam and looked over his shoulder. Panic seized him when he saw the collie racing towards him and he quickly ran through the gate leading to the car park, slamming it shut behind him.

Sam cleared the gate in one easy bound.

Neil felt his lungs burning as he and Dotty ran faster and faster. They had overtaken Emily, who had been caught up in the crowd, and Neil was in time to see Sam fly over the gate. He was just close enough to witness Sam's party trick.

The collie shot in front of the startled thief, neatly tripping him up, and snatched the "ball" which fell from the youth's grasp. Without a second thought, Sam turned and leapt back over the gate with the bag in his mouth and ran to meet Neil with it. He dropped the bag at Neil's feet and backed away, barking, asking to play again.

Dotty leapt around with excitement, trying to snatch the bag herself. Fortunately, Emily arrived, very out of breath, and picked it up out of harm's way.

The dazed thief scrambled in the dirt to get up and escape, but as two security men from the car park opened the gate, Dotty ran past them and jumped up at the thief. As the man staggered backwards, wasting valuable seconds, he was grabbed by the men from security.

Neil was quick to control the excited dog. "Down, Dotty!" he ordered firmly.

The Dalmatian obeyed immediately and dropped down on all fours.

Neil knelt down and smothered Dotty and Sam with hugs and praise, digging in his pocket for a couple of biscuits as reward, while Emily returned the handbag to its delighted owner.

"Oh, thank you. Thank you," said the woman,

clutching the bag to her chest. "What marvellous dogs you have! I'm so grateful. Wait till my husband hears about this!" She gave Sam and Dotty a pat, too.

There was quite a crowd around them now, eager to see and stroke the two dogs. Neil was bursting with pride, but felt a bit overwhelmed by all the attention. He was relieved to see his father and mother, with Sarah, making their way through the crowd towards him.

"Well done, both of you. That was quick thinking, Emily!" said Mr Parker. "And well done, Sam!" He stroked the dog gently. "Good dog."

Emily beamed with pleasure.

"You should have seen Sam go!" she said. "It's all those football matches we've played! They were *both* so fab."

The reporter Neil had seen earlier at the pet show ran over to them. "This is going to make a great story," he said. "Let's get a shot of you and your sister with your dogs."

The reporter took his photographs and then asked them questions, writing their answers swiftly in his notebook. He was interested to hear that Mr and Mrs Parker ran King Street Kennels.

"Brilliant bit of training, that," he said. "And did you teach the other dog special things, too?"

"Yes!" said Emily, before Neil could reply. "Neil taught Dotty everything. She's going to be brilliant! Only she's got to go away—"

She would have said a lot more, but her father coughed loudly. Standing on the edge of the crowd were Mr and Mrs Hamley, smiling at her.

"Oh!"

Mr Hamley laughed. "It's all right, Emily. She's quite right," he said to the reporter. "Dotty is our dog and we left her in the care of King Street Kennels while we looked for a new home for her. She was just a bit too boisterous for us to manage. But I'm proud to say that Neil has done a remarkable job of training her, and I'd recommend him to anyone who has a difficult dog!" He explained how Dotty had come to be entered in the Agility competition. "We appreciate what you did, Neil, but we didn't need a rosette to tell us that Dotty was special."

"And are you going to change your minds

about keeping her?" asked the reporter matter-of-factly.

The Hamleys looked at each other.

Neil held his breath. He could see the hope shining in Emily's eyes.

The reporter looked up at the sudden silence.

"Was it something I said?" he asked.

Everyone laughed.

"The truth is," Mrs Hamley spoke up, "Paul and I always knew that the house just wouldn't be the same without Dotty. When we saw her in the Agility arena, and then saw her break off just to come and join us, we knew that she missed us just as much. Now that we can see she can be controlled so well too, we think her proper place *is* back with us. Would you like that, Dotty?"

Dotty looked as if her tail might fall off, it was wagging so hard. She almost knocked over the reporter, who laughed and had to catch his camera before it fell off his shoulder.

Neil and Emily let out whoops of joy. They hugged their parents, and the Parkers grinned and shook hands with the Hamleys.

The reporter was just putting his notebook

away when a small group of show officials made their way through the crowd.

"Where's the dog who saved my wife's handbag?" asked a tall, elderly gentleman in a bowler hat and dark suit. He had a red and gold badge on his lapel which read: *Edward Harding, Chairman.*

"Over here, Mr Harding!" said the reporter, snatching up his camera. "Can I have a picture of you, please, for the *Compton News?*" The flash lit up Mr Harding's face before he could reply.

Mr Harding shook hands with Neil and Emily and smiled. Then he looked at Sam and Dotty.

"Two delightful dogs you have here. Which one is the big hero?" he asked.

"Sam is, sir," said Neil. "He tackled the thief and brought the bag back to us."

"Well, I think that's splendid," said Mr Harding. "And to show how grateful we are, I'm going to present Sam with this special rosette. For courage." He took a large red rosette from his pocket and fixed it to Sam's collar. Sam lifted his paw and Mr Harding shook it solemnly.

"Very well done, Sam."

The reporter's camera clicked and clicked.

Before they left the showground, the Hamleys arranged with Bob Parker for Paul to collect Dotty from the kennels the following morning.

The Parkers were making their way over to their own car, when Neil heard familiar voices shouting across the showground.

Chris and Hasheem caught them up. Hasheem was struggling with an enormous pink toy rabbit he had won at one of the stalls. They had seen everything that had happened.

"Sam's going to be famous," Chris said admiringly. "It was brilliant the way he caught that thief. Must have a good football coach, eh, Sam?" He stroked Sam's head.

"I was sure Dotty was going to win the Agility contest too," said Hasheem. "She looked like she had it sewn up. Man! Did you see her zip through that tunnel?" His hand swept down like a jet plane. "Zooom!"

"Yeah," Emily agreed. "She was doing great until she saw Mr Hamley and his wife." She sighed. "It's a shame – now we won't be able to collect the sponsor money for the RSPCA because Dotty was eliminated."

"Hey, I'll still sponsor the Puppy Patrol," said Chris. "They both deserve the money after all they've done."

"So will I," said smiling Mrs Smedley, who had just walked over to them as well. "Sam and Dotty did marvellously."

"And I will," said Tom Smedley, behind her. They both stopped to make a fuss of the dogs.

Emily was speechless with delight. Everything was working out perfectly!

Mr Hamley arrived promptly next morning to collect Dotty. He spent some time with Neil and his father while they gave him some useful advice about keeping Dotty in line.

"She's only a young dog, Paul," Bob reminded him, "and still learning. Once she gets older and wiser, she'll lose some of that boisterousness. "

"I'm sure you're right, Bob," said Mr Hamley. He turned to his dog, dancing impatiently at the end of her lead. "Well, Dotty, come on. Time to go home!"

They had only taken a few steps, though, before Mr Hamley stopped and turned back to Neil and his dad. Sam was sitting quietly beside them.

"I almost forgot. I wanted to ask you, Neil, if you're still serious about Agility work? Or has yesterday put you off?" Neil's teacher had an expression on his face which Neil couldn't read. What was he getting at?

"No, it hasn't put me off, Mr Hamley. I'm

going to try again with Sam, and this time hopefully get it right."

"Well, if you think you might like to try again with Dotty, let me know."

"Oh, wow! Mr Hamley!" Neil couldn't believe what his teacher was saying. "Do you mean it?"

"I certainly do. See you at the obedience lessons! Come, Dotty!"

Neil's dad stood beside him as they waved goodbye to Dotty and her owner. "Looks like you're going to steal away my business now, young man!"

Life at King Street Kennels went back to normal that week. At school, Neil had to suffer an embarrassing session in assembly, when the head teacher drew the attention of the entire school to the front-page article in the *Compton News* about the events at the county show and presented Neil with a leather-bound copy of *White Fang* by Jack London. But then things slipped into their usual routine, and Neil reckoned that he'd probably be famous until Friday if he was lucky.

Only one thing remained to be settled.

*

"Letter for you, Neil!" called his mother one morning.

Neil came down the stairs two at a time and snatched at the official-looking envelope lying on the kitchen table.

He ripped it open and pulled out a letter. A slip of paper edged in green fell out. Neil picked it up, his hand shaking slightly.

The Kennel Club, he read.

Registration certificate for: NEILSBOY PUPPY PATROL SAM. Owned by: Neil Parker.

There were other details too, but Neil didn't see them.

"They chose it!" he shouted at his family, all looking at him as if he'd gone mad. "They picked my first choice for Sam! Yeah!"

Sam charged into the kitchen when he heard Neil's shouts, looking for action.

"See that, Sam?" said Neil, waving the magic paper in front of the collie. "You're official. You can do anything now!"

He opened his arms with a whoop of happiness and Sam leapt into them and licked his face energetically.

"Neilsboy PuppyPatrol Sam: the name of a champion! Today, King Street! Tomorrow . . . the world!"

Tug of Love

1

"Sam is the best dog in the whole world!"

Neil Parker was standing in the middle of a field at the Padsham Dog Show, shouting at the top of his voice.

His nine-year-old sister, Emily, groaned and ducked down below the table in front of her to avoid being spotted. "Neil, you are *not* my brother. I disown you."

"But he won, Em! Sam came first in the Agility competition and he's *my dog*!" Neil jumped up and down on the spot, punching the air. In his excitement, he didn't care that he had suddenly become the centre of attention for the passing crowds. "Aren't you pleased for me?" Neil said, laughing. His short, dark, spiky hair was ruffled, and his T-shirt flapped as he leapt about. "This is Sam's first win. He came top in his category – by seven clear points!"

"OK, OK, I'm pleased for you! But will you stop celebrating! You're eleven, not five! And it's too hot to jump up and down. People are *looking* at us."

The day of the Padsham Dog Show was always busy and usually, like today, very hot.

Padsham was a small country town a few miles from Compton, where the Parkers lived at King Street Kennels. Neil, and his sisters, Emily and Sarah, sometimes felt they were the luckiest people alive. How many other dog-mad children got the chance of living at a boarding kennels?

King Street Kennels was sited in the grounds of their house. Bob Parker, Neil and Emily's father, hosted dog obedience lessons twice a week in their converted barn. The Parkers also ran a dog rescue centre. They took a stall at the Padsham Dog Show every year to help raise money for it.

Emily dipped her head even lower behind their trestle table so that only the very top of her brown hair was showing. The wobbly-looking table was piled up with T-shirts, sweatshirts and doggy stationery. Underneath, Neil's victorious black and white Border collie lay in the shade, panting.

Emily glanced at the dog beside her. "Poor Sam. Neil, you've worn him out!"

Sam raised his head from his paws and barked. The dog's feathery tail thumped the ground. Sam had been the Parkers' family pet for five years. He'd been abandoned as a puppy and was found in a very poorly condition. Neil had helped nurse him back to health, and he was now a wonderful example of his breed – and a promising contestant at every Agility competition in the area.

Neil had been training Sam on an obstacle course at home, and had already entered him in several local dog shows. He'd been improving with every event and was always highly placed. This was the first time he had actually *won* a competition, however, and Neil was over the moon. Sam had pushed himself over, round and through the obstacles like an expert.

"Have you got some more water for Sam?" Emily asked her mother, still looking at the tired dog.

Carole Parker was sitting in a green Range Rover parked on the grass behind the stall. All of the doors and windows were open in an attempt to let in some cool air. "After coming first in the contest, he deserves champagne rather than water!" Mrs Parker remarked. "Here, this is the last of the bottled water."

Emily emptied the water into Sam's tin dish and the collie lapped at it thirstily.

Carole Parker looked at her watch and then began counting sweatshirts. "Two, four, six . . ."

They had brought along two dozen, each with the distinctive King Street Kennels logo emblazoned across the chest, but had only sold one so far. "I might as well put these back in the box. Time's moving on."

"I told you not to bother bringing any sweatshirts! It's boiling!" Emily flapped her damp white T-shirt to try and cool herself down.

"I sold three notebooks all by myself, didn't I?" five-year-old Sarah said proudly. She was sitting on the grass, drawing a picture of a dog on some scrap paper.

Carole Parker smiled. "Neil, do you think you could get me some more mineral water before we pack up?"

"I want an ice cream!" Sarah piped up.

"Make that two," Emily said cheekily, suddenly standing up again.

"OK," Neil agreed. "I'll go. I know you can't cope with being in the presence of a superstar dog trainer!"

"Neil! Neil!"

Neil turned round and saw Chris, his best friend from Meadowbank School, coming towards him out of the crowd. Chris was wiry and had short dark hair like Neil's. Right now, he seemed to be in a hurry.

"I've just been to the main show ring," he gasped. "You won't *believe* what I've got to tell you."

"Who won the Cutest Pooch class, you mean? I bet it was one of Mrs Smithson's chihuahuas as usual," said Neil, groaning.

"Of course it was! But you'll never guess who came second!" Chris looked as if he was about to burst and he was trying hard not to laugh.

"Go on, tell me," Neil begged.

Chris dragged the silence out for as long as possible before announcing, "*Sugar and Spice!*"

"Never! I don't believe it!" said Neil, wide-eyed.

Sugar and Spice were two West Highland terriers who had recently stayed at King Street Kennels and caused a lot of trouble. They looked cute and harmless at first glance, but were actually very badly behaved.

"I think you can take all the credit for that, Neil," his mother said. "This time last year, they wouldn't have sat still on the judging table for five seconds."

"And they'd have bitten the judge!" said Emily.

"Too true. Sam, on the other hand . . ." Neil began.

Emily and Carole Parker groaned.

". . . did even better in the Agility contest," Neil continued.

Chris crouched down and fondled Sam's silky ears. "Can you escape for five minutes?" he asked Neil, straightening up again. "They've just started judging the Labrador class and it's so funny. Your cousin Steve has entered Ricky – he's causing a riot!"

"This I've *got* to see." Laughing, Neil hurried off with Chris in the direction of the show ring. He yelled back at his mother: "Won't be long. I'll get the water on my way back."

"And don't forget Sarah's ice cream!" Carole shouted after him. "It'll be torture if you forget!"

Neil and Chris shuffled into a gap between two spectators in the crowd surrounding the small show ring. The dogs were already in the ring, lined up beside a large table. It was quite a big class: Neil counted fourteen different Labradors, all sitting obediently beside their owners. They ranged from puppies to fully mature dogs, and were a mixture of different colours – mostly yellow and golden, but two were black.

At the end of the line, Neil's cousin, Steve Tansley, was doing his best to keep Ricky, his pet Labrador, sitting still. It seemed an impossible task. Even though Steve regularly took his wayward dog to Bob Parker's obedience classes, Ricky refused to behave. As Neil and Chris looked on, Ricky kept wanting to stand up and make friends with the dog next to him. Steve had to resort to holding him firmly in place with a hand clamped on the dog's head.

Two judges in long coats were examining a yellow Labrador in the middle of the line. Neil could see that it was a particularly sleek-looking young male. He had bright, eager eyes, an alert look, and seemed to smile at the crowd as his owner lifted him on to the table.

"He looks a potential winner to me," said

Neil, pointing towards the dog as the two judges examined him closely. "Well proportioned. Good grooming. Powerful hindquarters."

"Not too jumpy, either," chipped in Chris, nodding.

"It's all wrong, you know," said a voice, rising suddenly above the chatter of the crowd. "It's cruel putting the dogs through an ordeal like this."

"Eh?" Neil looked round to see who had spoken. The crowd was three or four people deep, and Neil could hear several animated conversations about who should win the competition. "That's rubbish," he whispered to his friend.

"I wish they hadn't entered him for the show. It's bad for their nerves. It's totally unnatural!"

It was definitely a woman's voice, Neil thought, but he was still unsure exactly who had spoken among the noisy crowd.

"She seems upset, whoever she is," Chris commented. "I wonder why she bothered coming to a dog show, if that's the way she feels about them."

In the centre of the ring, the young Labrador being judged was staring in their direction.

Something had caught his attention and his tail was wagging energetically. The two officials moved on to the next entrant, and the dog's owner moved forward to lift him down from the table.

"Nobody could say that dog isn't enjoying himself," Neil observed. "Just look at him! He's revelling in all the attention. That woman's got it totally wrong. Maybe there are one or two highly strung dogs who wouldn't like the atmosphere of a show, but most love all the fuss. They jump at the chance to show off."

The woman from the crowd didn't shout out anything else, and Neil and Chris were soon lost in conversation about the next dog being shown.

After making their own personal list of winners, they clapped and cheered when an impressive-looking black Labrador came first, with the happy yellow Labrador awarded second prize.

Remembering that he'd promised to go back and help his mother pack up the stall, Neil pulled Chris away from the show ring and they headed back in the direction of one of the many refreshment tents.

It was four o'clock when they reached the King Street stall again. In the distance, high in the sky above the Padsham showground, billowing black clouds threatened a thunderous end to the red-hot day. Neil was glad his mother had decided to leave an hour before the official end of the show. They had all had enough, and were soon busy packing their merchandise into boxes and loading the car.

"Help!" Emily yelped, staggering under the weight of one end of the collapsible table.

Neil and Chris grabbed the table just before she disappeared beneath it, and they helped Carole Parker manoeuvre the awkward object into the boot of the Range Rover. The car had the King Street Kennels logo emblazoned on both of the front doors. Everybody who knew Neil and his family called them the "Puppy Patrol".

Neil picked up another box of unsold sweatshirts. He was manoeuvring it round to sit awkwardly on the edge of the car boot, when Chris suddenly yelled, "Look out, Neil!"

A streak of yellow fur shot past Neil's legs and made him drop the box. Instinctively, he thought something was attacking him.

"What was that?" Neil looked in the direction that the speedy animal had fled. It was a dog, and its legs were moving at such a rate that they were a blur of motion.

"That was close. It almost ran into you, Neil!" said Chris, surprised.

Desperate to find out where the dog was going, Neil and Chris set off across the dusty field and into the car park to get a clear view.

"He's running after that car!" Chris yelled,

pointing. It was true. The racing dog, which looked like a young yellow Labrador, was pursuing a blue car that was bumping over the grass towards the exit gate. As the car turned left into the road, the dog continued to run after it. Both boys watched until a tall hedge obscured their view.

"I hope his owners catch him," Emily said anxiously, coming up and standing beside them.

"Right. *I* hope they get him back before he's involved in a road accident," said Neil, grimly.

"Poor dog," said Emily.

"Daft dog!" muttered Chris. "What on earth was he doing, chasing after a car like that?"

"Perhaps he'd fallen in love with a lady Labrador that was in it," sighed Emily.

"Don't be so soppy," Neil snapped.

Emily pulled a face behind his back, which made Chris chuckle.

Neil continued to look worried and watched the horizon as distant glimpses of the blue car flashed between the tall trees. "I hope he'll be OK."

2

"Carole, do we have a gold-plated dog dish?"

Emily dropped her fork and it clattered onto the plate in front of her. "Eh? What are you on about, Dad?"

"It's for the visitor who's arriving tomorrow." Bob Parker continued eating his evening meal at the big wooden kitchen table, acting as if he hadn't just said something extraordinary at all.

Neil and Carole Parker exchanged curious glances. Sarah giggled.

"OK. Think of a famous dog. One who's won his owners thousands of pounds recently . . ." prompted Bob.

"Muttley! It's got to be!" shrieked Emily.

Sarah clapped her hands and chanted, "Mutt-Mutt-Muttley!"

"Is he really coming *here*?" Neil was suddenly

excited at the prospect of such a famous dog staying at their kennels. Muttley had hit the local headlines a couple of weeks earlier when he had won his owners a big lottery prize. They'd been using a system of predicting numbers based on Muttley's erratic barking. The family had claimed their success was all down to him, and the chubby grey mongrel with his floor-mop hairstyle had become an overnight celebrity. He'd been on television and all over the daily newspapers. The media couldn't get enough of him.

"The Hendersons are spending some of their winnings on a cruise," explained Bob Parker. "We've having Muttley for three weeks, starting tomorrow."

"I'm not sure we can provide a gold-plated dog dish though, Dad!" Neil smiled.

The past few weeks had been quiet at King Street and Neil was already looking forward to the new arrival. "We didn't make much at the show today," he volunteered. "The sweatshirts were a *bad* idea!"

Bob laughed. "Never mind, I'm sure the Hendersons will pay their way and provide enough to keep Muttley in the manner to which he must have become accustomed!"

Neil pushed his empty plate away. "Right, talking about famous dogs. I've got my own superstar who needs feeding and walking. Haven't I, Sam?"

Sam had been curled up on the floor beside Neil's feet and jumped up as soon as he heard his name. He nuzzled Neil with his wet nose, sure that food was on its way.

"Congratulations, Neil. You've done well with Sam. I only hope today is the first of many glorious wins for King Street!" Bob Parker said, smiling.

"So do I!" said Neil, his cheeks reddening slightly. Then he tapped his leg and both he and Sam raced out of the kitchen door into the yard.

Neil's dream-filled sleep was shattered on Sunday morning by the insistent ringing of the front doorbell. He'd imagined that he too had won the National Lottery, correctly guessing the six winning numbers by basing his choice on Sam's own unique pattern of barking. The happy thought disappeared in an instant.

Listening carefully, Neil could just about hear his father talking to somebody at the front door. He couldn't stand not knowing what was going on so he jumped out of bed, threw on some jeans and a T-shirt, and rushed downstairs two steps at a time.

His father was talking to a policeman.

"OK, leave him with us. I'll find him a space in the rescue centre."

Rubbing the sleep out of his eyes, Neil saw his father take a blue nylon lead from the policeman. He looked down and saw that it was attached to a yellow Labrador. Rubbing his eyes again, Neil studied the dog closely. It looked familiar.

Bob Parker stepped outside with the dog, closing the front door behind him.

Neil snapped to attention, rammed a pair of trainers on his feet and followed his father outside.

"Dad! Hang on!" Neil skidded on the gravel path just in front of the rescue centre door. "This dog," said Neil breathlessly, pointing to the Labrador. "It's the one from the show yesterday."

"Are you sure?"

"I'm positive. Big happy grin, wagging tail, same yellow colouring. I think it won second prize in its section yesterday afternoon."

Bob Parker knelt down and ruffled the dog's ears. He looked at the Labrador's teeth and ran a hand across its back, then felt its flank and examined all four paws.

"He seems perfectly healthy. A police patrol car spotted him sitting in the middle of the main road between Compton and Padsham last night. It was about ten o'clock, they said. There was no collar."

"Another dog needing a good home?" Kate McGuire, the King Street kennel maid, arrived on her bike and pulled up alongside them. "Morning, all. Who's this then?"

"Morning, Kate. The police have just dropped this chap off. Neil thinks he's an escapee from the Padsham Show yesterday."

"He was doing a hundred miles an hour down a road the last time I saw him!" said Neil. "Chasing after a blue car."

Kate looked at the young dog and smiled.

"Well, give me two minutes and I'll help you kennel him. You can tell me all about it." She wheeled her bike away to lock it up.

Inside the rescue centre, Neil unhooked the mesh door to one of the pens. There were ten pens in the centre, five on each side of a central stone walkway. The pens were not that much different from those in the two kennel blocks next door. Each dog had an outside run to itself, a basket and a metal water dish.

"You'd think he'd have had the sense not to sit in the road," Neil said, trying to settle the dog down in his basket.

"He was probably very confused at being lost," Bob pointed out. "He was hungry and thirsty when they found him. He doesn't seem too upset by his ordeal, though, does he?"

The Labrador gave Bob Parker a friendly lick on the back of his hand.

"There we are." Kate returned and put a dish with some crunchy biscuit meal beside the dog's basket.

Neil described to her what had happened the previous day.

Kate looked thoughtful. "Do you remember what the dog's name was?"

Neil shook his head. "Sorry. It was one of those long, complicated, pedigree ones and I didn't buy a programme. When he ran past us, there were lots of people all shouting different things. If the owner had been calling him, we'd never have heard. You know how busy those shows can get."

"They probably don't print the names of all the entrants, anyway," Bob chipped in. "The Padsham Show's not really that big an event compared to others and there are always lots of last-minute entries. Pity. Otherwise it would have made it a lot easier to find his owner."

"You can call the show's organizers on Monday, Dad."

"Of course. I'm sure we won't have to wait long for the owner to turn up."

"They must be going frantic!" cried Kate. "I'd hate it if my dog ran off like that. Look, he's extremely well-behaved for a young dog. Can't be more than ten months old, I'd say. Anyway, if you'd like to hold him, I'll go and get the camera."

Colour Polaroid photographs were taken of

every dog that came to the rescue centre. The police station in Compton had a regular spot on its public noticeboard for displaying the details of lost dogs. So did the surgery owned by the local vet, Mike Turner.

The Parkers were experts at reuniting lost dogs with their owners, and finding good homes for them. If the pictures failed to bring an instant result, Mr Parker would sometimes give the local paper the details and a copy of the photograph. In the past, the *Compton News* had been great at bringing attention to lost dogs with desperate stories.

"Say 'cheese'!" A bright flash lit up the pen. Kate waited for the dog's photograph to develop, then handed it to Bob, who began blowing on it to help it dry.

"I'll put this in the office. How about some breakfast, Neil?"

"You bet! See you later, Kate." Neil said goodbye to the new arrival, then headed back towards the house with his dad for his favourite Sunday breakfast. He'd already worked up a huge appetite!

*

After he'd eaten, Neil went with Emily to the rescue centre. The Labrador sat up in his basket and whined when they entered his pen. Neil guessed he was overjoyed at seeing people again after his ordeal the night before.

"I'm sure he's the dog from the show. But it all happened so fast. I suppose I could be mistaken."

Emily was looking into the dog's eyes. She rubbed his ears and sighed. "He's wonderful. I hope his owners reclaim him quickly, Neil. He seems happy enough, but I bet he'd prefer to be at home."

"Too true," said Neil. "Right. Time to give Sam his morning walk, I think."

He walked back across the courtyard. Closing the garden gate behind him, Neil whistled in his special way – one long, continuous sound for about five seconds. At once, the lithe Border collie wriggled out from under his favourite leafy bush and came bounding up to greet him.

Neil ruffled Sam's head, and leant inside the kitchen door to grab his lead. "Race you to the field!"

Neil burst into a run and Sam belted after him into the clear blue morning.

That evening, just before dinner, Neil was busy tidying the pen of an English bulldog who was due to be picked up the following day. Tank had been a handful all week and Neil would be very glad to see him go. As he washed the floor, he decided bulldogs were one of his least favourite breeds of dog.

He was mentally adding the tenth item to his "Big list of things not to like about bulldogs" –

they always eat their food messily – when the sound of a car on the gravel front drive caught his attention.

Neil dropped his mop and went to investigate.

As he came round the side of the house, Emily and their mother were already engaged in conversation with a woman who was standing beside her vehicle, next to a girl and a boy. Neil guessed both were about nine – Emily's age rather than his own. They looked excited and the girl was tugging at the woman's arm.

"So, can we help you?" Neil overheard his mother ask. He wondered what they might want, calling so late in the evening. It was well past closing time and Kate had been gone for over an hour.

"Oh, I do hope so," the woman replied. She was short, and had blonde, wavy hair, with a fringe flopping down to her eyebrows. She looked at her bright-eyed children and then announced, "I think you have our missing Labrador."

3

"Oh, so he's yours!" Emily burst out. Sarah suddenly appeared behind her big sister's legs and squealed in delight.

Neil watched as Carole Parker ran a hand through her hair. "You've come about the yellow Labrador?"

"Yes. I'm Pam Weston. We've lost our dog, Jason. A policeman at the station in Compton told me that they'd brought a Labrador to you. I'm sure it'll be him. He belongs to Kirsty and Jonathan here."

Neil noticed that the boy was leaning back against the car. He spotted that there was a baby asleep inside, strapped into a baby seat in the back. As Neil got closer, the boy turned to look at him. "You're Neil, aren't you?" he said immediately.

"Yes?" Neil frowned slightly. He knew the face but couldn't place it.

"You don't recognize me, do you?" the boy said accusingly.

"I'm not sure," Neil replied. "Were you at the show yesterday?"

"I'm from school, you dummy! Jonathan Weston. Kirsty and I are two years below you!"

"Yeah, right. Is he your dog then? The Labrador?"

"We think it's Jason. We've had him for ages. We've got photos of him and everything!"

"I can't wait to get him home again." Mrs Weston's voice rose above Neil's conversation and distracted him. There was something about it that he recognized.

"Can I stroke Jason before you take him away?" Sarah asked anxiously.

"Hang on a moment, Sarah. It's not that simple!" Mrs Parker was beginning to get a little flustered. "It's quite late and, if it is Jason, there are certain procedures we must go through before we can let you take him, I'm afraid. Are you sure you want to do this tonight?"

"Please, Mrs Parker. The children missed him so much last night. We were devastated to lose him. And it would be quite difficult to come back tomorrow."

Carole Parker hesitated. "Well, it might be possible. Can you show the Westons to the rescue centre, Neil, while I get some of the paperwork." Carole Parker took Sarah's hand and together they headed off towards the office.

"This way." Neil led the visitors down the driveway at the side of the house. Emily ran ahead to get the Labrador out of his pen, and they met up in the courtyard.

Emily was holding the yellow Labrador by a lead. He began to bark enthusiastically as soon as the Westons approached.

"Jason! It is you!" Kirsty ran forward and threw her arms round the dog. "I've missed you so much!"

Jason's long, otter-like tail was thumping everybody's legs as they gathered round. The dog smothered Kirsty with enormous licks and then barked excitedly.

"That's our Jason all right!" Mrs Weston confirmed.

Neil could see that Jason was happy again and he breathed a sigh of relief that the dog had been claimed so soon. Often dogs went unclaimed, and Neil and Emily would have to spend a lot of time looking for suitable new owners.

"How did you lose him, Mrs Weston?" Neil asked.

"Oh, he just got free from us at the dog show," she replied. "You know how it is. One minute he was there, the next he'd disappeared into the crowd. I was so busy with baby Michael that I just lost track of him."

"How long did you—"

Mrs Weston interrupted him and pointed towards her daughter who was hugging the dog as if she was never going to let him go again. "Kirsty missed him the most, you know."

Emily laughed. "We can see!"

Kirsty held her slender arms round Jason's neck and kissed him on the head. It was a touching reunion.

Jonathan bent down, ruffling the hair on the Labrador's neck, and said, "Welcome back, trouble."

Neil was about to ask his question again when Carole Parker arrived with a clipboard in her hands. Despite the late hour, Neil's mum still looked as professional as ever. Neil would give anything to sound half as confident as her when *he* was talking.

"We'll need some details before I can release the dog to you. I can't let you take him just like that," Carole said apologetically. "I can see he knows you all, but I need some kind of concrete proof of ownership. Do you have any registration documents?"

Mrs Weston suddenly looked flustered. "Oh, no, I didn't think we'd need them. Isn't it obvious that Jason belongs with us? You can see how much he loves the children."

"Well, yes, I *can* see that, but perhaps you have something else? Photos of you with him, perhaps."

Carole glanced across at the dog and felt guilty. Jonathan and Kirsty looked so pleased to be hugging him again and their faces positively shone with happiness.

"Of course, I've got one here." Pam Weston

rummaged about in her handbag and produced a crumpled snapshot. "Do you think that's enough, though?"

"Please, Mum . . . can we take him home tonight?" Kirsty begged.

Carole Parker smiled and looked at the picture. Neil glanced at it, too, craning over his mother's shoulder so that he could see it properly.

The picture was of Jason and the two oldest Weston children. The Labrador was much younger, perhaps only four months old – but it was undoubtedly him. He had the same sparkling, deep brown eyes and distinctive colouring round his nose. In the middle of the picture, Jason had his paws flopping over the top of a grey drystone wall. Neil even recognized the field behind him. It was one of the poppy fields near Badger Farm on the other side of Compton.

"It's a lovely picture, Mum," said Neil.

"Yes, it is. I don't think there's any harm in letting you take Jason tonight."

Jonathan and Kirsty Weston cheered. Jason barked a couple of times as if he had understood the good news.

Carole Parker held out her clipboard and a pen. "If you could just write your full name, address and phone number in the book and sign it, we'll let him go."

"Thank you so much," exclaimed Mrs Weston as she hurriedly put the photo back in her bag. "We don't live that far away, actually. We're in Sycamore Drive on the new estate in Compton. Mrs Parker, you've made the children so happy again."

"Do you have your own lead for him?" Emily addressed her question to Jonathan but it was his mother who answered.

"Yes, of course, but it's back at the house. I'm sure he'll be OK in the car until then. Anyway, we'd better be going."

She finished writing her address with a flourish of the pen, and then handed the clipboard back to Carole Parker.

Everyone walked back round to the front of the house and Kirsty opened the tailgate of their car. Jason immediately jumped up and settled down onto some big, colourful tartan rugs. Jonathan slammed the tailgate shut and rushed to the front of the car.

Emily and Neil stood watching them all as Mrs Weston started up the car. Emily had a wide grin on her face. She had that familiar warm glow inside her which she always got when she was saying goodbye to a dog – especially when it was going home to its proper owners.

Mrs Weston wound down the front window and thanked them again for all their help. Carole Parker nodded.

Jonathan waved at Neil from the back of the car.

"See you at school tomorrow!" Neil mouthed at him through the glass.

Jonathan nodded and looked away.

With a screech of tyres on gravel, the car

pulled out of the drive and joined the main Compton road.

Neil turned to his sister, looking puzzled.

"What's up with you?" asked Emily, seeing the look on his face. "Aren't you pleased? Jason has found his owners again."

Something was bothering him, nagging away at the back of his brain, but it was nothing that he could identify. He made a mental note to find Jonathan Weston at school the next day and ask him a bit more about Jason. Neil hoped that would dislodge this weird feeling he suddenly had.

"You all right?" Emily asked again.

"Sorry, yes. It's great news about Jason, isn't it? See you later, I'm going to finish up in Kennel Block One. I was in the middle of cleaning a pen."

"OK."

Neil trooped back to the kennels, kicking at the gravel underfoot as he went. He was happy about the dog being back where he belonged, but he had the feeling that it was not the last he was going to hear about Jason, the friendly yellow Labrador from the Padsham Show.

*

"Are you looking forward to seeing moneybags Muttley tonight?" Chris Wilson rattled the loose change in his pocket and laughed. He and Neil were sitting under a tree in Meadowbank School's playing field before the start of lessons on Monday afternoon. "The dog with the amazingly large bank account?"

"You bet I am," said Neil, whistling. "I'm hoping the Hendersons will give Dad a huge tip for looking after their dog so well!"

"Do you think Sam could win the lottery?" joked Chris. "You always said he was one in a million. Now he has the chance to prove it by picking the right numbers for you!"

"I don't think so. Sam's talents lie elsewhere – like in winning Agility competitions at dog shows."

Chris groaned. He hoped Neil wouldn't go on about Sam's first competition win again. Chris decided to try and change the subject – fast. "I saw Emily this morning," he said quickly. "She told me you'd found the people who owned that crazy Labrador."

Neil's face clouded over. "Yes, we did. It belonged to Jonathan and Kirsty Weston –

they're two years below us. I thought I'd see them this morning but I guess they're not around. I've looked everywhere, though."

"Maybe they're off sick," ventured Chris.

"Both of them? Anyway, they were fine yesterday."

"Don't worry about it, Neil." Chris looked up as the bell went. He stood and brushed himself down. "Come on, we'd better get going."

"I do worry about it, though. I just can't help it."

"You and your dogs, Neil Parker. You can't stop thinking about them for one minute, can you?"

Neil sighed as he followed his friend towards the school building. "No. I can't."

As Neil turned his bike off the Compton road into King Street Kennels, his mother and two sisters overtook him in their big green Range Rover and pulled into the front driveway. The drive was already filled up with several other vehicles and Carole had to park the car in a different spot from usual.

Neil was confused. "Hey, what's going on? And what's all the racket for?" The unmistakably loud noise of about twenty dogs all barking at once filled the air.

Emily jumped down from the car and slammed the door behind her. "What do you think? Muttley's here! The other dogs must be going crazy!"

"Mutt-Mutt-Muttley!" Sarah grabbed her satchel and ran into the house. Emily rushed after her.

Neil hurriedly leant his bike against the front wall and followed the noise.

The courtyard between the back of the house and the kennels was full of people. The centre of everybody's attention was a proud-looking Mr and Mrs Henderson and their scruffy-looking mongrel dog, the lottery-winning Muttley. Mr Henderson was wearing an expensive-looking suit, and his wife a smart dress, completely inappropriate for visiting a working kennels.

Several newspaper reporters were crowded around asking them questions, each scribbling in a notebook or thrusting a hand-held recorder into Mr and Mrs Henderson's faces. Neil glimpsed Jake, a photographer from the *Compton News*, who had been very helpful to King Street in the past. He'd often featured stories in the paper about some of the rescue centre dogs which desperately needed homes. Above the frantic chatter, the dogs in the two kennel blocks were all barking loudly.

"Crikey! There's a TV camera as well!" Emily's jaw dropped.

"I've never seen so many photographers! I hope they don't scare the dogs," said Neil, looking concerned. He realized that Muttley's holiday at King Street Kennels was not going to be as easy as he had thought.

Neil approached the gaggle of people and made a "What's happening?" sign at Kate. She was standing beside his father to one side of the group. Neil saw Kate laugh.

Looking between the reporters' bodies, Neil studied Muttley more closely. He was a large, hairy, bumbling animal and Neil suspected he had lots of Old English sheepdog in him. He was being terrific. He was barking on cue and licking the reporters' hands. Muttley also had a way of shaking the hair out of his eyes which made everybody laugh.

The television camera recorded Muttley being paraded up and down the courtyard and then sitting in his basket in his pen in Kennel Block One.

"This is great publicity, isn't it?" Kate whispered in Neil's ear as they looked on.

"Fantastic!" Neil answered, beaming. "It's

the best thing we could have hoped for. They're bound to mention the rescue centre as well, aren't they?"

"I only hope we can cope with his expensive habits," Bob Parker chuckled. "He's already caused me one headache this morning."

"What do you mean, Dad?" asked Emily.

"Well, I had to move Dinky, the fat basset-hound, into another pen. Mrs H. insisted that Muttley go into pen eight. Apparently, eight was the first number he predicted on their winning lottery ticket."

"Oh," Emily commented, weakly.

"Oh, indeed. You know how much I hate moving dogs in the middle of their stay. It's disruptive. It unsettles them all over again."

"Do you think we need to increase security?" asked Neil. "Get a few more locks put on in case someone tries to steal him?" He could imagine that Muttley would be very desirable to someone who desperately wanted to win a lot of money.

Bob shook his head. "I'm not sure. Let's see how it goes. Do make sure any visitors have proper appointments, though. We don't want just anybody waltzing in so they can see a famous dog. Once the fuss has died down, I'm sure everything will settle back into the usual routine, and Muttley will be just like any other visitor!"

"I hope so," Kate added. "I can't be doing with all of these reporters under my feet when I'm trying to work."

Jake overheard her, turned round and winked.

"No offence," said Kate, turning pink.

"Bob! Bob!"

Neil's mother came rushing up to them. Her face was red and she looked hassled.

"What's up, Carole? What is it?"

"I think you should come to the office straight away. We've got another visitor."

"Can't it wait?" Bob Parker turned and looked back at the group of reporters, still busy snapping away and fawning over Muttley and the Hendersons.

"No. We've got a problem," Neil's mum insisted. "There's a man here who claims we have his dog. Or rather, *had* his dog."

Neil exchanged confused looks with Kate.

"What do you mean?" Bob Parker didn't understand either.

"He says Jason, the yellow Labrador, is *his* dog. And that he can prove it. Bob, I think we've given Jason to the wrong people!"

4

Grim and unsmiling, the man tapped his fingers impatiently on Mrs Parker's desk. He was in his late thirties and looked very smartly dressed in a dark green jacket and a brown peaked cap.

"Sorry to keep you, Mr . . . ?"

"Scott. My name's Scott," the man snapped back, whipping the cap off his head and scrunching it up in his hands.

Neil shuffled into the office behind his father and mother and tried his best to look inconspicuous.

"My wife tells me that you've come about a Labrador," Bob said calmly.

"Yes, I have. I was informed you were holding him here. But you appear to have given him away to a complete stranger – without checking out your facts first."

"I'm sure there's been some mistake, Mr Scott. We always check that a dog is being returned to its rightful owners before it is released. It's King Street policy."

"Is it also policy to get it so wrong, then?"

Neil could see that Mr Scott was working himself up into a furious temper.

Carole Parker tried to calm him down.

"Mr Scott, please. Are you sure we are talking about the same dog? I checked its details myself. There was photographic proof of Jason's ownership."

"Photographic proof? Is that all? And Jason? Who's Jason? The dog's name is Junior."

"Perhaps there *has* been a mistake then, Mr Scott," Neil piped up. "This Labrador definitely answered to the name Jason. I saw that for myself. He was lost at the Padsham Dog Show on Saturday."

"Yes, that's right: *I* lost him at the dog show! Look, we're wasting time. I *know* it was Junior. I saw his picture on your wall as soon as I came in!"

Everybody looked at the cork noticeboard on the office wall. In the middle of several small snapshots that were pinned up, Kate's picture of the Labrador was clearly visible. Carole Parker had forgotten to take it down once the dog had left them.

"I've got proof as well, you know. Here's his Kennel Club registration." Mr Scott produced a wad of paper from a metal briefcase. "I've got his ownership documents from the RSPCA Canine Sanctuary. And some photos of him outside his kennel on my farm. Do you want me to go on?"

Bob Parker took the documents and silently flicked through them. He handed them to his wife for her to look at, then flopped back into a swivel chair behind the desk, scratching his beard. "I'm sorry, Mr Scott. These papers are in perfect order and it does seem that we may have reunited Junior with the wrong people."

Neil couldn't believe it. Nothing like this had ever happened before.

The man looked triumphant. "So what are you going to do about it?"

Bob Parker paused, thinking about what options he now had. "I'll make some enquiries and get back to you as soon as I can."

"Is that *it*?" said Mr Scott, incredulously.

"If you'd lost your Labrador, Mr Scott, why didn't you come to us earlier?" Neil asked him. He didn't like Mr Scott's aggressive behaviour.

"Because I didn't know your rescue centre existed! I do live some distance away. I had to travel thirty miles to get to the Padsham Show. After Junior ran off, I rang round the local police stations yesterday, and eventually got your number. It was too late to call or come round last night, so I left it until today. I *thought* he was in safe hands, and didn't think another day would make any difference. Little did I know you'd give him away to the first person who came knocking on your door looking for a new pet!"

"It wasn't like that, Mr Scott," said Bob, reassuringly.

"How did you lose him, anyway?" Neil asked, pointedly.

"He'd just been placed second in the Labrador class when something excited him. He just took off! Straight through the crowd and away. I should have expected it. He's young and still in training."

"Why wasn't he wearing a collar?" asked Carole.

"Bad timing," replied Scott. "I'd just taken off his show collar and was putting his normal one back on when he dashed off. I did ask the officials to broadcast an announcement over the tannoy, but it was a very bad sound system and it was hard to make out what anybody was saying. My wife and I spent hours looking for him, but in that crowd it was impossible."

"I see. Yes, the show was very busy," agreed Carole Parker.

"Look, is this really getting us anywhere? All I want is my dog back! I'm sorry I sound so angry, but Junior means a lot to me. Who were the people who took him? Can you tell me their address?"

"I'm afraid not, Mr Scott," replied Neil's father firmly. "We can't give out personal details like that."

"Then I suppose I'm at your mercy, Mr Parker. I can't say I'm at all happy about it, but please get in touch as soon as you've made your 'enquiries'."

Mr Scott returned the dog's identity papers into his briefcase and clicked it shut.

Neil tried his best to sound hopeful. "I'm sure there's a simple explanation. Labradors do tend to look very similar, and—"

"I should know, I breed them!" Scott retorted sharply, thrusting a business card into Bob Parker's hand. "Here are my details. I shall expect to hear from you soon."

Scott pulled open the door and walked determinedly towards a muddy Land Rover parked on the roadside. He brushed past Kate who was just about to enter the office, and she paused to let him pass.

Neil watched through the office window and saw him drive away.

"Phew – thank heavens we've got rid of him!" exclaimed Neil.

Bob glanced down at the card and read out loud, "*Paul Scott, registered Labrador breeder, Four Gate Farm, Hadleigh St Mary.*"

"Who on earth was *that*?" said a confused-looking Kate as she tapped on the door and entered. "He looked mad!"

"He was! Absolutely fuming! We've lost his dog, Kate!"

Neil was wide-eyed and looked at his parents to see how they were taking it all.

"I can't blame him for being angry. It must be a very frustrating situation for him." Bob Parker swivelled in his chair to face his wife and put his head in his hands. It was the first time Neil had seen his father look really worried about kennel business.

"I can't help feeling a little guilty," confessed Carole. "I should have known not to let the dog go with just a single photo as proof. I should have asked for his purchase documents. But it was late, I'd had a long day, and the Weston children looked so over the moon to see him. I can't understand it. Jason, or whatever his real name is, looked so comfortable with them – as if he'd known them all his life. It doesn't make sense!"

Kate looked at Mr Parker. "This isn't going to look good for King Street's reputation, is it, Bob?"

"No. Not at all," Mr Parker agreed, thoughtfully. "All the more reason to sort it out quickly. We need to find out some more background about this dog. I think I'd better give Mrs Weston a ring straight away. I don't want to spoil her children's fun, but the sooner we find out what's going on, the better.

"And Kate. Can you get rid of those reporters? The last thing we need right now is for this thing to leak to the press!"

"So he was really mad then?" asked Chris, as he admired Muttley through the wire mesh of the dog's pen.

"Mad wasn't the word for it. At one point I thought I saw his veins popping out of his forehead!"

"I'm glad I missed him. I tried calling straight after school to see if I could come round, but the line was engaged. It took me ages to get through."

"It's all these reporters," sighed Neil. "They all want to see Muttley. It's been a madhouse round here ever since I got in."

Muttley responded to the sound of his own name with a series of loud barks.

"Hey! We should have noted those down, Neil. Maybe they would have won us a prize," chuckled Chris.

"Don't *you* start!" Neil retorted with a grin.

"Emily's been scribbling away ever since he got here. Anyway, I'm beginning to think the lottery is a waste of money. Dad never wins anything!"

"But it worked with the Hendersons," Chris reminded his best friend.

"Just a lucky coincidence, that's all," Neil snorted. "Dad reckons he's going to win us enough to build an extension on the kennels, but I can't see it ever happening. Our luck has just run out, anyway."

"Because you've lost the Labrador, you mean?"

"What a mess. Remind me to ask Dad how he got on phoning Mrs Weston."

"Remind me about what?" Bob Parker appeared over Neil's shoulder.

"Oh, Dad. I was wondering how Mrs Weston reacted when you told her about Mr Scott. What was her explanation?"

"'Fraid I'm still getting no answer. I couldn't get hold of her earlier on, and she doesn't have an answering machine. I've tried three times already."

"They might have just popped out," said Neil, hopefully.

"For this long? On a school night? No, I suppose I'll have to drive over there and drop a note through their door."

Neil and Chris immediately looked at each other. Maybe they could help?

"I'll see you later, boys," said Mr Parker as he left the rescue centre.

"Chris?" asked Neil, slowly.

"Yes, Neil?" replied Chris, innocently.

"Why don't we go for a bike ride?"

"Not out over the other side of Compton, by any chance? To a certain address where a fugitive dog is holed up avoiding capture?"

"Spot on. We can check out the Westons' house and see if they really are in. They might be deliberately not answering the phone. Come on."

"Hang on, Neil, I can't come!" Chris sighed. "I promised Mum I wouldn't be too long. I've still got homework to do."

"Oh. I'll get Emily to come with me. Shame, though. You're going to miss all the fun and excitement!"

"Don't tell me!" Chris said goodbye to Muttley and followed Neil outside. He waved to his friend and cycled off down the Compton road towards home.

Neil looked around for his sister and spotted her in the back garden with Sam.

"You're coming with me!" Neil said as he pulled his sister away, out of view of the kitchen windows.

"Oi!" protested Emily. "Where are you taking me?"

"You'll see!" said Neil mysteriously, thrusting Emily's bike into her hands. "Come on!"

Dodging past the office window on their bikes, the two riders cycled down the Compton road, pedalling as fast as they could.

The Westons' home was in one of the newly developed parts of Compton, where estates with rows of modern houses had been built.

Neil and Emily rode round looking for the right street. All around they could see pocket- handkerchief-sized front gardens with bushes and flowers that were struggling for survival in the dying heat of the day. After five minutes, they turned left at the end of Hazel Street and found themselves in Sycamore Drive.

"Do we know what number it is?" Emily asked, leaning over her handlebars and surveying the long road in front of her.

"Sorry, Em. Couldn't give the game away by asking Dad for the address, could I? He'd never have let us come here on our own. Let's pick a house and ask."

Neil approached the nearest front door and knocked. Seconds later it was answered by an elderly woman with curlers in her white hair. "Yes? Can I help?"

"Excuse me, we were wondering if you knew where the Westons live?" explained Neil.

The woman looked blank.

"They have three children. Two kids about our age and a baby," he added.

The old woman still looked blank. Neil was beginning to think she was a bit deaf.

"And they have a dog. A yellow Labrador," Emily added. She looked at Neil hopefully.

"Ah, of course! Jason. He's been playing in the road with them two kids all day."

Neil and Emily both breathed huge sighs of relief.

"But you'll have to be quick, mind you," the woman continued.

"What do you mean?" asked Emily.

"Why, they're moving today – if they haven't gone already. Look, that's them going now!"

Neil followed the woman's bony finger in the direction she was pointing. At the other end of the street, a large white van was just pulling away from a small bungalow.

"Oh, no! Hurry, Emily!"

Quickly thanking the old woman, they set off up the street.

But it was no use. Even before they'd reached halfway, the van was picking up speed and turning the corner out of sight. They'd never be able to catch it.

They stopped outside the bungalow, panting from their efforts – which all seemed to have been in vain.

"I don't believe it!" groaned Emily.

"No wonder Dad couldn't get hold of them. They were in the middle of moving!"

Emily stooped down and picked something up off the ground. "Neil, look, it's a dog's rubber bone. From what that old woman said about seeing Jason, and with finding this bone . . ."

". . . It all confirms that he was here, Emily. And you know what? I think they've stolen him!"

Bob Parker was not in the best of moods when Neil and Emily arrived back at the kennels. The first thing Neil heard was his father complaining about Muttley.

"Having that dog here is an absolute nightmare!" he grumbled, pacing up and down the kitchen. "The phone hasn't stopped ringing today. The whole world seems to want to come and see him!"

"Calm down, Bob," said Carole Parker, soothingly. "Eat your dinner. It'll be quieter tomorrow."

Emily looked at Neil and smiled. "*You're* telling Dad about the Westons moving house, Neil, not me!" She grabbed both bikes and wheeled them away towards the garage. "I'll put the bikes away!"

Neil rolled his eyes. "Thanks a lot."

He breathed deeply and went inside the house to give his dad the bad news.

Carole Parker looked up from eating her dinner. "The wanderers return. Where have you two been all this time?"

"Sycamore Drive," he replied sheepishly.

"Sycamore Drive? Isn't that where the Westons live?" Carole asked, giving Neil a concerned look.

"It *was*."

"Explain yourself, Neil," said his father, sternly. "Why did you go out there? I thought you'd taken one of the dogs out."

Neil sat down at the table and began to eat his food, freshly served up from the oven.

"You were so busy with Muttley, we thought we'd see where they lived. See if anyone was around. But when we got there, we'd just missed them."

"They were off out again? I was going to go round there this evening," said Bob, incredulously.

"No, they were moving. As in *moving house*!" It was Emily who answered as she came in and sat down at the table.

Bob Parker's expression clouded over. "Are you sure? You actually saw them leave?"

"In a big removal van! We looked in the windows of their bungalow and it was completely empty. Signs were they left in a hurry, too," confirmed Neil.

"Great. This is all I need. I'd better phone Mr Scott immediately and let him know it's going to take a little bit longer than we thought to get his dog back." Bob pushed back his chair and left the room.

Moments later the rest of the family could hear the sound of Bob Parker's soothing tones on the telephone in the hallway.

"How did he take it, Dad?" Neil asked tentatively when he returned.

"He wasn't exactly pleased, but then I didn't *exactly* tell him what we'd found out about the Westons, either. He's definitely holding King Street responsible though, which is my biggest worry."

Emily shook her head. "I still think Jason belongs to the Westons. He looked so at home with them, didn't he, Neil?"

Her brother frowned. "I'm not so sure, Em. Mr Scott seemed to know what he was talking about. He was the one who was showing Jason on Saturday, after all. Mrs Weston didn't even mention the Labrador class. Chris and I didn't pay much attention to Jason's owner when we were watching – but it was definitely a man. And the Westons' behaviour is a bit dodgy, isn't it? Moving house the day after they dog-nap Jason."

"Absolutely," said Bob, sighing. "Anyway, Mr Scott wants me to go out and see him at his farm. I said I'd go tomorrow."

That night, Neil lay exhausted on his bed with Sam curled up beside him. He kept thinking about what might happen to the missing Labrador. As he stroked the Border collie's ears, Neil tried to picture how affectionate Jason had been with the Weston children. He tried to conjure up the picture they had showed his mother to prove that he was theirs. He heard Mrs Weston's voice again, thanking his mother for letting them take the dog home the previous night. Her voice sounded familiar . . .

Neil rolled over and drifted off to sleep. The last picture in his mind was the image of Mr Scott's angry face. Mr Scott wanted his dog back very badly indeed. But now the Labrador had disappeared. How on earth was King Street Kennels going to get out of this mess?

"The Westons? They're no longer with us, Neil. They've moved house and they've been withdrawn from school."

It was Tuesday morning and Neil couldn't believe his ears. The school secretary's words were confirming his worst fears. "So they're not coming back? Ever?"

"No. They've moved out of our area," she replied, turning away.

"Oh. Thank you, Miss Thorn." Neil trudged back outside into the morning sun. He found Chris sitting underneath their favourite tree in the school playing field.

"Any luck?" Chris asked, hopefully.

"They've gone all right. Thorny said it was a bit sudden, but they've definitely gone. Jonathan and Kirsty have been withdrawn from classes. Their teachers have all been told about it!"

"So you're stuck then," concluded Chris.

Neil scratched his head and looked thoughtful.

"Looks like it."

"Do you think your dad will go to the police?"

"As a last resort," Neil replied. "I think he wants to see this Scott bloke first at his farm. He's driving out there tonight, after we close, and I'm going to see if I can go with him."

Chris nodded. "He might not be the sort of man you'd want to give the dog back to, anyway. Pretend you've found the dog, but that you don't think Scott is suitable. If he breeds them, and takes them to shows as well, he might be in it just for the money. You know – a bit cruel."

Neil wasn't so sure. "No, I think he's fairly professional. He seemed to know what he was talking about when he came to see us. Anyway, we'll see tonight. I'll give you a ring when we get back."

"Good luck!"

6

The Parkers' Range Rover pulled off the main road and turned onto a side lane that led to Mr Scott's farm. A large wooden sign at the entrance was painted with the words: *Four Gate Labradors – Breeding, Sales and Purchase. Proprietor: Paul F Scott.*

At the end of a short driveway stood a large Victorian farmhouse. It had rough white walls and tiny windows. Mr Scott appeared in the doorway before the car had come to a stop.

Neil noticed that he looked more casual and relaxed than when he had visited King Street. He was wearing brown cord trousers, green Wellington boots and a checked shirt. He took off his cap and welcomed them. Out of sight, Neil could hear the loud cacophony of several dogs barking together.

"Glad you could make it," said Mr Scott. "Come through the house. I'll show you round the place while we talk."

"Thank you." Bob Parker turned to Neil and Emily and smiled, indicating that they should follow him in.

Mr Scott introduced them all to his wife, who was in the kitchen. She was a plump, pleasant-looking woman with curly brown hair and an infectious smile. She immediately insisted on making refreshments for the three visitors and promised that they wouldn't take more than a few moments to prepare.

"I'm sorry my husband shouted at you on the phone," she said to Bob Parker. "He doesn't often lose his temper. The dogs are his life, you know. He's very protective of them."

Paul Scott coughed. "This way." He led them outside to where the dogs were housed.

As Neil approached two low, brown buildings, he could sense that the farm was a very professional establishment and very well run. There were fences everywhere, and neat drystone walls with not a rock out of place. The fields surrounding them on all four sides were luscious and green, thick with trimmed grass.

"These are the kennels. I don't think you'll find my dogs are lacking basic comforts and the freedom to run about." Mr Scott opened the main door and led them down a sandy walkway between two long rows of pens.

All the dogs were out of their baskets and barking at the visitors. Some of them pressed their wet, black noses up against the wire mesh and whined.

Neil noticed Labradors of several different colours – almost as many shades as he had observed at the Padsham Show. They were kept in light, clean and spacious pens with generous outdoor runs – twice the size of the ones at King Street. They had comfortable baskets, too, and all looked healthy and very well cared for.

Emily poked her fingers through the mesh door of one of the pens and cooed. Inside was a litter of puppies, all chocolate-coloured – one of the rarest shades of the Labrador breed.

Emily was entranced. "Aren't they gorgeous!"

"These little chaps are only one week old,"

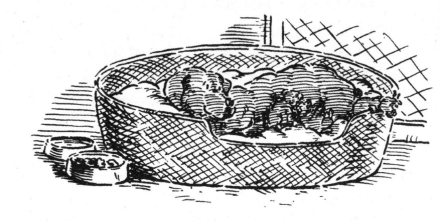

said Mr Scott, affectionately. Neil sensed that he was very proud of them.

The mother lay sleepily in her basket. She lifted her head and her bright brown eyes shone. The three little puppies tumbled over each other and bounced playfully off their mother.

Neil's father was visibly impressed. "The whole place looks very efficient, Mr Scott. I've been working with dogs for twenty years now, and I've rarely seen anywhere as well run as Four Gate Farm."

"Thank you, Mr Parker. I'm sure King Street usually runs very smoothly too. Let's go back inside and discuss our small . . . problem."

Bob Parker's face reddened a little as they followed Mr Scott back into the house.

Mrs Scott announced that the refreshments were ready and led them over to a big wooden kitchen table covered in a summery cloth.

"How long have you been in business, Mr Scott?" said Neil, tucking into a slice of cake. Mr Scott wasn't at all how Neil had expected him to be.

Mr Scott thought for a moment. "My parents have always kept Labradors. My mother started breeding them, so I could say I've been in the business all my life. I managed to get this place started up based on her reputation. We have a good track record for breeding pedigree dogs. I also train them for showing, too. I get a lot of fun out of it, and it helps the business."

"Are dogs just a business for you, or do you keep any as pets?" Neil wanted to know.

Mr Scott let out a throaty chuckle. "Drop any crumbs under the table and you'll soon get your answer to that question!"

Emily pulled up the tablecloth and peeped underneath. "Neil, look! It's a fat dog!" She couldn't resist pulling off a small chunk of cake and holding it under the table.

The greying muzzle of an elderly black Labrador came into view, and he greedily ate the cake from Emily's hand.

"We don't normally let our animals become house dogs – but Barney here's a bit of an exception, isn't he, Paul?" Mrs Scott remarked to her husband.

"He was our most successful stud dog. He sired several champions. When we retired him, we just couldn't let him go. He's the only one I've ever kept. He had such a lovely personality, so we invited him indoors to share our lives. He's a bit on the heavy side now, as you can see. Cake is his biggest downfall, as Emily has already found out! But we all love him to bits . . . don't we, Barney?"

Mr Scott fondled the dog's ears and stroked him under the chin.

"The other dogs all stay outside. They're well trained, get good diets and have lots of exercise. We spend a fair amount of time just giving them love and attention, too. It's my secret ingredient, if you like. I have three paid members of staff here most days. Happy dogs breed happy puppies, don't you think?"

He addressed the remark to Mr Parker, who nodded in agreement.

"I couldn't agree more. We have one house dog, like you," answered Bob. "But we never bring our rescue dogs indoors. We don't want them to get attached to us when they're destined to be adopted by other people. It's not fair on the dogs."

Neil started to relax, and he decided to tackle the thorny subject of the missing dog before his father did. "When did you get Junior, Mr Scott?"

"Ah, Junior. He's one of my favourites. If it had been any other dog but him, I don't think I'd have made half as much fuss. We didn't breed him. In fact, we got him from the RSPCA. My cousin's son happens to work at one of their canine sanctuaries and he let me know that they'd got a pedigree Labrador pup in. He knew I'd be interested.

"We're always on the lookout for new blood for our breeding stock and, rather than always going to the same places, we thought we'd try something entirely different."

"A random factor," said Neil, understanding what Mr Scott was getting at.

"That's it, exactly. Sometimes it works and you get champions out of it. Sometimes it doesn't – and you get pups that can only be sold as pets."

Bob Parker nodded.

Mr Scott continued. "Junior was about four months old when we got him. It was earlier this year. I could tell he was going to be a large dog, and he was completely untrained. But he had good conformation, super looks and a lovely character – so I decided to take him on. After a bit of training he fitted in quite well, though he was never very happy in a pen. He preferred to be running round free."

Neil was thinking that the description sounded exactly like Jason.

Mr Scott continued the story of Junior's background. "He was too young to start his career as a stud dog. As you know, they need to be fully mature and that won't be till he's two or so. Junior is a dog who is easily bored. As he loves people so much, and enjoys showing off, Maggie persuaded me to start showing him in the meantime. The Padsham Show was his first big public appearance . . . The rest, you know."

Mr Parker coughed. "Indeed. Yes, we do."

"I can see why you were so upset to lose him." Neil was touched by the man's devotion to his newest dog.

"And you've not had any luck contacting the people who've taken him?" Paul Scott looked Bob Parker in the eye.

"Not yet. I'm having difficulty getting through to them."

"I'm not surprised. I bet they were professionals. They probably spotted Junior at the show and deliberately lured him away. If I ever find them, I'll definitely prosecute."

Neil and Emily exchanged anxious glances and both looked at their father.

"I don't think it's like that, Paul," said Bob, quietly. "It was actually a young family who claimed the dog. The children obviously knew him."

"Whatever. Whoever it was, I think they've stitched us both up, Bob."

Their discussion was interrupted by the shrill ring of Bob Parker's mobile phone.

"Excuse me, Paul. I'll just have to get this." He got up and stepped outside.

As Neil and Emily continued chatting to Mr Scott about Junior, they could hear their father's voice outside, talking into the phone. It was getting louder with every sentence.

Everyone turned to look at Bob Parker when he came back into the kitchen. His face was pale.

"Neil, Emily, get in the car. We've got to get back to King Street. Immediately!" His voice was stern and serious.

"Dad, what's up? What's wrong?" Neil was immediately very worried.

"Anything I can help with, Bob?" Mr Scott added, obviously concerned.

"No, it's too late. The police are already there."

"Police? Dad, what's happened?" Emily was frantic with worry.

"There's been an incident at the kennels. Some lads tried to take Muttley. Kate has been hurt."

7

As the green Range Rover approached King Street Kennels, Neil felt the blood drain from his face. Blue flashing lights lit up the sky above the Parker house and sent a thrill of anticipation down his spine. Emily gripped his hand tightly on the back seat.

Everybody was in the kitchen. Kate was sitting at the table, clutching a mug of hot tea. She was in tears. Most of her blonde hair had escaped from its normally neat ponytail and tumbled down over one shoulder. There was an unsightly red mark on her forehead where somebody had hit her, and the beginnings of a large bruise on her left wrist. She wiped her eyes with the back of her other hand. Carole Parker had a comforting arm round Kate's shaking body.

Two uniformed policemen stood behind them. One was scribbling in a notebook.

"Are you all right, Kate?" Bob Parker rushed towards Kate and sat in the seat next to her.

Carole Parker tried to fill them in as quickly as she could. "They forced the side gate, Bob. Luckily, Kate was able to set off the alarm, and they ran away."

"I think it confused them," Kate added, with a sniffle.

"Sam was a big help, too. He never stopped barking at them." Carole stroked the frightened girl's shoulder.

"It was terrifying," Kate gasped. "I've never been so scared. There were about five of them. Sam was brilliant. He knew there was danger straight away and wouldn't give them a moment's peace. They rushed at me while I was in Kennel Block One. I tried to keep the door shut but they all shoved past me. One of them hit me." Kate lifted a hand to her sore forehead.

"We've taken a statement, Mr Parker."

Neil recognized Sergeant Moorhead and smiled weakly, then he bent down and gave his Border collie a scratch on the head to say "Well done".

"Did you catch any of them?" Emily asked, anxiously.

Sergeant Moorhead shook his head. "I'm afraid they all escaped. Sam gave one of them a few teeth marks on his arm, though. It sounds like they were drunk and didn't care who they hurt. They definitely weren't local – Kate heard their voices. Probably came down from Manchester after hearing about Muttley."

Neil was shocked. "Trying to steal him, you mean?"

"And they just had to pick the very time when none of us were here," Bob Parker said grimly. "The main thing is that Kate is safe."

"We might still get them," said the other policeman, trying to sound confident. "There's a patrol car combing the area now. With a bit of luck they won't get far."

"I hope not," said Bob.

"Those locks in the kennels will be needing some attention, though. They made a right mess of a couple of them."

Carole Parker agreed. "There's at least two that will need replacing completely. We wouldn't want anybody trying to steal Muttley again!"

Emily was horrified at the prospect that somebody might try to grab their prize canine visitor again.

"Muttley! This is all his fault!" Bob Parker slammed his fist down onto the kitchen table and startled everyone.

"Dad?" Neil said quietly. "What do you mean?"

"He'll have to go. I'm not putting Kate or anybody in this family at risk again."

"But where will he go?" asked Neil.

"To Uncle Jack's. He and your aunt can keep him shut up in the house until his owners get back."

Neil was confused. "You mean hide him?"

"Exactly. The Hendersons will understand. We're just not geared up to taking phone calls from journalists every minute of the day, and to having people traipsing through the place all the time. King Street is a working boarding kennels, and having Muttley is too much. It's upsetting everything. Can you understand, Neil?"

Neil stayed silent.

"I agree with your father, Neil," said Carole, soothingly. "Look at Kate. Look what she's been through! We don't want this happening again, do we?"

"I understand. It's tough on Muttley – but I understand." Neil fought to control his mixed emotions. He was upset that Kate had been frightened, but sorry to see that Muttley had to suffer because of it. The dog would be unhappy locked up in a house all day. He wouldn't be able to go out for long walks in case somebody spotted him and told the newspapers where he was.

"I'll call the emergency locksmith," said Carole.

"And I'll give Jack a ring. I'm sure he'll help out." Bob turned to Kate. "And if you're OK, we'll have Sergeant Moorhead give you a lift home."

The police sergeant nodded. "No problem. We're done here. I'll get one of the boys to give you a ring if we catch those thugs."

As the kitchen slowly emptied of people, Neil was left sitting at the table with Emily. Tired

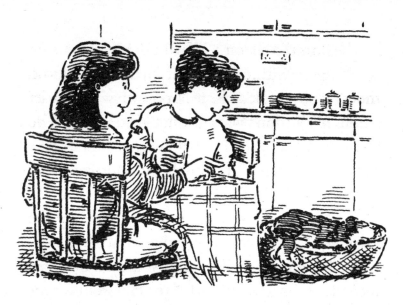

from all the evening's excitement, Sam lay curled up in his basket. His legs began to twitch.

"Look, he's dreaming!" said Emily, smiling.

Neil grinned weakly. "Good old Sam. He must be worn out. I wonder how Junior's getting on – wherever he is."

"Neil, you've started calling him Junior!" exclaimed Emily.

"Oh, I suppose I have. I think it's because I was so impressed by Mr Scott's place tonight, Em. I really believe he loves that dog."

"So do the Westons, Neil. We both saw that," Emily replied.

"It's confusing, isn't it? All I do know for sure is that we've got to move fast on this," Neil said thoughtfully. "Otherwise Mr Scott will feel let down. He'll think we're just not bothering. We've got to find that Labrador before the Westons take him too far away. It'll help Dad too – he's so busy with this Muttley thing already."

"But what can we do?" Emily asked. "Try the local paper?"

"Not a good idea. I think we'd best keep reporters out of Dad's sight right now, don't you?"

Emily managed a laugh.

Neil looked thoughtful. "Dad's going to be wrapped up with getting the locks sorted, repairing the damage those thugs did *and* getting Muttley away tomorrow, isn't he? So it's up to us to find out where the Westons have gone. Agreed?"

Emily nodded.

"Meet me tomorrow straight after school. Tell Mum that you have athletics practice or something."

"OK, but why? Where are we going?"

Neil suddenly looked very sly. "We're going back to Sycamore Drive."

The Westons' old bungalow on Sycamore Drive wasn't as empty as Neil and Emily had thought it would be. As they rounded the corner at the bottom of the road, there was another big removal van outside the house.

"Neil! They've come back!" cried Emily, astonished. It was the last thing she had expected to see.

Neil didn't reply at first and studied the van closely. He wasn't so sure. "False alarm, Em. It's a different van! It looks like somebody else is moving *in*."

"Oh. But that's good, isn't it?" Emily replied. "They might have a forwarding address for Mrs Weston."

Neil knocked on the door of the bungalow and a young man answered. He was wearing paint-spattered dungarees and had a dusty cloth in his hand.

"Sorry to bother you," Neil began. "But the people who lived here before, the Westons, do you have a forwarding address for them? It's quite, er, important that we get hold of them."

The man shook his head. "Sorry, mate. They didn't leave anything – except mess."

Emily was disappointed and her face clouded over.

"You could always try the agency that rents the house out," continued the man, trying to be helpful. "They might know. But I doubt it. The place was in a bit of a state when we got here. They seem to have left in a hurry." The man rummaged about in his pockets and brought out a card with a telephone number on it. "Here. Try this number. Good luck – you'll need it!"

Neil took the card and thanked him. The door closed behind them as they stood looking down at the number on the card.

"It's a chance, Neil."

"A *slim* chance. Come on. Let's get back home before they miss us. I'll sneak a call from the upstairs phone while everybody is having dinner."

"Neil! What have you been doing upstairs all this time? Your dinner is nearly cold!"

Neil slipped into his seat at the kitchen table and avoided looking at his mother. He looked up momentarily and winked at Emily. He wanted to let her know that he'd successfully made the call to the agency.

Bob Parker was talking about Muttley.

"What about Muttley?" asked Neil. "Where is he? Has he gone?"

Across the table, Sarah giggled. "Cloth ears!"

Carole Parker looked exasperated. "If you'd been here on time, Neil, you'd know that Uncle Jack came over today and took Muttley away with him."

"It certainly cheered Kate up, Neil!" Emily laughed.

"Why? Was it funny or something?" asked Neil.

"Hysterical! Apparently, Dad had to cover him with a blanket and smuggle him into the back of Uncle Jack's van." Emily laughed again, imagining how silly it had looked.

Bob Parker couldn't help but smile.

"Dad? Is this true?" Neil was having trouble believing that they had gone to such lengths in trying to move Muttley.

Bob's smile grew larger. "There was somebody

hanging round outside. Near the gates. I thought he was a reporter, spying!"

"It was probably some perfectly innocent man walking into Compton and stopping for a breather!"

Everybody burst out laughing.

Carole Parker cleared the plates from the table. "It did look very strange, I must admit."

Neil took the opportunity to signal to Emily that she should follow him upstairs. They left the kitchen without anybody asking them about their after-school activities and rushed upstairs to Emily's bedroom.

Neil flopped down onto the bed below a huge poster of some TV animal show presenter that Emily had pinned to the wall.

"Well?" asked Emily, breathlessly. "What did the agency say?"

Neil's face didn't give anything away. "There's good news and bad news. Which do you want first?"

"Stop messing about! Give me the bad news."

"OK. The agency don't have an address for the Westons, either. I think the woman I spoke to was hoping I would tell *her* where they were. She got very excited when I told her why I was calling."

"What did she say?"

"Only that Mrs Weston *did* leave in a hurry. She left owing rent and the place was a mess. There were dog hairs everywhere! I think she was a bit miffed because there was a 'No Pets' rule."

"Then we're still no nearer to finding the new address, Neil. So what's the good news?"

Neil hesitated and raised his eyebrows. "The good news is that I've thought of another sure-fire way of getting it."

"I'm waiting," said Emily, tapping her foot.

"We can get it from school. Thorny is bound to have it, isn't she? Mrs Weston can't just pull her kids out of school without telling them where she's off to."

"Neil, you're brilliant!" Emily clapped her hands in pretend admiration.

"True. But the bad news is—"

"Hey! We've already had the bad news!" Emily cried.

"I know, but there's more. I lied. Old meany Miss Thorn will never give us it, will she?"

"She might."

"She won't," said Neil, forcefully. "Not in a million years. I'll try, of course. But you can imagine what she'll say." Neil began to mimic the school secretary's voice. "I couldn't possibly give you that information, Neil Parker. It's confidential. It's more than my job's worth. Blah blah blah."

Emily started laughing.

Neil suddenly looked serious. "So . . . we'll probably have to break in to the school and get it!"

8

Neil tapped nervously on the school secretary's door and waited. The longer it took for Miss Thorn to answer the door, the bigger the mood Neil suspected she would be in.

"One, two, three . . ." He tried counting to make the time pass quicker.

"Anything I can do, Neil?"

Neil's blood froze at the sound of the headmaster's cutting voice. He turned and looked up.

"I was looking for Miss Thorn, sir. I needed . . . an address."

"She's not here this morning, I'm afraid. Or tomorrow. She'll be back Monday. I'd help you myself, but that filing system of hers is a monster. It's positively Jurassic. I'd get lost in there if I tried. No, it'll have to wait till next week. Sorry!" The headmaster was off down the corridor before Neil had had a chance to reply.

Emily shuffled out from her hiding place in one of the caretaker's broom cupboards and rushed over to him. "What did *he* want?"

"It doesn't matter," said Neil hurriedly. "What matters is that he's told me Miss Thorn is going to be off for the rest of the week. Paul Scott hasn't given Dad that long to find out about his dog. So . . ."

Emily hesitated. "So . . . we go to plan B."

"We do. We break in and get it ourselves. It's the only way."

"When?"

"Saturday morning. There's a cricket match on. The school will be open but there'll hardly be anybody about."

"What if we're caught, Neil? Dad will flip."

"I know. I'm terrified, Em. But this is the only way I can think of getting this address so quickly. We'll take Sam with us. If anybody stops us, we can say we were looking for our dog!"

"It *sounds* as if it might work. You're right,

Neil. We've got no choice. If we don't find the Westons, Mr Scott will find *us,* and King Street will be in even bigger trouble!"

The next evening, Neil and Emily dropped their bikes onto their cousin's lawn and shouted through the letter box.

"Anybody home? It's the Puppy Patrol!" they chorused.

The door opened and out onto the porch came a bedraggled-looking Steve Tansley. He was thirteen, two years older than Neil, and went to a different school.

Steve shook his dark floppy hair out of his eyes and grunted. They both assumed he had said hello.

Behind Steve's legs, his wayward Labrador, Ricky, panted energetically, his big pink tongue lolling out of the side of his mouth.

"Are you OK?" Neil asked, looking concerned.

Steve looked at him and sighed, "Sure. Just tired, that's all."

"Ricky worn you out again?" enquired Emily. "I'm not surprised. My dad tries so hard with that dog. I think you've got to face it, Steve. Ricky is beyond hope!"

"No, no, it's not Ricky. It's Muttley! Come and see, he's in the garden." Steve stepped outside and pulled the door shut behind him. He led Neil and Emily round the side of the house and into the large garden beyond.

Neil was suddenly struck by an alarming thought. "Hang on a minute. If Muttley's in the garden, won't people be able to see him? They might recognize him!"

"Not any more, they won't."

"What do you mean?" asked Emily.

"See for yourself." Steve pointed towards a

grey, hairy animal with two magenta-coloured bows tied on its head, kicking up turf on the lawn. His coat was trimmed and beautifully groomed and the hair on his head neatly parted.

Emily stared at the dog and frowned. "Muttley?"

"Er, Muttella, actually." Steve looked sheepishly at Neil.

"Steve! What have you done to Muttley? You've turned him into a girl!" Neil's jaw dropped.

"It was the only way we could get him out of the house without people recognizing him, Neil. He ran riot inside – breaking everything that wasn't nailed down. You didn't tell us that he was so clumsy!"

"Sorry, Steve. I didn't know. He was fine in the kennels while *we* had him."

"Anyway, he may be out of the house, but now he's digging up the garden all the time. I've been running round like a madman trying to get him to stop, but he just keeps doing it somewhere else. I can't win!"

Muttley looked up from his digging and barked. The bows on his head flopped down in front of his eyes, and the dog had to shake his head to flick them away again.

"How's Aunt Mary taking it?" Emily asked tentatively.

"Not very well. I think she's going to phone your dad tonight and ask if he'll take Muttley back."

"Oh no!" cried Neil. "She can't! I can help sort out his digging problem if she likes. If you shake a really noisy tin in his ear every time he digs, he'll soon begin to associate the sound with digging – and he should stop. I've seen Dad do it with other dogs."

"It's no use, Neil. Mum's made up her mind. The dog's got to be out of here this weekend at the latest."

Neil looked at Emily and shrugged. "Your turn to tell Dad!"

Neil and Emily skirted the edge of Meadowbank School playing fields, trying desperately not to look too conspicuous. Every now and again, Neil threw a short stick for Sam to chase after and retrieve. The black and white Border collie scampered back and forth collecting it and dropping it obediently at Neil's feet.

In the middle of the school playing field, a cricket match was in progress. Emily and Neil pretended to watch, and cheered every time somebody scored a run.

"Are we going in the front way or the back way, Neil?" Emily whispered, attaching Sam's lead to his collar.

"I thought the side door near the hall. It'll be unlocked and there shouldn't be anybody hanging about around there," replied Neil.

They reached the school buildings without incident. Before they went in and set off down the long corridor which led to the school secretary's office, they both took a careful last look round. The school was silent, and there was a faint smell of polish in the air, mixed with cleaning fluid.

"Quiet now, Sam. Shh!" Neil held his finger to his lips, and the dog knew that this signal meant he wasn't to bark.

Treading softly, with their hearts racing and nerves tingling, and alert to the slightest sound of anybody who might be approaching, Neil and

Emily began what felt like an endless journey down an ever-lengthening corridor.

Finally, the door of Miss Thorn's office was in front of them, and they came to a stop. Neil felt a jolt of nervous excitement run through him.

"On guard, Sam!" Neil whispered.

The lithe black and white dog sat down outside the door, his ears cocked and alert. Neil turned the handle and the door swung open.

"How did you know it was going to be unlocked?" Emily asked incredulously.

"It's never locked. Too many of the teachers need to go in and out of here all the time. It's the filing cabinets we have to worry about. Quick! Inside!"

He and Emily ducked into the room and closed the door behind them.

"We mustn't knock anything over, Em." Neil whispered. "As long as we stay quiet and don't let anyone see us through the window, we should be all right. Sam'll bark if he sees anybody coming."

"Where do we start, then?" whispered Emily.

Neil looked around and took in the layout of the room. He'd been in here a few times before, on errands, but he'd never stopped for more than a minute. Nobody stopped longer in Miss Thorn's office than they absolutely had to.

Behind a large, flat, black desk with a cluttered top was a whole wall of grey filing cabinets. Various sets of stacking trays stuffed full of paper and textbooks were on top of the cabinets.

"You start that end, and I'll do this end. Read out what it says on all the labels," Neil instructed.

"OK." Emily skirted round the desk but then noticed a framed photograph propped up in one corner. "Hey! Old Thorny's got a dog! Look, Neil, it's a Dobermann pinscher!"

Neil quickly looked at the picture his sister was holding up of Miss Thorn with her arms round a powerful black and tan guard dog. "Somehow, I'm not surprised at her choice of breed. Dobermanns can be quite vicious as well, sometimes."

Emily laughed and carefully put the picture back on the desktop – exactly as she found it. She started to read out the file names. "Suppliers A-Z, Book Clubs, Personnel Agencies, Requisition Forms, Staff Records—"

"I bet that one's locked!" interrupted Neil. "Go on, try it."

Emily tugged on the top drawer and it rattled noisily.

"Told you. Nothing here," said Neil, scanning the cabinets in front of him. "What's next your end?"

"Lost Property, Pupil Records! Yes!" Emily let slip a little cry.

"Excellent!" Neil moved over to join her in front of two five-drawer filing cabinets standing side by side, each labelled *Pupil Records.*

"How do we get into these things, anyway?" asked Emily, giving each of the drawers a fruitless tug. "We don't have the keys."

"Aha! No problem. Miss Thorn keeps the keys in one of her desk drawers," Neil said, grinning triumphantly.

Emily was astounded. "How on earth do you know that?"

"Hasheem told me."

"You told Hasheem we were breaking into Miss Thorn's office? The whole school will know about it by Monday! One of the teachers is bound to find out, and we'll be expelled. Neil, how could you?" Emily put her face in her hands and moaned.

"Keep your hair on, Em! Hasheem told me ages ago. He'd been in her office last term and seen her get them from her desk. Look, I'll show you." Neil stood behind the desk and bent down. "They're in one of those thin, funny drawers." He felt underneath the lip of the desk. "They don't have handles. Ah, here it is. You just push it," he said, giving a rectangular section of one panel a shove. "And out it comes. *Voilà!*"

Emily looked up. "Brilliant! But hurry up, Neil – I'm getting worried."

Neil quickly picked up a ring with six or seven thin silver keys on it and rapidly tried each of them in the first lock. Eventually, one was a perfect fit, and the top drawer slid effortlessly out on its rollers, revealing a dense collection of files and folders.

"The W to Z files are in here," Neil said, sliding open the bottom drawer. "Wallis, Warwick . . . Weston, J! Yes, this will do!" He pulled out a bulging manila file.

"It's Jonathan Weston's confidential file. Miss Thorn would go crazy if she knew we were doing this." Emily peered out of the window. She glanced nervously back at the closed office door. "I hope Sam hasn't fallen asleep."

"Look, it's here! Jonathan's old address has been crossed out and a new one written above it. It's in Colshaw, on the other side of Padsham. They must be going to Colshaw All Saints School."

"They haven't moved *that* far, then. Is there a telephone number?"

Neil flicked on a few pages. "No, but did you know what position he came in last year's Geography test? He only—"

"Neil! We haven't got time!" Emily was getting more nervous the longer they stayed in the office.

Neil wrote the address down, swiftly replaced the file in its correct place, and closed the filing cabinet drawer. He locked it and replaced all the keys in Miss Thorn's desk.

Suddenly they heard a bark outside the door.

"Someone's coming!" Neil tucked the piece of paper with the Westons' new address on it into his back pocket, and rushed towards the door.

Emily only just managed to close it behind them before an authoritative voice snapped, "Neil Parker? Emily? What are you two doing in here with a dog?"

It was the headmaster.

Emily's face turned white and Neil had trouble stopping himself from shaking.

"Nothing, sir," Neil mumbled. "Our dog got

into the school and we were trying to get him back."

Emily looked down at Sam, and slid her foot over next to his flank. She nudged him gently, and the dog stood up and scampered off towards the door they'd used to enter the building.

"He's off again, sir! Sorry about this! We'll just go and get him!" Emily glared at Neil and set off after the collie.

"Er, yes. We've got to go and get him back, sir," Neil mumbled again. He started running after Emily and Sam, who was streaking away down the corridor.

"Make sure he doesn't get into the kitchens, Neil!"

Neil could hear the headmaster shouting something at him, but he didn't care. They overtook Sam, crashed through the double doors at the end of the corridor, and tumbled onto the edge of the playing field, laughing.

"Phew! That was close!" Emily cried.

"Good dog, Sam!" Neil ruffled the Border collie's fur and praised him, then clipped his lead onto his collar.

"Sam was great, Neil. He did everything perfectly."

"He's an absolute star, more like."

Emily was still panting from having run so fast. "Mr Scott will be dead impressed when we tell him we've found his dog, won't he?"

"He sure will," Neil agreed. "This time tomorrow we might even have Junior back where he belongs. Wherever that is!"

9

Colshaw was a fifteen-minute cycle ride from Compton town centre. Neil and Emily set out from King Street on Saturday afternoon, calculating that the whole journey would take them no more than about half an hour.

Emily glanced across at her brother as they free-wheeled down a hill on the Compton road. "Do you think we should have told somebody where we were going?"

"This is something we've got to sort out ourselves, Em," Neil shouted back into the wind. "You saw how Dad reacted when Uncle Jack phoned and told him he was bringing Muttley back. He looked so stressed."

"He did look kind of preoccupied, didn't he?" Emily couldn't help but agree with him. "Did you bring the street map?"

Neil tapped one of the bulging pockets of his jacket.

They rode on in silence for the rest of the journey, only stopping twice: once to get their breaths back after a particularly steep climb, and the other when they were so lost in the maze of streets in the middle of town that they had to consult their map.

"We're nearly there. It won't take long." Neil folded up the map and put it back into his pocket.

Emily bit her lip. "What are we going to say to them when we get there?"

"We'll tell them what Mr Scott told us," Neil said matter-of-factly. "He got Junior from the RSPCA and has certificates to prove it. Then we'll tell them that they've got to bring him back to King Street."

"What if we've come all this way and they're not in?" Emily asked.

"There's a fifty-fifty chance that they are," Neil began. Suddenly his eyes lit up. "But it doesn't matter either way. Look over there!"

Walking down a tree-lined street, Neil had spotted a woman with a pushchair. Alongside her was a familiar-looking girl, a boy, and a yellow Labrador dog.

"It's the Westons! And Junior!" gasped Emily.

"Jonathan!" Neil shouted across the road. "Over here!"

Jonathan Weston stopped in his tracks and his mouth gaped open like a guppy fish. He tugged at the sleeve of his mother's baggy blue shirt. She shot Neil a horrified look, and then immediately looked down at the Labrador. Junior, meanwhile, was tugging on his lead and pulling in Neil's direction. The dog had spotted a familiar face and wanted to say hello.

Neil and Emily pushed their bikes across the road and walked slowly up to the Westons. There was a stony silence for what seemed an eternity to Emily before somebody spoke.

Mrs Weston's blush rose up to meet her blonde fringe. "Neil Parker, isn't it?" She looked down at the Labrador again and half smiled. "Have you come about Jason?"

"Yes. I'm not sure that what you told us about Jason is true, Mrs Weston," said Neil, quietly.

There was a silence as the woman stared at

him. Then she ran her hand through her blonde hair and sighed.

"OK. You win. Come back with us, Neil. I'll explain everything."

Pushing their bikes, Neil and Emily accompanied the Westons back to their new house in the adjacent street. Jonathan described it as a "proper house"; they had more bedrooms, a bigger kitchen, and a large back garden as well as a small front one.

Neil and Emily settled themselves on the comfy sofa in the Westons' living room. Emily kept glancing at Neil and wondering how they were going to say what they knew they had to say. Two large patio doors opened out on to a sunny, unkempt garden. It was ideal for the dog to run about in.

"Sorry the place is such a mess," said Mrs Weston as she entered the room. "We've not been here a week yet, and there's still so much to do." She placed two mugs of tea and a plate of biscuits down on a low table and said, "Help yourselves."

"Thanks." Neil leaned forward and picked up a mug.

Jonathan and Kirsty Weston sat cross-legged on the floor. Both had their hands on the Labrador, who sat calmly between them. The dog seemed sad and was strangely quiet. He stared straight ahead at Neil and Emily, unsettling them a little.

"Does Jason really belong to you, Mrs Weston?" asked Emily, looking away from Jason.

Neil stared at his sister. She'd just said exactly what was on his mind.

Mrs Weston chewed her lower lip. Her eyes left Emily's and darted awkwardly round the room. "Yes – and no," she replied at last.

"You obviously weren't total strangers to him," said Neil. "He knew you all. Otherwise he wouldn't have been so happy to go off with you the day you came to claim him."

"It's very complicated, Neil," Mrs Weston said, sighing. "You see, Jason *used* to belong to us. When he was a puppy."

Neil nodded. It made sense that there was already a special bond between them. No dog could pretend to know people when he didn't.

"We got Jason because Jonathan and Kirsty wanted a puppy," continued Mrs Weston. She sat back in her armchair. "I didn't know at the time that I was pregnant with Michael. When he was born, Jason wouldn't leave him alone. He was always licking the baby's face and trying to play games with him. I think he thought Michael was another puppy. Jason was such a lively pup – far *too* lively for that tiny house we were in. He was always knocking things over and breaking them."

Neil thought of Muttley and his aunt. Some dogs just weren't designed for cramped houses containing lots of ornaments. Or babies!

Mrs Weston continued her story. "One day, I went into the baby's bedroom. I'd left the door open so that I'd hear him if he cried. Jason had got in. When I arrived, he looked as though he was trying to climb into the cot."

"You must have been very frightened," said Emily, sympathetically.

"I was. I know he was only trying to play with Michael, but I was worried in case he accidentally hurt him. I panicked, rushed down to the RSPCA, and explained that we just couldn't keep Jason. Naturally, the kids were very upset."

Jonathan and Kirsty both nodded.

"So what happened then?" Neil asked.

"Well, a few weeks after Jason had gone, I spoke to a friend about it and she told me that there are things you can get to put over cots to stop animals getting near a baby. She also said that he could be trained to be better behaved, and not lick faces and throw himself at people."

"That's true. I could have done that for you," agreed Neil.

"I might well have come to you if I'd known King Street was so close! Anyway, seeing how upset the children were, and knowing that there were things I could do to protect Michael from Jason, I decided that we should get him back again. I suppose I missed him, too. He's the most lovable animal I've ever known."

"And the most loving!" Kirsty said, beaming.

"Yes, he is. However much affection you give that dog, he gives even more back. He's one big love factory, aren't you, Jason? You know we're talking about you, don't you?"

The yellow Labrador padded over to Mrs Weston and rested his head against her knee. His eyes closed in bliss as she fondled his silky ears and scratched his head.

"See what I mean?" said Mrs Weston, in a voice husky with emotion.

How are we ever going to take him away from them? thought Neil. It would be a huge wrench for them all.

Emily was touched by their story too. "Why couldn't you get him back?"

"Weeks had passed by then. When I went back, he'd gone. I went spare! I decided we should get another Labrador puppy quickly, to help us forget Jason. That was how I found Mr Scott."

Neil was astonished. "You know Mr Scott?"

"Yes. I'd heard about Mr Scott being a breeder, so we went up there – and found Jason, penned up in a cage. He wasn't for sale, though. Oh, he looked so miserable. He went wild when he saw us. I didn't dare reveal that we were his previous owners, in case Mr Scott thought I was irresponsible. The kids had trouble not letting on we knew him."

"I almost called him Jason at one point. Right in front of Mr Scott!" said Jonathan, laughing.

"Anyway, having seen Jason again," said Mrs Weston, "we couldn't bear to have any other dog. I must admit, Mr Scott's dogs were all rather expensive, too. I didn't expect them to be that much."

"We didn't know what to do, did we, Mum?" said Kirsty, excitedly.

"Then we went to Padsham Show," said Mrs Weston, "and saw Jason there. It was the last straw.

Jonathan and Kirsty really had to drag me there, too. I usually hate dog shows. I think they're an ordeal for the dogs."

Neil's mind was racing. He remembered watching the Labrador class being judged, and a woman shouting out from the crowd. It must have been Mrs Weston!

"It was wonderful that he came second, of course," she continued. "Though I couldn't bear to look at him being examined like that—"

"And we just wanted to take him home with us," Kirsty interrupted.

"At the end of the show, I gave him my special whistle, and I know he recognized it. He looked straight at us!" Jonathan said. "But then Mum said we had to go. I looked back and Mr Scott was doing something to Jason's collar. He was still looking at us. I was sure of it."

"Then we went to the car park," concluded Mrs Weston.

"So Jason must have got loose and run after you," said Neil.

Emily guessed the next bit. "But he got there a bit too late because you were already driving off."

"If only we'd known!" sighed Mrs Weston. "We could have simply opened the car door and he'd have jumped in. I was so desperate to get Jason back at that point, I really would have done it. We could have avoided getting King Street Kennels involved."

Neil was serious for a moment. "You know that would have been wrong?"

"You really would have been accused of stealing him, then," Emily told her.

Mrs Weston gave a guilty grimace. "It wouldn't have been very honest, no. But I was thinking about Jonathan and Kirsty. And I wanted what was best for Jason. I was confused."

Neil looked puzzled. "But how did you find out that King Street had him in the first place? You didn't know he'd run off from Mr Scott when you drove away."

Mrs Weston nodded. "No, it was an absolute stroke of luck. The following day I was talking to my neighbour, who'd also been at the show. She'd seen a Labrador run off into the crowd and knock a show judge over in his excitement. She thought it was the funniest thing she'd seen all day. That's the only reason she mentioned it. I called the police stations straight away and, sure enough, a Labrador had been found and taken to King Street."

"We knew it was Jason," said Jonathan, enthusiastically. "He's so clever! He was looking for us!"

"If you'd loved a dog as much as we love Jason, Neil, wouldn't you have been tempted to do the same thing?" Mrs Weston looked pleadingly at Neil and Emily.

Neil took a sip of his tea. "I suppose I might," he admitted. "But claiming Jason as yours *was* wrong. Dad's in trouble with Mr Scott, and I know he's going to want answers."

"Mr Scott is coming to the kennels tomorrow morning, Mrs Weston," said Emily. "When he finds out we know where the dog is, he'll want him back, I'm afraid."

"No! He can't! Jason's ours!" Kirsty Weston cried, and flung herself at her mother, sobbing. Jonathan grabbed hold of Jason and held him defiantly.

"We have to sort this out properly," Neil said

quietly. "I think you should bring Jason round to King Street tomorrow at eleven-thirty."

The Westons looked glum. They sat quietly and let the news sink in. Kirsty moved over to Jason and patted him affectionately on the head.

By that time the following day, Jason's fate would be decided. And Kirsty Weston might have to say some painful goodbyes to her dog all over again.

10

"Where did you find the Westons' new address, Neil?"

Carole Parker sat at her desk in the kennels' office on Sunday morning. It was judgement day and Jason's fate would be decided before noon.

Neil turned away from his mother, looking guilty. "From school."

"We should have thought of that. But you know how it's been this last week, Neil. Having Muttley has been a nightmare. I thought we'd solved the problem, but now he's back again! And the calls from reporters have started all over again."

Neil was relieved that his mother had accepted his vague answer to her question, and was more than happy to move on to a new topic of conversation! "I think I'll go and see him now," he said hurriedly. "I know he was trouble and caused Dad a lot of headaches – but I'm glad he's back."

"Don't tell your father that!" laughed Carole. "Anyway, well done, Neil. You and Emily have been brilliant. I'll see you later when Mr Scott arrives."

Neil left his mother to her work and walked over to Kennel Block One. On his way, he stopped by the barn and looked in on the obedience class which was in full swing. He stood just inside the entrance and spotted Emily watching her dad putting an American cocker spaniel through its paces.

"Ugly things, aren't they?" whispered Neil, and Emily giggled.

"I can't understand why anybody would want one!" she said, grinning. "Anyway, where have you been all morning?"

"I took Sam over the ridgeway. I've hardly walked him all week. I suppose I was feeling a bit guilty," Neil replied, shoving both his hands in his jeans pockets. "I'm just popping in to see Muttley before the fireworks start!"

"It's going to be awful, Neil. What's going to happen?"

Neil looked blank. "Search me. I just hope everybody does what's best for Junior. Or Jason. Oh, I'm so confused about who owns that dog I keep calling him different names!" Neil shrugged and stomped off. "Oh, I'll see you later."

*

Muttley's pen had more locks and chains on it than Neil had ever seen before. He was surprised that the weight of metal and iron hadn't already been too much for the wire mesh and torn right through it.

Neil poked his fingers through the holes and said hello. Muttley's thick tail thumped on the wicker base of his basket and the dog whined gently.

"Poor Muttley. You've been through the wars a bit lately, haven't you?" Neil said sympathetically.

The dog responded with two quick barks and more thumps of his feathery grey tail.

"At least we got rid of the bows, old boy!" Neil waved goodbye, stood up and left the kennel block chuckling. Having Muttley at King Street had certainly been an experience. There was never a dull moment while he was about.

Neil stopped smiling as soon as he got outside. Turning into the Parkers' front driveway was Mr Scott's Land Rover.

Neil froze and hoped the visitor couldn't see him yet. He wanted to see the look on Mr Scott's face as he got out of the car, in order to judge what sort of mood he was in.

Neil studied the man's face closely but couldn't interpret his expression at all. He was relieved when Mr Scott's wife also emerged from the car. He'd liked her; she had been so kind and friendly when they had visited Four Gate Farm.

Carole Parker greeted the Scotts on the driveway and took them through into the office. Neil followed and hoped his father's obedience class would finish soon. They were going to need all the help they could get.

"You've found Junior! That's excellent news." Neil entered the office just in time to hear Mr Scott's delighted voice.

"The Westons should be arriving with him any minute now," Carole Parker assured him, glancing at her watch.

"Are you sure they'll turn up?" Mr Scott asked suspiciously.

"Of course they will," said Neil, firmly. "They're not *bad* people, Mr Scott. They love

Jason . . . I mean Junior," he corrected himself quickly. "Probably as much as you do."

"That may well be true, Neil. But Junior is *my* dog. There's no escaping that fact."

Bob Parker popped his head round the office door and smiled. "Morning, Paul. Thanks for coming. Mrs Weston and the children have just arrived. Let's go through and meet them out the back."

"Oh, good. Yes, let's sort this out once and for all."

Neil followed the Scotts and his mother outside. He didn't like the sound of Mr Scott's voice and immediately feared the worst. The Westons didn't stand a chance of keeping their old dog.

Pam Weston was standing in the middle of the stone courtyard. She had one arm round Jonathan, and was holding Kirsty's hand. Jason, the yellow Labrador, sat obediently in front of them, panting.

"Junior! Here, boy!" Mr Scott knelt down on one knee and called his dog.

Junior pricked up his ears and looked in Mr

Scott's direction. There was only a brief moment of hesitation before the dog rushed over to greet him.

Kirsty Weston began to cry. She wiped her eyes with her sleeve and turned her head away.

"Be brave," her mother whispered, and handed her a paper hanky.

Mrs Scott looked at her husband affectionately hugging the Labrador, and then at Kirsty. "Don't cry. You'll be able to see . . . Jason again, I'm sure." There was warmth in Mrs Scott's eyes and Neil knew she meant what she said.

Bob Parker stood back with his arms folded. He seemed happy to let Mr Scott and Mrs Weston solve their problem by themselves. Neil looked on too, but had a different feeling – one of helplessness. Suddenly he knew he had to speak up. He had to make sure Mr Scott knew how it would affect the Westons if he took Jason away from them.

"Tell them why you gave him up, Mrs Weston," Neil said quietly. "Tell Mr Scott how much it means to Jonathan and Kirsty. Before he decides what to do."

Mr Scott stood up and addressed Mrs Weston. "I can see you're all upset. It must be difficult for you. Yes, tell me what did happen? Why did you get rid of him?"

Mrs Weston told him the whole story. Bob and Carole listened too, hearing the full details themselves for the first time.

Neil and Emily exchanged anxious glances. What would Mr Scott do? Surely he wouldn't just walk away and take Jason with him?

Mr Scott took a deep breath when he had finished listening to the story, then looked across at Neil's dad. "What do you think, Bob?"

Bob scratched his chin. "Usually, in cases where two people claim the same dog with legitimate reason, the rule is to let the dog decide. Whoever he appears to know and like best is judged to be his owner. But in this case . . . there's really no question of a legal dispute." Bob Parker looked at Pam Weston. "The dog belongs to Paul. And he has every right to take him back."

"I know that what I did was wrong. And I'm sorry," Mrs Weston said with emotion. "But you see, we all loved him so much."

A loud sob came from Kirsty. Jonathan was staring hard at his feet, trying not to look at Jason standing obediently by Mr Scott's side.

For a moment, Mr Scott looked in two minds, and Neil suddenly knew he had the chance to influence his decision. "Mr Scott? Can I say something?" he asked. Everyone looked at him.

"What are you up to, Neil?" whispered Emily, nudging him in the ribs with an elbow.

Neil ignored her and cleared his throat. "Let

me get this straight, Mr Scott. I know you bought him legally – I don't think anybody is doubting that. But can you tell me why you really want him?"

The directness of Neil's question surprised Mr Scott. "Pardon?" he said.

"Do you just want to use Junior for breeding and showing?"

"Well, yes. That's right," Mr Scott confirmed, still looking a little confused.

"Did the judges at the Padsham Show tell you why they didn't award Junior first prize in the Labrador class?"

"Yes, of course," Mr Scott replied, matter-of-factly. "They said it was because of that kink towards the end of his tail. It's not genetic. We think he was bitten by another puppy from his litter, and it caused a bit of damage."

Neil stared at Junior's wagging tail. He'd never noticed it before, but there *was* a kink in his tail which shouldn't have been there.

"It's enough to ensure he'll never qualify for Crufts in that case?"

Neil waited for a reply. If only he could make

the Scotts agree to this point, then the next part of his plan might work.

"I suppose he'll never be up there with the best, no," said Paul Scott at last. "I think he won the second prize at Padsham on the strength of his personality. But it's precisely that happy, outgoing nature of his that I'd like to introduce into my future Labrador pups."

"So there *is* a solution here to keep everyone happy! One that nobody seems to have thought of. It might be best for Junior, too. After all, isn't that what everybody wants?" Neil said, looking round the sea of faces, all hanging on his every word.

"What is it, Neil?" asked his father. He looked mystified. "What are you suggesting?"

Neil took a deep breath. "Sharing him," he said.

Mr Scott frowned. "What do you mean?" he enquired, frostily. "I'm not sure I like the sound of that at all."

"But Mr Scott, it makes sense. You want Junior to help with your business. Mrs Weston wants Jason as a pet. Well, there's no reason why he can't be both things to both people!"

Mrs Weston was gazing at Neil with her mouth half open. Mr Scott glanced at his wife and raised his eyebrows.

"I don't quite see how it would work, Neil," said Carole Parker.

"It's simple," Neil explained. He was sure the answer was more straightforward than everyone seemed to think. "Let the Westons look after Jason for the time being. You know they'll do a brilliant job, Mr Scott. You've seen for yourself how much they love him, and how much he loves them. You said Junior isn't old enough yet for you to breed from him. When he *is* old enough, why can't you just borrow him back?"

Neil turned to Mrs Weston, without waiting for a reply. "You would let the Scotts have him for a couple of days every so often, wouldn't you? If it meant you could keep Jason?"

"Of course!" Mrs Weston confirmed with delight.

"How do you feel about it?" Neil asked Mr Scott.

"Yes, how does Neil's plan grab you, Paul?"

Mrs Scott asked her husband, placing a hand on his arm.

Bob Parker looked at Neil and winked.

"I'm not sure. He needs to be kept in top breeding condition. He mustn't be overfed, or given the wrong diet for that matter," said Mr Scott, sounding uncertain.

"You could devise a nutrition programme for them to follow," suggested Emily.

"Yes. We don't mind doing that," Mrs Weston said hopefully.

"Mr Scott . . . ?" Neil gazed expectantly at the man from Four Gate Farm, and held his breath. Would he agree to the plan?

Mr Scott was thinking hard. His brow was furrowed and he twirled his cap round in his hands. Then he cleared his throat.

"You were right about Jason, Neil."

Neil exploded inside. It was the first time Mr Scott had called the yellow Labrador by his original name, Jason, and he knew that he was about to hear good news.

"Jason has a fantastic character and is a lovely dog. That's why I'm so attached to him. He loves human company and I must admit, we probably can't give him as much of that as young Jonathan and Kirsty might." He smiled at Kirsty and she brightened up, drying her eyes with the paper hanky.

Emily sensed Mr Scott was going to give in, too, and gave the thumbs-up sign to her older brother.

"I think your plan is perfect, Neil," said Mr Scott.

Everybody cheered and Jonathan and Kirsty rushed over to throw their arms round Jason.

Mr Scott looked at Mrs Weston. "I'd like you to consider having Jason on permanent loan. I'll give you plenty of warning when I think I'll need Jason at the farm. Until then, I think having such loving owners and a superb home will be the best possible thing anyone could do for him. And that includes me!"

Mr Scott gave Jason a final pat on the head and smiled.

Bob Parker stepped forward and put an arm round Neil's shoulder. "Good work, Neil."

"Thanks. It *was* the best plan, wasn't it?"

"Definitely!" chorused Jonathan and Kirsty.

Jason swished his long pink tongue sideways and licked Mr Scott on the wrist.

"He's saying thank you!" cried Emily.

"Does this mean we really can keep him, Mum?" asked Kirsty, still bewildered by the unexpected and happy outcome of their visit to King Street Kennels.

"Yes, for ninety-nine-point-eight per cent of the time, it does," confirmed Mrs Weston, beaming.

"Oh, wow!" yelled Jonathan. "Jason's really ours again!"

Mrs Weston blushed. "Thank you very much, Mr Scott. I know I was a bit hasty letting Jason go in the first place and it was wrong of me to steal him. But thanks for giving us a second chance with him."

"Hey! Wait up, everyone! I forgot to tell you my good news!" Everyone turned and looked towards the barn. It was Neil's cousin, Steve Tansley, pulling his Labrador, Ricky.

"Steve!" gasped Neil. "What are you still doing here? Ricky's lesson finished ages ago!"

"I know. But I was trying to get him to stop chasing mice in the barn. You know how he's always doing stupid things!" Steve looked down at Ricky, who was sniffing at Jason, trying to make friends. Steve rolled his eyes. "Anyway, I forgot to tell you about yesterday!"

"Yesterday? Good news? What are you talking about, Steve?" said Neil, puzzled.

"Dad got Muttley to bark for him yesterday – before he brought him back here," said Steve, still grinning.

"Oh, no, Steve, not you as well?" Emily groaned. She knew exactly what was coming next!

"I know, I know. It was a crazy idea. But guess what? Five of the numbers came up in last night's draw! We're not millionaires, but we've won enough to keep my mum happy!"

"That's great!" said Neil, excitedly.

"It certainly is. Mum says it'll pay for all the things Muttley broke in our house last week!"

Neil laughed. "You're incredible, Steve!"

"I know. But not as incredible as dogs sometimes are. You should know that, Neil. I never understood why you were so interested in dogs. Now I'm beginning to understand."

Ricky barked loudly and Jason responded with a series of barks of his own. Suddenly the kennels behind them erupted in an uneven cacophony of barks and whines.

"Oh, no! You've set them all off!" Emily cried.

Everybody laughed.

"Dogs. Don't you just love them?" shouted Neil above the noise.

"Yes!" cried Kirsty and Jonathan Weston. "They're brilliant!"

Posh Pup

1

"Jake! Come here!"

Neil Parker dashed after his excitable black and white puppy. But he was too late; Jake had spotted a skipping rope and he eagerly grabbed one end of it. He began to shake it from side to side, growling, and Neil felt a blush creeping up into his cheeks as everyone else in the barn began to laugh. All the other dogs, who were there with their owners for a Sunday morning training session, started to get excited too. Chaos was in the air.

"He thinks it's a snake!" Neil's little sister, Sarah giggled. "Stop it, Jake!" She tried to pull the rope free, but Jake hung on determinedly.

"I didn't know you were going to teach Jake how to attack skipping ropes, Dad!" Emily, Neil's nine-year-old sister, remarked with a grin.

"He's pretty good at that already!" Bob Parker said drily.

Bob and Carole, Neil's parents, ran King Street Kennels, a boarding kennels and rescue centre just outside the small country town of Compton. Bob also held regular twice-weekly training sessions for local people and their dogs in Red's Barn, which was next to the kennel blocks on the land at the back of the Parkers' house. Neil loved his life with the dogs at King Street, and he couldn't imagine ever wanting to live anywhere else.

"Come on, trouble!" Neil scooped Jake up

into his arms, and the Border collie immediately let go of the rope so that he could lick Neil's nose. "You're going to start learning how to behave yourself, so you can be just like your dad."

Sam, Neil's black and white collie, wagged his tail furiously, his eyes bright and alert. Neil gently ruffled the older collie's ears. He was always careful to show Sam as much attention as possible whenever Jake was around, even though Sam had shown no signs of being jealous of his son. Jake was Sam in miniature – they both had the same silky coats and shiny black noses.

"Right, shall we try again?" Bob asked with a smile.

Neil told Sam to sit. Sam immediately did so, and Neil couldn't help feeling proud of the way the collie responded to him. Sam was a brilliant dog and Neil had spent most of his free time training him to take part in agility competitions. But when Sam collapsed at the end of a competition, Neil's life had changed. Sam had a heart murmur, and Neil now knew that his beloved dog was living on borrowed time.

"I hope you're watching this, Jake!" Neil

murmured to the wriggling puppy in his arms, "Because you've got a lot to live up to!"

Neil put Jake down, this time keeping a firm hold on his collar. But before the session could get started, there was another interruption. Carole Parker, Neil's mother, put her head round the open door of the barn.

"Bob? There's a phone call for you."

Neil glanced up, surprised at the tone of his mother's voice. Carole, tall and dark-haired, was usually unflappable even in a crisis. But right now she looked rather pale and sounded nervous.

"Well . . ." Bob glanced round the barn. There were eight people and their dogs waiting for the training session to begin, plus Neil and Jake. "Can't it wait?"

Carole shook her head. "It's urgent."

Bob frowned. "OK, I'm on my way." He turned back to the owners and their pets. "Sorry, I won't be long. While you're waiting, try those sit and stay techniques we practised last week."

"What do you think *that* was all about?" Emily said in a low voice to Neil, as Bob hurried out.

Neil shrugged. "I'm not sure. Mum looked a bit wound up, didn't she?"

"Maybe it's just because the kennels are almost full," Emily suggested. "You know how busy we get at the beginning of the holidays, and Kate's not here this week."

Neil grinned and nodded. The school holidays were always King Street's busiest time of the year, and their kennel maid, Kate McGuire, was on holiday herself at the moment.

"What are you going to do?" Sarah asked, as Neil put Jake down on the floor.

"Teach him to sit," Neil replied confidently.

Emily and Sarah grinned. Jake was now dancing round Neil's feet, trying to pull the laces out of his trainers.

"You'll have to get him to stand still first!" Emily pointed out.

"That's what these are for." Neil took out a packet of the dog treats he always carried. "You wait, by the end of these school holidays Jake'll be on his way to being as well-behaved as Sam – *ow*!"

Jake had pounced on the trailing end of one

of the laces, and had accidentally dug his claws into Neil's ankles. Emily and Sarah burst out laughing.

"You mean the holidays *next* year, don't you?" Emily asked wickedly.

"Ha ha, very funny." Neil pulled a face at her. "Let's get started, Jake." He showed the puppy a dog treat, and Jake immediately looked interested. Keeping the titbit in view, Neil then raised his hand slightly above the puppy's black nose.

"What're you doing?" Sarah asked curiously.

"Watch." Neil held his hand a little higher, and Jake, who was staring eagerly at the food, raised his head higher too. As he did so, his chubby little bottom hit the ground.

"Good boy!" Neil said quickly, and gave the puppy the treat. Jake swallowed it down greedily. Then Neil repeated the action, not giving Jake another treat until the puppy's bottom was firmly on the floor.

"See?" He turned to Sarah and Emily. "In a little while Jake'll sit whenever I raise my hand, whether I give him a treat or not."

"Neil?" Carole looked round the door of Red's

Barn again, and beckoned to him, her face excited. "Quick! Your dad wants to see you and the girls in the office!"

"Why?" Neil asked curiously, but his mother had already disappeared.

"Something really weird's going on!" Emily said, as Neil picked Jake up. "I wonder what's happened?"

"Well, we won't find out by standing here!" Neil said, giving Emily a push. "Come on!"

They all hurried outside, Sam at their heels, Jake in Neil's arms, and headed for the office, which was built onto the side of the Parkers' house.

Bob Parker was sitting in front of the King Street Kennels computer, looking slightly dazed, while Carole was perched on the desk, her eyes shining. They both smiled widely as Neil, Emily and Sarah rushed in.

"Don't look so worried!" Bob told them, swivelling round to face them. "I've got some good news for you!"

"What's going on?" Neil asked curiously, as he put Jake down on the floor. The puppy immediately went off to explore underneath the desk, but Sam stayed close to Neil's side, his doggy instincts obviously telling him that something important was happening.

Bob took a deep breath. "A solicitor in Melbourne, Australia has just phoned to tell me that my Great-Aunt Victoria has died."

"*Who?*" Neil, Emily and Sarah said together.

"Great-Aunt Victoria, my grandfather's sister," Bob explained. "She emigrated to Australia years ago, when I was just a boy."

"You've never mentioned her, Dad," Neil said, fondling Sam's silky head.

"Well, to be honest, she didn't really get on with the rest of the family," Bob explained,

sitting Sarah on his knee. "So after she moved to Australia, she didn't keep in touch."

"Were they asking you to go over for the funeral?" Emily asked.

Bob shook his head. "No, the funeral's already taken place, but they've been trying to trace me for the last few weeks. They needed to contact me because . . ." he took another deep breath, "Great-Aunt Victoria left me some money in her will. Quite a lot of money, as it happens."

Neil's eyes opened wide. "How much, Dad?"

"Well . . ." Bob cleared his throat. "Ninety-eight thousand pounds, to be exact."

"*Ninety-eight thousand pounds?*" Neil and Emily repeated in stunned voices.

"We're rich!" Sarah squealed, bouncing up and down on her father's knee.

Neil and Emily stared at each other, their mouths open in amazement. Ninety-eight thousand pounds? Neil couldn't even imagine what a quarter of that amount of money would look like. "It's like winning the lottery!" he gasped.

"What are you going to do with it all, Dad?" Emily asked, her eyes like saucers.

"Give me a chance to get used to it first!" Bob glanced at Carole. "You can see why I was so shocked. I didn't have a clue that Great-Aunt Victoria would leave me anything."

"Daddy, can I have another hamster?" Sarah piped up again. "Fudge needs a friend!"

Bob laughed. "We'll have to see, sweetheart."

"I still can't believe it!" Carole exclaimed, her face breaking into a smile. "Ninety-eight thousand pounds! Thank you, Great-Aunt Victoria!"

"It's a shame the solicitors couldn't get in touch in time for me to go to the funeral," Bob said soberly. "I don't suppose any of the family was there."

Neil wondered what it was like to move thousands of miles away from your family, and never see them again. He couldn't help feeling sorry for Bob's Great-Aunt Victoria. "I wonder why she left the money to you, Dad?" he said.

Bob smiled. "The solicitor said it was because of Winston. He was Victoria's dog. And I used to take him for walks before they left for Australia. The solicitor said that she'd never forgotten that."

"Dad, *what* are you going to do with all the money?" Emily repeated impatiently.

"I haven't a clue." Bob looked at Carole. "We'll have to talk it over, and decide a few things."

"We could have a swimming-pool!" Emily suggested, her eyes shining.

"One pool for us, and another for the dogs!" Neil added. "Dad, you could build more kennel blocks, so we can take in loads more dogs! And you could expand the rescue centre, and—"

"Hang on a minute!" Bob held up a hand. "Don't get carried away! We need to think about all this carefully."

"Yes, we might be a lot richer than we were ten minutes ago, but we've still got a crowd of dogs waiting to be trained in the barn, plus there's only one empty pen left in the kennels!" Carole added, with a twinkle in her eye. "So, it's all hands on deck!"

"This is brilliant!" Emily said happily to Neil as they went across the courtyard to Kennel Block One. "We're rich – we can buy anything we want!"

"I know," Neil agreed. He was already imagining all the extra dogs that King Street Kennels would be able to help . . .

"Did you say *ninety-eight thousand pounds?*" Chris Wilson stared at Neil, with his mouth open.

Neil grinned at the look on his best friend's face. "Yep. Brill, isn't it?"

It was the following morning, and Neil had taken Sam and Jake for a quick walk in the surrounding fields. On their way home, they had met Chris, on his way to King Street. Neil had wasted no time in giving his friend the amazing news about Great-Aunt Victoria's legacy. His mum and dad hadn't been too keen on anyone outside the family knowing about it at first, but Sarah hadn't been able to keep it quiet, and was telling everyone she met, so now the secret was out anyway.

"You lucky thing!" Chris said enviously. "What is the Puppy Patrol going to *do* with all that cash?" Neil and his family were used to being called the Puppy Patrol. The nickname had come about because they were seen around Compton so often in their Range Rover with the King Street logo on the side.

"Well, it's Dad's money, not mine." Neil turned to check on Sam and Jake, who were sniffing around in the hedgerows.

"So what is your *dad* going to do with it then?" Chris went on.

Neil frowned. "I'm not sure. I think he's still getting used to the idea. He and Mum have been talking about it non-stop since yesterday morning."

"I bet I know what you want to do." Chris grinned. "You'll want to make King Street Kennels ten times as big!"

Neil grinned back. "Well, why not?" he said, as they arrived back at King Street. "I can't think of a better way to spend Great-Aunt Victoria's money than on dogs!"

Neil unlocked the front door, and Jake charged in first, pelting full tilt down the hall towards the kitchen. Sam followed at a more sedate pace, and Neil checked, as he always did, that the older dog hadn't got too tired. But he seemed fine.

"Well, I don't think we can decide anything

straight away, Bob." Neil glanced upwards at the sound of his mother's voice. She was on the landing overhead, with his father. "We've got to think this through properly."

"I agree." Bob Parker said in a low voice. "But we're going to have to tell the kids what we're considering as soon as possible. They're involved in this as much as we are."

"I know," Carole replied softly. "I'm just not looking forward to it very much, that's all—" She stopped abruptly as she caught sight of Neil and Chris in the hall below. "Hello, boys. I didn't hear you come in."

"I met Chris on my way back from walking the dogs," Neil said, staring hard at his parents. Both of them looked tired and strained, and they certainly didn't look like two people who'd just inherited an enormous sum of money. He couldn't help wondering what his mum had meant when she'd said she "wasn't looking forward to telling the kids". He didn't like the sound of that at all. Telling them *what?*

At that moment Emily and Sarah appeared in the kitchen doorway.

"Chris, we're rich!" Sarah told him breathlessly. "We're millionaires!"

"Not quite, Squirt," Emily said. "You need a million pounds to be a millionaire."

"Well, we've got lots anyway!" Sarah informed Chris. She grabbed his hand. "Come upstairs and see Fudge! I'm teaching him to do Meccano!"

Chris raised his eyebrows. "This I've got to see!"

He followed Sarah upstairs, and Neil went into the kitchen, where Jake and Sam were waiting patiently by their empty bowls. As Neil gave his dogs some food, he couldn't help worrying about what he'd overheard. What on earth was going on? He was about to ask Emily if she knew anything, when their father came into the kitchen.

"Your mum and I would like to talk to you and Emily, Neil," he said quietly.

Neil frowned, as Carole hurried in too, closing the door behind her. "What about?" he asked warily.

"About what we're going to do with Great-Aunt Victoria's money," Bob said. There was a brief pause, then he went on. "Obviously, it's wonderful to be handed thousands of pounds out of the blue, but we do need to discuss exactly how we're going to spend it." He paused again, looking from Neil to Emily. "And it might mean a few changes to our lifestyle."

"Changes?" Neil repeated, his insides churning.

Carole nodded. "We haven't made up our minds one way or another yet."

"But we think it's only fair to discuss it with you two first," Bob continued. "Because one of the options we have to consider is selling King Street Kennels, and moving on."

2

Neil stood as still as stone, feeling as if he'd been punched very hard right in the middle of his stomach. He couldn't believe what he'd just heard. His parents were thinking of selling King Street Kennels? How could they even *consider* it? He glanced at Emily, seeing the shock he felt mirrored in her face.

"You don't mean it," Neil said in a shaky voice. "You wouldn't sell King Street Kennels. You *couldn't*."

"Neil, we didn't say we were *going* to." His mother rushed to reassure him. "It's just one of many things we've got to consider."

"Why?" Emily demanded, almost in tears. "We're happy here! We don't want to live anywhere else!"

Neil could feel himself shaking all over. He

couldn't envisage a life in which King Street Kennels, and all the dogs who passed through as boarders or as strays, did not play a major part – and he'd always thought his parents felt exactly the same way. Obviously, though, they didn't.

"I don't understand," Neil muttered, staring at his father. "I thought you loved the dogs . . ."

Bob sighed. "Neil, we do. Nobody could do this job if they didn't love dogs. But it's backbreaking work, you know that."

"The money's given us the option to think about doing something different," Carole went on gently. "We're not saying we're *going* to sell – just that we have to think about it very carefully."

"Basically we've got three options," Bob continued. "We can carry on as we are, perhaps with some extra help so that we can have an easier time of it. Or we can use the money to expand King Street. Or . . . we can sell up, and do something different."

"But where would we go?" Emily asked miserably. "Would we have to leave Compton?"

"Emily, we haven't got that far yet," Bob said quietly. "Ninety-eight thousand pounds might *seem* like a lot of money, but it's not enough for your mum and me to retire on. We'll need to keep working. It just may not be at King Street."

"But it'll almost certainly still be with dogs, one way or another," Carole added, looking anxiously at Neil and Emily.

"When will you decide?" Neil asked dully, feeling as if his whole world had turned upside down.

"We're still discussing it," Bob replied. "But as soon as we've reached a decision, you'll be the first to know, I promise."

"What about Sarah?" Emily asked.

"We don't want Sarah to know until we've made up our minds one way or another," Carole said firmly. "And remember, even if we *do* decide to sell up and leave, we'll still have Sam and Jake, and dogs will always be an enormous part of our lives."

But it wouldn't be the *same*, Neil thought wretchedly. Nothing on earth could beat living at King Street. Nothing. Why couldn't his parents understand that?

He glanced at Emily, and read the same

determination in her eyes. Together, they would have to try to change their parents' minds if they decided to do the unthinkable, and leave King Street Kennels.

"You look as bad as I feel," Neil whispered to Emily, as they met on the landing the following morning. Neil had tossed and turned for hours the night before, his mind going over and over everything that his parents had said. Emily, too, looked pale and heavy-eyed.

"I can't stop thinking about what Mum and Dad said yesterday—" Emily whispered. But she broke off abruptly as Sarah's bedroom door opened, and went off to the bathroom.

Neil hadn't felt like getting up early this morning, but he knew that Sam and Jake and the other dogs at the kennels would be expecting their morning walks. However bad he felt, he couldn't let the dogs down. But how many more mornings would he be getting up to help out with the King Street dogs? Not many, if his parents decided to leave.

Carole and Bob were already in the kitchen

when Neil went in, Sam and Jake immediately rushing over to greet him. It was early for visitors, so Neil was surprised to see his uncle sitting at the table.

"Hello, Neil." Jack Tansley, Carole's brother, gave him a friendly grin.

Neil frowned. "I thought you were supposed to be in London, Uncle Jack."

"Slight change of plan, Neil. Aunt Mary and Steve have gone, but I've stayed behind." He glanced towards Bob and Carole.

Neil felt sick inside. What was it now? He stroked Sam and Jake gently, grateful for the dogs' warm, comforting presence.

"That's right, Neil. Your dad and I have

decided to get away for a few days ourselves. To think things through."

"We obviously need to make a decision as quickly as possible," said Bob. "Jack has agreed to step in and take over."

Jack nodded. "I don't like London much, so I'm glad to have an excuse not to go! And I've run the kennels before, when you went to Cornwall. Remember?"

"Kate was here then," added Carole. "But she'll be back on Friday. You and Emily will give him a hand, won't you?"

"Sure we will!" Neil said eagerly. It was a huge strain, waiting to hear what decision his parents would make. If they went away for a while, it would ease the pressure on all of them. And maybe his parents would realize how much they would miss King Street if they moved.

"I'm just going to try and book somewhere to stay now." Bob was already heading for the phone. "Thanks, Jack. We really appreciate this."

After breakfast, things moved quickly. Within an hour, Bob had arranged for himself and

Carole to spend a week in a cottage in the Scottish Highlands. There were all the dogs to be fed and walked, then Neil and Emily helped their mother to pack, and also to pacify Sarah, who had burst into tears when she found out their parents were going on holiday without them.

Just before midday, they were ready to leave and Bob popped his head round the front door. "All set?"

Carole nodded, and everyone went outside, followed by Sam and Jake. Carole gave Sarah a big hug, then kissed Neil and Emily.

"Bye then," she said quietly. "And don't worry. We'll tell you as soon as we've come to a decision."

Neil nodded, trying not to show how worried he was. Would it be good or bad news?

Bob hugged Sarah and Emily, and squeezed Neil's shoulder. "I know you'll give your uncle Jack all the help he needs," he said. "See you next week."

Neil couldn't trust himself to speak. As his parents climbed into the car he stroked Sam, who was pressed reassuringly close against his side, sensing his distress. They all waved as the car pulled away, until it was out of sight.

"Well, shall we go and have some lunch?" Jack suggested.

Before anyone could answer, another car pulled onto the drive. Mike Turner, the local vet, leaned out, and grinned at them.

"Hi, you lot. Bob asked me to pop in and see one of the rescue dogs who's got an eye infection."

"Yes, that's Robbie," Neil said. He pushed the thought of his parents firmly out of his mind. All that mattered now was that the kennels were run properly, and the dogs were kept safe and happy. Moping around wondering what his parents were deciding wouldn't help anyone.

"Right." Mike opened the car door, and reached for his bag.

"Shall I give you a hand with your stuff?" Jack moved towards him. Unfortunately so did Jake, who had just stopped chasing his tail, and was charging towards the vet's car, barking a welcome.

"Jake!" Neil yelled. "Uncle Jack, look out!"

Uncle Jack looked round just as the excited

puppy tried to weave through his legs to get to Mike Turner. Jack was knocked off-balance, and fell heavily to the ground, landing awkwardly on his arm.

"Uncle Jack!" Neil, Emily and Sarah rushed over. Mike was already kneeling down, examining Jack's twisted arm.

"Don't try to move it, Jack," Mike said quickly. "I think it might be broken!"

"They're back!" Neil jumped up from the sofa as he saw the vet's car pulling onto the drive later that afternoon, and Jake, who was lying next to Sam, jumped up too. "Oh, no, you don't!" Neil said sternly, tucking the wriggling puppy firmly under his arm. "You've done enough damage for one day!"

After the accident, Mike Turner had driven Uncle Jack to the local hospital to have his arm X-rayed. Uncle Jack had been in a good deal of pain, and if Mike hadn't been there, they would have had to call an ambulance. Mike had also refused to leave Neil, Emily and Sarah at King Street on their own, so Neil had rung Chris, and he and his mum had hurried over to stay with them.

"You'll have to ring your parents and tell them what's happened, won't you?" Chris said to Neil, as they all went outside.

Neil shook his head. "No way. They need this holiday to sort things out. Anyway, Em and me want to show Mum and Dad that we'll work hard to keep the kennels going. Then they'll realize how much we want to stay."

Chris nodded, looking sober. He was still reeling from the shock of discovering that the Parkers might be leaving King Street.

Jack Tansley climbed out of Mike Turner's car. He had a plaster cast on his arm, but Neil was glad to see that he wasn't quite so pale.

"Are you all right, Uncle Jack?" Emily asked anxiously.

"I've been better," Jack said drily. He reached out, and scratched Jake's head. "For a little fellow, you've certainly caused a lot of damage, Jacob Parker!"

"Does it hurt?" Sarah asked sympathetically.

Jack pulled a face. "Yes, but the doctor's given me some painkillers to take."

"It was quite a bad break," Mike Turner said, as they all went inside. "And I hate to say this, Neil, but I think you'd better ring your parents, and ask them to come back—"

"No!" Neil and Emily said together. Mike looked taken aback.

"Mum and Dad really need this time away," Neil explained quickly. "Em and I can manage."

"Here, I've still got one good hand, haven't I?" said Uncle Jack indignantly, as Mrs Wilson handed him a cup of tea. "Between the three of us—"

"Four!" Sarah interrupted crossly.

"Between the four of us, we can manage. And Kate's due back on Friday."

"But that's four days away." Mike frowned. "Are you sure you can cope till then?"

"I'll come over every day to help," offered Chris.

"And I could give a hand with the cooking," Chris's mum added.

"Well, if you're sure . . ." Mike shrugged.

Uncle Jack nodded. "We can manage."

Neil could tell that Mike had sensed there

was something going on, but he wasn't the sort to pry.

"Well, I'll pop in as much as I can this week too." Mike stood up. "Now I'd better have a look at Robbie's eye infection."

"Thanks, Mike," Neil said gratefully. He knew how busy the vet was, and he must have had to cancel some of his afternoon appointments to take Uncle Jack to the hospital. Mrs Wilson and Chris, too, were giving up their holidays to help them out. If they did move away from Compton, they would be leaving all these good, loyal friends behind.

"Phew! I never knew looking after the kennels was such hard work!" Chris staggered out of Kennel Block One carrying a pile of dog dishes. "I'm tired out from walking all those dogs!"

"Don't be a wimp!" Neil was behind him, carrying another load of dishes. "Come on, the dogs want their food!"

"So do I!" grumbled Emily, who joined them from Kennel Block Two, also laden down with dog bowls. "I'm starving!"

Neil and Emily had only realized the extent of the task that they'd taken on when evening came, and it was time for all the dogs to be fed and walked. Uncle Jack had helped at first, but his arm had obviously been hurting, so he'd gone inside to take some painkillers. Neil was extremely grateful that Chris was there to lend a hand.

"Look!" Chris stopped so suddenly that Neil almost cannoned into him. "What's the matter with your uncle?"

Uncle Jack was standing near the back door of the house, staring around him as if he couldn't remember where he was, and swaying slightly from side to side.

Neil frowned. "It must be those painkillers the doctor gave him. Those pills can be pretty strong!" He hurried over to his uncle. "Uncle Jack, are you all right?"

"What?" Jack Tansley stared blearily at Neil. "Yes, I'm fine."

"You don't look it." Neil guided him gently back into the house. "Why don't you go and lie down?"

"All right." Uncle Jack yawned hugely. "I *am* feeling a bit woozy."

"A bit woozy!" Chris repeated, when Neil came back. "He was totally out of it!"

Emily looked worried. "Poor Uncle Jack. He's not going to be much use to us in that state, is he?"

"Mike Turner's definitely going to want you to ring your parents now," Chris pointed out.

Neil looked defiant. "We'll just have to keep Uncle Jack out of everyone's way, if he's taking those pills," he said in a determined voice. "All we've got to do is keep our heads down and play it cool, and we'll make it through to Friday, when Kate gets back."

Chris stared at him. "But that means we're going to be running the kennels on our own!" he gasped.

"Well, we can do it!" Emily said stubbornly.

"Yes, of *course* we can!" Neil agreed with more conviction then he secretly felt.

The telephone in the office rang just then, and Neil hurried over to answer it, while Chris and Emily went to wash the dogs' bowls.

"Hello, King Street Kennels," he said politely, wondering if it would be his father. Bob had promised to ring home as soon as they were settled in Scotland.

"Hello, my name is Rachel James, and I'm looking to board a dog for one week from tomorrow," said a brisk voice. "Do you have a vacancy?"

Neil hesitated. Maybe he shouldn't take in any more animals with things as they were? But one more dog wasn't going to make that much difference, and they did have a pen available.

"Yes, we do."

"Good," Rachel James said, pleased. "The dog's called Molly, and she's . . ." she paused, "yes, she's a terrier cross."

Neil frowned. Didn't Rachel James know what colour and type her own dog was?

"We're open from nine-thirty, Miss James, so you can bring your dog along any time you like after that."

Rachel laughed. "Oh, Molly isn't *my* dog. She belongs to Kerry, my employer."

"Oh," said Neil. There was a pause, then

Rachel James said sharply, "You *do* know who Molly is, don't you?"

"Yes, you just said she was a terrier cross," Neil said, even more puzzled by now.

"Oh, don't you ever read the papers?" Rachel asked, with a little laugh. "Pictures of Molly have been in the tabloids for the last few weeks!"

Neil frowned. He didn't read the newspapers much, but he usually took notice of any doggy stories. Then slowly it began to dawn on him. He remembered Emily mentioning something about a famous dog . . .

"You mean—?" he said faintly.

"Yes, Molly is Kerry Kirby's dog!" Rachel snapped. "You *have* heard of Kerry Kirby, haven't you?"

"Yes," Neil said weakly. Kerry Kirby was the lead singer of All Spice – Emily's favourite band. They were one of the most successful groups in the world! Kerry was in the news because she was dating Liverpool and England footballer, Michael Newman. It was Michael who'd adopted the dog from a rescue centre in Liverpool, and given her to Kerry just a few weeks ago. The

press were already speculating wildly that Molly might be a secret engagement present, and that the famous couple were planning to get married.

"All Spice are touring in the North for the next week or so," Rachel explained. "And Kerry wants Molly close by so she can collect her at the end of the tour. We'll need to drop the dog off at about eight-thirty tomorrow morning because of our schedule. Is that all right with you?"

"Er – yes." Neil was still too stunned to object.

"Kerry will be bringing Molly along herself tomorrow," Rachel went on cheerfully. "So you can expect the press to be out in force – they'll want lots of pictures!"

Neil felt himself turn white. So much for keeping a low profile. Tomorrow one of the most famous dogs in the country would be moving into King Street Kennels, and if anything went wrong, the whole world would soon know about it.

3

"I can't believe it! Kerry Kirby and her dog coming to King Street Kennels tomorrow!" Emily said ecstatically. "You could look a bit more excited, Neil!"

"At any other time I would be," Neil said grimly. "But if anyone finds out we're running the kennels on our own, we're sunk."

Neil, Emily and Chris were in the Parkers' living room. Sarah had bounced off to bed to tell Fudge the exciting news, and Mrs Wilson, who had popped over with a casserole for dinner, was tidying the kitchen. Luckily, Uncle Jack had stayed upstairs, fast asleep, while Chris's mum was in the house.

"But why should Kerry Kirby's dog coming to stay make any difference?" Chris asked.

"Well, for a start, Uncle Jack's got to be there to book the dog in," Neil said.

"I see what you mean." Chris nodded. "People will start getting a bit suspicious if there's only kids around!"

Emily frowned. "So that means we've got to persuade Uncle Jack not to take any painkillers!"

"Exactly," Neil said. He could just see the headlines now: KIDS RUN KENNELS WHILE UNCLE IS OUT FOR THE COUNT! He didn't know if his parents were bothering with newspapers up in the Scottish Highlands, but if they saw any stories like that, they'd race straight back home.

"We've got to make sure *nothing* goes wrong," he said urgently. "Because if it does, we'll be in big trouble—"

The phone in the hall erupted into life.

"I bet that's Dad," Emily said, nervously.

Neil went to answer it, his heart pounding. If it was his father, he would have to make sure he didn't give anything away.

"Hello, Neil?"

"Hello, Dad!" Neil hoped he sounded cheerful. "Did you have a good journey?"

"Yes, we arrived safely," Bob told him. "How's everything at home?"

"Fine," Neil said calmly. "Don't worry about anything here, Dad."

"Good. I'm ringing from the nearest village, because the cottage doesn't have a phone. If you need to contact us urgently, you can leave a message with the owner, Mrs MacDonald." Bob gave Neil the number. "Is Jack around?"

Neil gulped. "No, he's out with some of the dogs."

"OK, I'll speak to him next time I phone. Give my love to the girls."

Neil couldn't help feeling guilty as he hung up, but he hadn't *really* lied. All the dogs had been fed and walked, despite Uncle Jack's injury, so everything *was* fine. He just hoped things would stay that way when Kerry Kirby and Molly arrived tomorrow.

"Look at all those photographers!" Emily gasped, staring through the living room window the following morning. "And there are more arriving!"

"Maybe they'll want to photograph us as well!" Sarah said, her eyes as round as saucers.

Neil joined his sisters at the window. There

were five photographers hanging around outside King Street already, loaded down with cameras and flashguns, and a couple more cars were pulling up at the side of the road. Emily nudged Neil.

"There's Jake Fielding." Jake was a photographer with the local *Compton News*, and had often covered stories about King Street dogs.

Neil glanced at the clock. "I'd better go and wake Uncle Jack up."

"And don't let him take any painkillers!" Emily reminded him.

Just as Neil was about to go upstairs, the doorbell rang. He opened it cautiously, thinking it might be one of the photographers, but it was Chris, along with Hasheem Lindon, their friend from school, and Emily's friend, Julie, all looking very excited.

"Have you seen the photographers?" they all said together.

Neil nodded, as he let them in. He and Emily had phoned Hasheem and Julie the day before, and they'd both offered to come over and help out when they heard about Uncle Jack's accident. Neil was hoping that, with so many willing hands, the day would run smoothly. Once they'd got over the tricky business of booking in a pop star's dog, of course.

"Em and Sarah are watching for Kerry and Molly to arrive." Neil headed for the stairs. "I've got to go and wake Uncle Jack – he's still snoring his head off!"

But Neil was in for a shock. When he went into the guest bedroom, Jack was already up and dressed.

"Morning, Uncle Jack." Neil glanced anxiously at the bottle of painkillers on the bedside cabinet. Had his uncle taken one yet or not? "How's your arm?"

Jack grimaced. "Still painful. I had quite a good night's sleep though." He frowned. "I don't remember much about yesterday. Did we get all the dogs fed and walked last night?"

"Yes, we did," Neil assured him. "Er – do you think you'll need to take any of those pills today?"

"Oh, I've just taken a couple," Uncle Jack said. "I can't manage without them yet."

Neil's heart plummeted. That meant they only

had about twenty minutes or so before Uncle Jack started going all woozy again.

"Neil!" That was Emily, shrieking at the top of her voice. "They're here!"

Neil glanced out of the bedroom window. A white Mercedes was pulling onto the driveway, and the photographers were already surrounding it eagerly.

"Who's here?" Uncle Jack asked, puzzled.

Neil quickly explained as he hurried his uncle downstairs.

"Oh. I don't remember taking the call yesterday," Uncle Jack remarked, still puzzled.

"You didn't, I did." Neil told him.

"Rather exciting, looking after a pop star's dog, isn't it!" Uncle Jack said. Then to Neil's dismay, he yawned widely. "Oh dear, must be those painkillers that're making me drowsy."

Neil's heart begin to thump nervously. *Please keep awake long enough to book Molly in, Uncle Jack,* he thought silently.

Emily and the others were already waiting in the driveway, their eyes out on stalks. The Mercedes drew smoothly to a halt, and a slim, red-headed woman got out, followed by a burly bodyguard.

"Hello, who's in charge here?" the woman asked briskly.

Uncle Jack hurried forward. "I am. Welcome to King Street Kennels."

"I'm Rachel James." She frowned. "You're not the person I spoke to yesterday."

"That was me," Neil said, conscious of all the photographers around them.

"Oh, right." Rachel glanced at the plaster cast on Uncle Jack's arm. "You look like you've been in the wars. Are you sure you're well enough to look after Molly properly?"

Neil felt a thrill of horror run down his spine. "Of course we can," he assured her quickly.

"Great!" said a familiar voice, and Kerry Kirby climbed out of the Mercedes. She wore a zebra-print mini-skirt, and big platform shoes, and her hair was in blonde dreadlocks. In the last All Spice video, her hair had been long and jet black.

"Kerry, over here!" All the photographers on the drive started snapping away immediately. "Give us a smile, Kerry!"

Kerry grinned and waved at them. Then she reached into the car, and picked her dog up.

"And this is Molly!" she told Neil and the others. Then she turned to pose for the photographers, who began firing off shots as fast as possible.

Neil inspected Molly more closely. She was small and sturdily-built, with a golden-brown, shaggy coat, and had the typical lively, alert look of a terrier. Her big, brown eyes were full of interest as she stared round at the photographers, and she barked loudly every time a flashgun went off. Neil couldn't help smiling when he saw that the dog was wearing a red velvet collar and a large gold identity tag.

"Can we have one of the kennel kids in the frame?" Jake Fielding called out. "Come on, Neil, what about you?"

Neil turned pink.

"Yes, go on, Neil!" Emily said eagerly.

Feeling rather embarrassed, Neil went over to stand next to Kerry Kirby. Molly immediately leaned towards him, barking with delight, and sniffing Neil's scent. Neil put out his hand,

and Molly licked it enthusiastically, pawing at his shoulder, as the cameras clicked. She was certainly one of the liveliest dogs he'd ever met, Neil thought.

"That's all, folks," Rachel called, ushering Kerry and Molly away. "Jeff, will you bring Molly's things in?" The bodyguard immediately went round to open the boot, and Rachel turned to Uncle Jack. "Can we get Molly settled in quickly, please?"

"Of course," he said politely, stifling a yawn. Neil's heart began to thump nervously. He just hoped Uncle Jack wouldn't fall asleep in the middle of booking Molly in!

Uncle Jack led Kerry, Molly and Rachel into the office, and Neil and the others crowded inside too.

"There seems to be rather a lot of you!" Kerry remarked, raising her eyebrows. "Surely you don't *all* live here?"

"Our friends like to come and help out in the holidays," Neil explained quickly. The others all seemed tongue-tied, especially Emily, who was staring at Kerry Kirby as if she couldn't believe she was really there. Only Sarah didn't seem fazed by the pop star's presence.

"My sister's got all your CDs," she told Kerry Kirby. "But she won't let me borrow them!"

"Sarah!" Emily hissed, mortified, but Kerry Kirby laughed.

"We *are* in a hurry, so could we make this as fast as possible?" Rachel glanced impatiently at Uncle Jack.

Neil kept a sharp eye on his uncle while he was entering Molly's details onto the computer, but fortunately Uncle Jack managed to get everything down correctly. Meanwhile the bodyguard had brought Molly's things into the office.

"These are her toys." Kerry pointed at a sports bag, bulging with rubber bones and frisbees. Next to it was a basket as big as a baby's cot, and lined with soft blankets and velvet cushions. "Molly *can* have her own basket in her pen, can't she?"

"Yes, of course." Neil stared at a pile of gold dog dishes, which had *Molly* engraved on them. "What does she eat?"

"Chicken's her favourite," Kerry said. "There should be enough frozen meat here for the whole of her stay, but if you need more, just add it to my bill. Oh, and Molly likes to have this with her." Kerry held up a large, gold-framed publicity photograph of herself. "Can you put it in her pen?"

"Sure." Neil tried not to smile. He'd never seen a more pampered dog!

Kerry hugged Molly. "Be a good girl for your mum, won't you?" She turned to Neil. "She's very well-behaved, you know."

Molly barked, and began chewing Kerry's dreadlocks.

"Would you like to come and have a look at

the kennels?" Neil asked. Most owners wanted to check that the place they were leaving their pet in for the first time was clean and well-kept.

Kerry hesitated.

"Kerry," Rachel James said urgently, "we really must go."

"No, that's all right," Kerry told Neil. "King Street was recommended to me by a friend of mine, anyway. Jeff Calton – he produces *The Time Travellers.*"

"Oh." Neil remembered Jeff. When his favourite TV show, *The Time Travellers*, had come to Padsham Castle on location, he and some of his friends had been cast as extras. It was good to know that Jeff remembered him, and King Street Kennels.

Kerry hugged Molly again, then handed her over to Neil. "Look after her, won't you?" she said with a shaky smile, and hurried out with Rachel. Cameras clicked again as they got into their car.

"She was nice, wasn't she?" Emily sighed, as they all crowded round the window to watch the Mercedes pull away. The photographers began to drift away too. "And she's mad about Molly."

"You know what? I reckon this dog's the poshest pup in England!" Hasheem said with a grin.

"And the daftest!" Neil groaned, trying to stop Molly from licking his ear off.

"Who's snoring?" Sarah asked.

They all turned round. Jack had dozed off with his head on the computer keyboard.

"I thought you were going to stop him from taking any painkillers, Neil!" Chris said.

"I didn't quite make it!" Neil sighed, leaning over to shake his uncle's shoulder. "Why don't you go back to the house and have a lie-down, Uncle Jack?"

"Eh?" Uncle Jack said, dazed. "Is it time for bed?"

"Yes, it is," Neil assured him. Uncle Jack yawned, and staggered out.

"That was close," Emily said. "Another minute, and he'd have fallen asleep in front of Kerry Kirby!"

"Yeah, that would have been *great* publicity for the kennels!" Neil groaned. "Let's go and get Molly settled in. We've still got all the morning jobs to do yet. And Mike said he would stop by. Everything must look normal."

He put Molly down, intending to put her lead on. But as soon as the dog's paws touched the ground, she bolted towards the back door, which Uncle Jack had left open.

"Molly!" Neil yelled. "Come back!"

Molly took no notice. She darted out into the back garden, snuffling eagerly around, her eyes darting everywhere. As Neil and the others raced after her, she dodged them easily, racing around at top speed.

"This is all we need!" Neil groaned, as they chased after her. He had nightmare visions of another newspaper headline: INCOMPETENT KENNELS LOSE POP STAR'S DOG.

"I thought she was supposed to be well-behaved!" Chris gasped.

Just then Jake trotted out of the kitchen door. He took one look at Molly, and charged over to her, tail wagging furiously.

Molly eyed Jake with interest. While the two dogs were sniffing at each other, Neil and Emily sidled over, and managed to clip Molly's lead to her collar. Molly immediately grabbed it in her teeth, shaking it from side to side, and growling playfully.

"Phew!" Neil gasped. "I think we've taken on a whole lot of trouble here!"

4

"Hey, Em!" Neil said indignantly, as he stuck his head round the office door to find his sister sitting in front of the computer. "Come on, I need some help to lock up the kennels for the night!"

"Sorry." Emily looked up, as Neil came in, followed by Jake. "I was just checking some of the All Spice websites to see if I could find anything about Molly."

"Good idea!" Neil went into the office, and looked at the computer screen. "Have you got anything?"

"There's bits of stuff here and there, but this one's the best." Emily clicked the mouse, and accessed a site which had the title *The Molly Zone!* After a few seconds, a large picture of Molly appeared too.

Neil grinned. "You mean there's one site that's just about Molly?"

Emily nodded. "Some nutty All Spice fans must have put it together. Look, it's got lots of information about Molly in it."

Neil scanned the screen. "Molly's two years old, and she's a terrier cross," he read out. "No one knows where Molly came from. Three months ago, she was left tied to the railings of a dogs' home in Liverpool. Then she was adopted by the footballer, Michael Newman, and given to his girlfriend, Kerry Kirby of All Spice."

"How could someone have treated Molly like that!" Emily exclaimed angrily.

Neil nodded. However many neglected or abandoned dogs he saw, it always shocked him that anyone could hurt a dog. His own dog Sam had been an abandoned puppy when he first came to King Street.

"It's amazing that she still trusts humans after what she's been through," said Neil. Jake was standing on his hind legs, trying to climb up the desk to see what was going on, so Neil picked him up. "What else is there, Em?"

"This looks interesting!" Emily pointed to a section entitled *Amazing Facts About Molly*.

"Molly's got twenty different collars," she read. "Her favourite is a gold one with silver tassels on it!"

"She probably likes chewing the tassels!" Neil remarked with a smile. "How do they know all this stuff anyway?"

"I've seen some of these stories before, so I suppose they've copied them out of the newspapers." Emily skimmed down the list of "amazing facts", and read aloud: "Molly once chewed up a pair of Kerry's designer shoes, which cost £500!"

Neil laughed. "I wonder why Kerry told us Molly was well-behaved? She obviously isn't!"

"Maybe she thought we wouldn't take her if we knew the truth!" Emily pointed at the screen. "Check this out! Molly has her own playroom in Kerry's mansion in London, complete with an intercom, so that she can bark for the housekeeper when she wants her lunch!" Emily logged off the computer. "It must be a bit of a comedown for her, staying at King Street Kennels!" she giggled.

"She doesn't seem to mind!" Neil said. "Come

on, let's go and lock up, and we'll take Jake in to see her."

"Yeah, they certainly seem to like each other!" Emily commented, as she, Neil and Jake went over to Kennel Block One.

"That's probably because Molly came from a rescue centre, so she's used to loads of other dogs being around," Neil pointed out. They went into the kennel block, and as they made their way down the aisle towards Molly's pen, he and Emily checked that the dogs were all safely locked in. Most of them were asleep, although some of them looked up sleepily as Neil, Emily and Jake went by.

"I'm worried about Daisy." Emily stopped by one of the pens which had a little white poodle in it. "She seems a bit off colour."

"She's not ill, is she?" Neil asked, alarmed.

"I think she's just missing her owner," Emily said. "She's never been to a kennels before."

Daisy was lying in her basket, but she wasn't asleep. She stared mournfully at Neil with her big dark eyes, but she didn't move, not even when he held a dog treat through the wire mesh.

"We'll have to keep an eye on her," Neil said, worried, as they went on down to Molly's pen. He was always concerned when dogs didn't settle in well at the kennels, but as he felt as if he was in charge at the moment, it was up to him to make sure Daisy was happy. It was a big responsibility.

Molly, unsurprisingly, wasn't asleep. When Neil, Emily and Jake went into the pen, she hurled herself at them joyfully.

"She's a right handful, isn't she?" said Emily, as Molly and Jake ran round each other in circles, nipping affectionately at each other's tails.

"Yeah, she's pretty crazy!" Neil said. "I guess the kind of lifestyle she leads doesn't help either. Kerry's away from home a lot, so I suppose Molly travels around with her most of the time."

Emily nodded. "Perhaps Molly hasn't really had a chance to settle down in one place."

"*And* she's got bags of energy!" Neil stroked Molly's head, then was nearly knocked over backwards as Molly launched herself at him enthusiastically. "No wonder she gets overexcited. Did you see her with Mike earlier? She nearly licked him to death!"

"How was Uncle Jack when Mike came round?" Emily asked anxiously.

"He was all right," Neil said thankfully. "The painkillers he'd taken this morning had almost worn off by then. And I told Mike the real reason why Mum and Dad are away."

"What did he say?"

"He was shocked," Neil admitted. "But at least it took his mind off Uncle Jack yawning!"

Emily grinned. "So we're still managing to get away with it?"

"Just about. And maybe Uncle Jack won't need to take those pills for too much longer." Molly pounced playfully on Jake again, and Neil smiled. "I think I'd better take Molly for a really long walk tomorrow morning, and tire her out a bit!" He looked thoughtful. "Maybe I'll include her in Jake's training sessions too."

Emily glanced at the photo of Kerry Kirby, propped up in one corner of the pen. "Do you think Kerry would mind?"

"I don't think so. It must be difficult taking Molly around with her if the dog's not trained." Neil looked determined. "Anyway, it can't hurt."

Emily shrugged, and yawned.

"You're as bad as Uncle Jack!" Neil teased her.

"I'm really tired," Emily complained. "And we haven't finished feeding all the dogs yet."

"I know." Neil was suddenly conscious of feeling exhausted himself. Hasheem, Chris and Julie had helped out with all the feeding and walking of the dogs that day, but there had been plenty of other things happening too – people had been ringing to make bookings for their pets for the next few months, a van had arrived with a delivery of dog food, which Neil had had to take charge of and check carefully, and Robbie's eye infection had suddenly got worse. Neil had always known that running the kennels was hard work, but now it was really being brought home to him. He was beginning to understand why his parents might be considering changing their lifestyle. Even if they could afford extra help, life at the kennels would never be easy. "I wonder how Mum and Dad are getting on?"

"Well, they can't have decided anything yet, or they would've phoned. It seems ages to wait until they get back next Tuesday, doesn't it?"

"It seems ages to wait until *Friday*, when Kate gets back," Neil pointed out. Once Kate returned, things would be a lot easier. But there was still another long, hard day to get through before that would happen.

Neil forced himself to open his eyes, then blinked in the sunlight which was streaming into his bedroom. He had been woken up by the noise of barking. He was so used to hearing the dogs that it didn't usually bother him, but now it sounded as if they were all barking at once. He checked the time. Quarter to nine! He should have been up over an hour ago to start the morning walks! Groaning, Neil rolled out of bed, and grabbed his jeans. As he hurried out onto the landing, pulling his sweatshirt over his head, he bumped into Emily, who was dashing downstairs too.

"We're late!" she gasped. "All the dogs are going crazy!"

"I know!" Neil's voice was muffled as he fought to get his sweatshirt on. "Are Uncle Jack and Sarah up?"

"Sarah is," Emily replied. "Uncle Jack's still asleep."

"We'd better take Sarah with us then," Neil decided. "She can walk Barney, the little Yorkie – I'll take Molly and Jake. You take Scooter the Labrador and Daisy – it might cheer her up a bit. We'll give the other dogs a run round the exercise field when we get back."

Neil hurried into the living room where Sarah was stretched out on the carpet, watching a cartoon. "Come on, Squirt! We need you to help with walking the dogs!"

Sarah jumped up eagerly. "Can I walk Molly?"

"We'll see," Neil said vaguely. He had no intention of letting anyone except himself handle Molly – she was such a handful.

"Have you seen all those people outside?" Sarah asked as she followed him out, but Neil wasn't listening. He went into the kitchen to collect Jake, who was curled up under the table next to his father. Both dogs jumped to their feet when Neil came in, and rushed up to fuss over him as if they hadn't seen him for days. Neil clipped Jake's lead to his collar, and shook his head gently at Sam, who was staring up at him hopefully.

"Not today, boy," he said, stroking the collie's silky ears. "We're going for a *long* walk. I'll take you into the field when I get back, OK?"

"Emily, did *you* see all those people outside?" Sarah asked impatiently, as Emily arrived at the back door with a black Labrador called Scooter, Daisy and Barney. But Emily wasn't listening either.

"Molly's up and running round her pen already!" Emily grinned at Neil. "I think you're going to have to walk to Padsham and back to tire that one out!"

"Or maybe I should just give her one of Uncle Jack's painkillers!" Neil said, as he headed towards Kennel Block One. "By the way, Em, you'd better leave a note for him to say where we've gone."

Molly was amusing herself by dragging all the cushions out of her basket, but she stopped as soon as she saw Neil, and started whining and pawing at the pen door.

"Good girl!" Neil clipped the lead firmly to her collar. "Let's go for a walk, shall we?"

Molly barked gleefully, and dragged Neil along, almost pulling his arm from its socket. For a small dog, she was strong, and she rushed Neil across the courtyard, to where Emily and Sarah were waiting with the other dogs. Molly sniffed round them all in a friendly way, but she nearly went mad with joy when she saw Jake.

"They love each other!" Sarah said, delighted.

"Maybe we should suggest to Kerry that she gets another dog to keep Molly company," Neil said, as they all went round to the front of the house.

"You can't tell *Kerry Kirby* of All Spice what to do!" Emily gasped, scandalized.

"Why not?" Neil shrugged, "If it means Molly will be happier, she should be pleased."

A bark behind him make him look round. Sam was trotting towards them, looking very pleased with himself. Neil groaned.

"Oh no, how did *he* get out? Go home, Sam! Home!"

"Neil!" Emily suddenly nudged him hard in the ribs. "Look!"

Neil turned round, and his eyes widened in amazement. There was a crowd of about fifteen people standing on the drive in front of the house. Most of them were teenagers, and they were wearing All Spice T-shirts and badges, and carrying All Spice scarves.

"See?" Sarah piped up triumphantly. "I *told* you there were people standing outside!"

"What're they doing?" Emily whispered to Neil, but before he had a chance to say anything, one of the girls in the crowd saw them.

"That's Kerry's dog!" she shouted, and Neil's heart began to race with fear as everyone dashed towards them. Before they could move, he, Emily and Sarah were surrounded by excited people, all fighting to try and stroke Molly.

"Get out of the way – please!" Neil yelled, feeling really scared as the crowd of fans pressed in on them. He could hear Sam barking frantically, although he couldn't see the collie. "You're frightening the dogs!"

Jake was cowering against Neil's legs, terrified. Molly thought this was all great fun, and barked loudly, jumping around and getting tangled up in her lead. Meanwhile, Sam, knowing that Neil

was upset from the tone of his voice, was running desperately round the edge of the crowd, trying to get to his master. Neil could hear the collie's barking becoming hoarser, as if he was coughing. Emily looked pale and scared, and Neil couldn't even see Sarah and Barney. Desperately he looked around for help, and, miraculously, it came.

"What on earth is going on here!" thundered a loud voice. Everyone fell silent, even the excited All Spice fans, as Uncle Jack strode out of the house, put his good arm round Sarah, who was crying, and glared at them. "This is private property, and you're trespassing!"

"We just wanted to see Kerry's dog," muttered a couple of the fans sheepishly.

"And now you've seen her, I think you'd better go." Uncle Jack fixed the fans with a beady stare, as they trailed away down the drive, looking rather embarrassed.

"Thanks, Uncle Jack," Neil said gratefully, picking Jake up. The puppy still looked scared to death, although Molly was taking it in her stride, as usual. He glanced round, worried about Sam. "Is Sam OK?"

"Neil!" Emily's anguished shout made Neil spin round. What he saw made his heart turn over sickeningly in his chest.

"Sam!"

Sam was lying on the ground. His whole body was heaving as he panted and coughed, trying to get his breath.

5

"All right, Sam." Mike Turner spoke in a soothing voice as he gently put his stethoscope against the collie's heart. "Good boy."

"Is he—?" Neil swallowed hard, not able to finish the sentence, staring at his dog stretched out on the sofa. Uncle Jack, who was watching anxiously with Emily and Sarah, put a comforting arm round his shoulders.

Mike Turner made a thorough examination of Sam's abdomen, before straightening up to look at Neil.

"It's all right, Neil. Sam's going to make it this time. This was just a scare."

Neil felt his legs buckle with relief, and he sat down with a thump on a nearby chair.

"But it does go to show that he's got to be kept quiet, and avoid getting overexcited," Mike went on. "Getting frightened or excited raises Sam's heart rate, and then, because his heart's faulty, it can't cope."

"I know," Neil muttered, feeling guilty, although it wasn't his fault. The minutes which had ticked away while they waited for Mike Turner to arrive had been the worst of his whole life.

"I think I ought to keep Sam at the surgery for a few days," Mike went on. "Just to keep an eye on him. I'm pretty certain he'll be OK, but I'd like to be sure."

Neil nodded, reaching out to stroke Sam's head. The collie pushed his muzzle into Neil's hand, acting a little more like his old self.

"I'll take him with me now," Mike said, as he packed his stethoscope away. "Get his lead, will you, Neil? He should be all right to walk to the car."

Mike gently urged Sam to his feet, and led him very slowly down the hall, while Neil and the others followed. Just as Mike opened the front door, Hasheem and Chris raced up the drive, looking very excited. Both of them were carrying several newspapers, which they waved at Neil and the others.

"Hey, Neil! You and Molly are all over the papers!" Chris yelled.

"Sorry we're late – we both overslept!" Hasheem added. Then he stopped as he saw Neil's face.

"Sam collapsed," Neil explained quietly. "But Mike thinks he's going to be OK this time."

"What happened?" Hasheem asked anxiously, as Mike made Sam comfortable in the back of his car.

Neil told them about the All Spice fans, and the way they'd tried to get to Molly.

"What a bunch of idiots!" Chris said angrily.

Neil leaned into Mike's car, and rubbed his head against Sam's.

"'Bye, Sam," he whispered.

"I'll keep you posted, Neil," Mike Turner said, as he started the engine. "And drop in to see Sam at the surgery whenever you like."

Neil nodded. He stood and watched as Mike's car pulled onto the main road, and set off in the direction of Compton.

"Hey, listen to the dogs back there!" Hasheem said, as the sound of barking intensified. "What's going on?"

"We haven't fed or walked them yet!" Emily explained, pulling a face, "And it's after ten o'clock!"

"Well, we'd better get on with it then, hadn't we?" Chris said briskly.

Neil was the last to go back into the house. He felt tired and drained, as if he had all the problems of the world on his shoulders – well, all the problems of King Street Kennels, anyway. Now he had Sam to worry about too. And it was still five days before his parents would be home. They hadn't phoned again either, which meant that they still hadn't come to a decision about the fate of the kennels.

Neil sighed. Why had he ever thought they could run the kennels on their own? So far he felt as if he'd made a complete mess of things. He didn't even care that his picture was in the papers. If he hadn't let Kerry Kirby's dog come to stay at King Street, then none of this would have happened. The press wouldn't have turned up, neither would the fans, and Sam would still be all right. He'd been right when he'd said that they'd taken on a whole lot of trouble by boarding Molly at King Street Kennels.

Just as Neil thought he couldn't get any more depressed, things started to improve. For one thing, Uncle Jack decided that he would try to manage without his painkillers from now on, and he helped out with the walking and feeding that morning.

"My arm's still a bit painful, but I think I can put up with it," he said cheerfully, spooning dog food into dishes with his good arm. "Anyway, I don't think I was much use when I was popping those pills!" He glanced at Neil, who was opening a bag of dog biscuits. "You should have told me, Neil."

"Oh, we managed all right," Neil assured him, but Uncle Jack grimaced.

"Your mum and dad would have forty fits if they knew you kids had been doing everything around here for the last few days!"

"Well, I won't tell them if you won't!" Neil

managed a smile. He was feeling much better how that Uncle Jack was getting back to his old self. Grown-ups could be a pain at times, but they did have their uses! And even a one-handed Uncle Jack was a help while they were so busy.

Neil cheered up even more when Mike rang just after lunch to say that Sam was improving.

"His heart rate's back to normal, and he's just had a small meal," Mike told him. "He's doing fine."

"Thanks, Mike," Neil said gratefully. "I'll come over and see him later this afternoon."

Now he was assured of Sam's recovery, Neil could relax a little. But he knew very well that a time would definitely come when Sam would fall ill, and he *wouldn't* get better. That was the hardest thing of all to bear.

To take his mind off Sam, Neil decided to give Jake another training session that afternoon, and let Molly join in too. Whatever had happened, he was glad, really, that Molly had come to King Street. He wouldn't have missed getting to know her for anything – she was one of the most loveable doggy personalities he'd ever come across.

"So you reckon you can train her?" Chris asked doubtfully, as Neil led Molly into Red's Barn. Molly was doing her favourite trick of hanging on to the lead with her teeth, and trying to wrench it out of Neil's hand, and even Neil had to admit she didn't look particularly trainable. Chris was holding Jake in his arms, and as soon as Molly saw the puppy, she dragged Neil across the barn towards him.

"Hasheem had to go," Chris said. "But he promised to be back tonight."

"Brilliant," Neil said gratefully. He could hardly believe how all their friends had rallied round to give them a hand. He didn't know how he would ever repay them, giving up their holidays like this.

"Here, hold Molly for me, will you?" Neil made sure he had Jake's attention, then he raised his hand, and the puppy immediately plumped down on his bottom, then looked expectantly at Neil. "Good boy, Jake!"

"He's very obedient. He obviously takes after his dad!" Chris said admiringly.

"Well, he's had the best training available

since he was tiny," Neil laughed. "But he *is* a fast learner."

Molly, for once, was sitting perfectly still, ears pricked and eyes alert, watching what was going on.

"Now it's your turn, Molly." Neil positioned the dog in front of him, and took a dog treat from his pocket. Molly's attention was immediately riveted on Neil's hand. As Neil raised it, Molly sat down on her haunches, her bottom going down as her head moved upwards.

"Good girl!" Neil said, as Molly wolfed down the treat. He took another one out of his pocket, and this time Molly sat down as soon as he raised his hand. Neil blinked in amazement.

"Wow!" Chris said, impressed. "She's got it already!"

Neil tried again, several times, in case it had just been a fluke. But it wasn't. Molly was proving to be an exceptionally intelligent dog.

"She might have had some basic training before she went into the rescue centre, I suppose," Neil said, thrilled at the way Molly had responded to him. "I reckon I might be able to teach her quite a lot before Kerry Kirby comes back for her next week!"

So the day had ended a lot better than it had started, Neil thought drowsily, as he snuggled down under his duvet. Sam had been looking

more lively when Neil had visited him, and Mike had said that he could come home in a day or two. Uncle Jack was back to normal now he wasn't taking so many of those painkillers, and Molly, contrary to all expectations, was proving a delight to train. Also Kate would be in bright and early tomorrow morning. Neil smiled to himself as his eyes began to close. Maybe he hadn't made such a bad job of running the kennels after all . . .

"Neil! Neil, wake up!"

Squirt's voice rang in Neil's ears as he lay fast asleep in his warm bed. He struggled to open his eyes, and dragged himself upright. Sarah was standing next to his bed, her eyes wide with fear.

"What – what's up, Squirt?" Neil mumbled, rubbing his eyes. It didn't feel as if he'd been asleep for very long, but the luminous dial on his alarm clock read 2:20am. "Can't you sleep?"

"There are two people in the back garden!" Sarah whispered fearfully. "And they're trying to get into the kennels!"

6

Neil stared at Sarah in disbelief. "Are you *sure*?"

Sarah nodded vigorously.

"Fudge was running round in his wheel, and he woke me up," she explained. "I got up to go to the bathroom, and I saw them!"

Neil climbed out of bed, and went over to the window. There was a security light in the corner of the courtyard, but he couldn't see anyone. Then he stiffened. Two shadows were moving around outside Kennel Block One.

He turned urgently to Sarah. "Why didn't you get Uncle Jack?"

Sarah pouted. "I tried to, but he wouldn't wake up!"

Neil's heart sank. He guessed his uncle must have taken one of his pills before going to sleep. Despite Uncle Jack's brave attempts to do without the painkillers, he had looked exhausted and pale by the end of the day.

"Sarah, go and wake him up," he said, groping for his trainers. "Pour a glass of cold water over him if you have to, but do it somehow!"

Sarah nodded, and hurried out.

"What's going on?" Emily stumbled into Neil's room, rubbing her eyes.

"Intruders," Neil said briefly, pulling a sweater on over his pyjamas.

"What, you mean burglars?" Emily gasped.

"They're trying to get into Kennel Block One." Neil drew Emily to the window, and pointed across the courtyard. The shadowy figures could just be seen, hovering around the door of the kennel block.

"But what *for*?" Emily asked, puzzled.

"I don't know," Neil began. Then he stopped, the colour draining from his face. "Maybe they're after Molly! I think we forgot to switch the alarm system on."

"Molly!" Emily repeated, horrified. "You don't think they're trying to kidnap her?"

"They might be," Neil said grimly, as he

brushed past his sister and hurried downstairs. "Kerry's rich, isn't she? She could afford to pay a big ransom. You'd better call the police, Em. I'm going to try and stop them."

"Neil, you can't!" Emily dashed after him. "Let's get Uncle Jack—"

"Sarah's trying to wake him now." Neil put his jacket on, and slipped a torch into the pocket. "I think he must've had one of his painkillers, because he's fast asleep."

"Well, I'm coming with you then!" Emily said in a determined voice, grabbing her coat.

"Somebody's got to ring the police—" Neil began, but Emily was already opening the front door.

"If we wait any longer, it might be too late!"

Neil gave up arguing, and followed his sister out into the cool night air. Emily was right – they couldn't wait for the police in case the intruders got away with Molly, assuming that Kerry Kirby's dog *was* their target.

"What shall we do?" Emily asked Neil in a low voice.

"Try and frighten them off," Neil answered,

hoping he wasn't going to be confronted by two large, burly dognappers. He switched his torch on, and played the beam across the courtyard to Kennel Block One. "Who's there?" he shouted bravely.

The two figures outside the kennel block froze in the sudden blaze of light. Neil and Emily's mouths fell open in amazement as they saw two teenage girls, wearing All Spice T-shirts and cameras round their necks, staring back at them sheepishly.

"We just wanted to get some photos of ourselves with Kerry's dog," one of the girls muttered, as Uncle Jack glared at them. "We didn't mean any harm—"

"Didn't mean any harm?" Neil exploded. "You almost frightened us all to death!"

Luckily Sarah had managed to shake their uncle awake, and he had hurried out into the courtyard just as Neil and Emily were confronting the two girls. He had brought them into the kitchen to find out exactly what had been going on.

"All right, Neil, I'll handle this," Jack said,

staring grimly at the two girls. "You've behaved very irresponsibly. You know that, don't you?"

Both the girls looked highly embarrassed, and nodded.

"And I suppose your parents don't know where you are either?" Uncle Jack raised his eyebrows at them.

"They think we're staying at each other's houses," the girls mumbled together.

"Well, I think you'd better give me your names and phone numbers," Uncle Jack said sternly. One of the girls was called Lucy Jackson, the other was Natalie Webb, and they both lived in Compton.

"How did you get in?" Emily asked.

"We cycled over from Compton," Natalie explained sheepishly. "Then we climbed over the gate in the field at the back."

"You're lucky we didn't call the police!" Neil pointed out. Although the girls were just harmless All Spice fans, he was still upset. They'd given everyone a real scare. And it had started him thinking about whether Molly was really safe at King Street or not.

The two girls turned pale, and Neil couldn't help feeling a bit sorry for them. He glanced at Emily, who looked as if she felt the same. "Uncle Jack, can I talk to you for a minute?" Neil said, as his uncle headed off towards the phone.

Uncle Jack stopped. "What is it, Neil?"

"I was thinking, maybe we could let those girls meet Molly," Neil said in a low voice. "Just for a few minutes."

Uncle Jack looked surprised. "I'm not sure that's a good idea, Neil. After all, they've been very silly, and caused a lot of trouble."

"I know," Neil admitted. "But their parents are going to be really annoyed, so I can't help feeling sorry for them."

Uncle Jack smiled. "I know what you mean – I wouldn't like to be in their shoes when their parents get here either! All right. Go and get Molly then."

Neil went over to Natalie and Lucy. "My Uncle Jack is phoning your parents," he said, and the girls' faces fell even further. "While you're waiting for them to get here, would you like to meet Molly?"

Lucy and Natalie looked as if they couldn't believe their ears.

"You mean it?" Lucy said breathlessly. "We can *see* Molly?"

Neil nodded. "Just for a minute or two."

"Thank you!" Natalie stammered, looking as if someone had just told her she'd won a million pounds.

"Good idea, Neil!" said Emily approvingly, giving him the thumbs up.

Neil grabbed the keys to Kennel Block One, and went outside. All the dogs were asleep in their baskets as he hurried down the passageway, but they stirred as they sensed his presence, and some of them started barking. Molly was already standing by the door of her pen, poking her muzzle through the wire mesh. She was delighted to see Neil so early in the morning, and leapt up at him, barking.

"Come on, Molly," Neil said, clipping the lead to her collar. "Time to go and meet some of your fans!"

As Neil led Molly into the kitchen, the two girls looked as excited as if Kerry Kirby herself had just walked in. They stared at Molly, their faces full of awe.

"Can we stroke her?" Natalie asked eagerly.

"Of course," Neil replied. Molly was beside herself with joy at seeing Jake again, as well as so many people crowded into the kitchen, and she was rushing from one person to the other, and pawing at their legs. She sniffed at Natalie and Lucy with interest, then launched herself at them, barking a welcome.

"Oh, she's gorgeous!" said Lucy, kneeling down so that she could give Molly a hug.

"I think that's enough," Jack said, as they heard a couple of cars pulling onto the drive. "It sounds like your parents are here to collect you!"

Lucy's parents and Natalie's parents came in together, full of apologies for their behaviour, and making threats of grounding them for life. Neil was glad that he'd let the two girls see Molly – they were obviously going to be in big trouble for sneaking out without their parents' knowledge!

"Well, I think that's enough excitement for one night!" Uncle Jack groaned, as he closed the door behind them. "And tomorrow I'm going to see Doc Harvey, to ask him to prescribe me some weaker painkillers!" He glanced at Neil and Emily. "I'd never have forgiven myself if anything had happened to you two tonight. It was my own fault for not checking the alarms. You should have called the police, not gone out there on your own."

"We thought someone might be trying to kidnap Molly," Neil explained.

Uncle Jack turned pale. "Good heavens! You mean to get ransom money out of Kerry Kirby? I never thought of that!" He frowned. "I'm beginning to wish we hadn't taken Molly in – she's been nothing but trouble so far!"

"It's not Molly's fault," Neil put in quickly.

"But I think we should be extra careful from now on."

Uncle Jack nodded. "Well, I'll take Molly back to her pen now, and I'll double-check that everything's locked up safely."

Neil frowned. He still wasn't happy. What had happened tonight had brought home to him the fact that Molly might need extra protection. "Uncle Jack," he said slowly. "I think we should move Molly into the house with us!"

Uncle Jack raised his eyebrows. "I thought your parents had a strict rule about that?"

"This is a special case, though," Neil argued. "We have to be sure that Molly is safe."

"It would be awful if anything happened to her," Emily chimed in. "And it would be really bad publicity for the kennels too."

"Yes, maybe you're right," Uncle Jack said slowly. "Do you think she'll settle in here though?"

"She'll be fine, as long as she's with Jake." Neil let Molly off the lead, and she immediately dived under the table where Jake, who was tired out after all the excitement, had curled up for a snooze. Molly nudged the puppy gently, and Jake opened a sleepy eye, then snuggled up against the older dog. "See?" Neil knelt down, and patted both dogs on the head. He was sure that this was the best solution for everyone, especially for Molly. "Night, you two. See you in the morning."

7

"Molly!" Neil stared round the kitchen, aghast. "Molly, what have you *done*?"

It was the following morning, and, after the excitement of the previous night, Neil had slept in. Again. So had everyone else, except for Molly and Jake, who were very much awake. Molly rushed over to greet Neil, just as Jake emerged from under the remains of the tablecloth, which had been dragged off the table and ripped to shreds. The rug had been chewed, and somehow the two dogs had got hold of a roll of kitchen paper, and torn it to bits. The room looked as if it had been hit by a snowstorm.

Just at that moment Emily came in, yawning. She stopped dead when she saw the mess. "Oh, *Molly*!"

"I think we'd better get it cleaned up fast,

before Uncle Jack sees it!" Neil threw the ruined tablecloth in the bin. "Or he might change his mind about having Molly in the house!"

A tap on the back door made them both look round. Kate McGuire was standing there, smiling at them.

"Kate!" Neil hurried across to unlock the door, and Kate came in, looking relaxed and tanned, her long blonde hair tied back in a ponytail.

"What's the matter with all you sleepy-heads?" she asked teasingly. "Lucky I've got my own keys to get in – I started work an hour ago!"

"Did you have a good holiday?" Emily asked her.

"Fantastic, thanks." Kate glanced around the kitchen. "But it looks as if you've been having even more excitement here! Oh, hello – who's this?" Seeing someone new in the room, Molly had rushed over to investigate, and was jumping up at Kate to get her attention. "Don't tell me – I think I know! I've heard all about you and a certain pop star! But what's Molly doing in the house?"

Neil explained briefly about the two intruders, and Kate frowned.

"I don't suppose Bob and Carole were too pleased about that!"

Neil glanced at Emily. "Mum and Dad aren't here at the moment, Kate. A lot's been happening since you were last at King Street."

While the three of them cleared up the kitchen, Neil told Kate about Great-Aunt Victoria's legacy, their parents' holiday, Uncle Jack's injury and Sam. He didn't mention the fact that their parents were thinking of selling up – after all, Kate's job was on the line, and he didn't want to worry her. But Kate was too sharp not to see the implications.

"If Bob and Carole have gone away at one of the busiest times of the year, they must be thinking about making some major changes to their lifestyle." One look at Neil and Emily's faces told Kate she'd hit the nail on the head. "Are they seriously thinking about leaving the kennels?"

Neil nodded miserably. "It's an option. They haven't made up their minds yet though."

Kate looked upset. "Well, maybe I'm being selfish, but I love working here. I hope they decide to stay."

"So do we," Emily and Neil said together. Then, as they heard footsteps overhead, Neil added urgently, "Sarah doesn't know yet, so don't say anything to her."

"I won't," Kate promised. "And, Neil – I'm really glad Sam's going to be OK. This place wouldn't be the same without him."

Neil felt as if a huge burden of responsibility had lifted from his shoulders, now that Kate was back. She was efficient and capable with the dogs, and even though he and Emily still had to help out, they didn't have to run around quite as much as they'd done before. It was lucky Kate was back today, Neil thought. Hasheem's parents were taking him to see his grandmother, so he wouldn't be able to come to the kennels at all, and Chris had phoned to say he'd be along later that morning, as he had a dental appointment to go to first. With Kate around though, he wouldn't need to rely on his friends so much.

"You look tired, Neil." Kate eyed him critically as they went into Kennel Block One. "Why don't you take a break? I can manage."

Neil hesitated. He *did* feel exhausted. The events of the last few days had knocked him for six.

"I don't want to leave you on your own—" he began, but Kate grinned at him.

"Go on, I've already sent Emily packing! If you two don't have a rest, you'll be tired out by the time you get back to school! Your uncle and I can manage."

Neil felt a sudden urge to get out into the countryside, and take Jake for a good, long walk to relax. "All right," he agreed. "I think I'll take Jake up to the ridgeway."

"Why don't you take Molly too?" Kate

suggested. "She looks like she could do with letting off some steam!"

Neil frowned. He had been reluctant to take Molly out of the kennels again, but Kate was right. The dog needed to release some of her pent-up energy – and they'd survived the press, the fans and the intruders so far. What else could possibly go wrong?

"All right," he said. "But, Kate, could you check on Daisy, the little poodle? She hasn't settled in very well, and she's been missing her owner."

"Will do," Kate agreed.

"Oh, and Robbie's had an eye infection. Mike left some drops for him, so could you—?"

"Neil, relax!" Kate told him with a grin. "I'll handle it all. Now will you *please* go?"

Twenty minutes later, as Neil headed up the path which led to the ridgeway, Jake and Molly bounding along at his side, he realized that he was enjoying himself for the first time in days. The sun was shining, and the air was crisp and fresh. Neil wondered what the weather was like in Scotland, where his parents were. He hoped it was good and that they were making the most of long walks to clear their heads and discuss the future properly. Neil pushed the thought aside. He didn't want to spoil the beautiful morning, and whatever happened, he'd just have to learn to deal with it.

He let Jake off his lead, and the puppy raced happily off, then came back to see if Molly was joining him. Molly stared pleadingly up at Neil with her big brown eyes, and barked.

Neil hesitated, but he couldn't really see any harm in letting Molly run free too. After all, she probably wouldn't go off anywhere while Jake was around, and she needed the exercise. He knelt down and unclipped the lead. "Off you go, Molly!"

Molly raced after Jake, quivering all over with joy, and the two dogs began to race each other along the ridgeway. Neil laughed, and walked slowly after them. He would have time to give Molly and Jake a longer training session today, now that Kate was back, and he was definitely going to suggest to Kerry Kirby that she get another dog to keep Molly company, whatever

Emily said. He was sure Kerry would agree, once she saw Jake and Molly together—

A loud bark interrupted Neil's thoughts. He glanced up and his heart sank as he saw a rabbit racing off along the ridgeway, with Molly in hot pursuit, ears back, her shaggy body trembling with eagerness. Jake, too, was running along behind her as fast as his short little legs could carry him.

Neil gave a groan, as he set off after them. "Molly, come back!" he shouted, knowing full well that she wouldn't.

True to form, Molly took no notice. All her attention was fixed on the fascinating, furry brown creature that was running along in front of her, and she wasn't going to stop until she caught up with it.

"Molly!" Neil called again, panting as he chased after them. "Molly, will you come here!" He shouldn't have let her off the lead, Neil told himself, feeling guilty, but at least it was fairly safe up here on the ridgeway. It wasn't as if they were near any busy roads – they were surrounded by fields and countryside, so neither of the dogs were in any real danger. As long as Neil kept them in sight, he would be able to catch up with them when the rabbit disappeared down a convenient hole. If only the rabbit would hurry up and do just that, Neil thought crossly, as he gasped for breath. He wasn't sure he could run at this pace for very much longer.

As if the rabbit was reading Neil's mind, it suddenly swerved sideways, and disappeared down one of the many narrow potholes that littered the surface of the ridgeway. The ground beneath the ridgeway contained a labyrinth of caves and tunnels, and was a favourite area with potholers, although most of the holes on the surface were too small for anyone to access.

"At last!" Neil thought triumphantly, as he saw Molly and Jake skid to a halt beside the hole, and start barking. "Molly!" he yelled with what little breath he had left. "Jake!"

Jake obediently started trotting back towards Neil, now that the rabbit had disappeared, but Molly was sniffing around the pothole, and barking with all her might. Then, to Neil's horror, he saw the dog stick her head down the hole, and start to wriggle her body through too, in an attempt to follow the rabbit.

"*Molly!*" Neil shouted, turning white with fear. "*Molly!* Stay there, girl! Don't move!" If Molly went underground, and got lost in the tunnels, she might never be seen again. Neil forced himself to run faster, although his lungs were almost bursting. He had to reach Molly before she went through the hole. *He had to.*

Molly was halfway into the hole, as Neil pounded desperately up the ridgeway towards her. She wasn't interested in Neil, but was staring down into the hole, as if she was trying to spot the rabbit.

"Good girl, Molly!" Neil panted, as he rushed up to her. "Now just stay there."

But then, just as Neil reached her, Molly lunged forward, and disappeared. Frantically Neil launched himself forward like a rugby player, trying to catch hold of her shaggy tail, but it whisked tantalizingly out of his reach just before he could grab it. He was too late.

Molly had vanished.

8

"Molly!" Neil yelled at the top of his voice, bending over the pothole. He couldn't see a thing because it was pitch-black down there. He couldn't even see how deep the hole was, and he hoped that Molly hadn't injured herself scrambling through it. "Molly, come back!"

Jake whined and pawed at the ground around the pothole, sensing that something was wrong. Neil clipped the puppy's lead on quickly, just in case he decided to follow Molly.

"Molly!" Neil shouted again. "Where are you?"

Then Neil heard a ghostly bark coming from underground. He leaned over as far as he dared into the pothole, his nerves stretched to breaking point. Then the barking died away, and there was silence.

"Molly!"

This time there was no answer. Neil felt dizzy with fear as he imagined Molly heading deeper and deeper into the labyrinthine cave system, and never being heard of again. There was only one thing he could do. He'd have to follow her. But what about Jake? He didn't want to take the puppy into what might be a dangerous situation.

Neil hesitated, then made a quick decision. He reached out, and looped the end of Jake's lead over a jagged piece of rock. He wasn't sure if it would keep Jake there for long, but it was the best he could do, and he and Molly might be back soon anyway.

Suddenly, with a surge of hope, Neil remembered that he still had his torch in his jacket pocket from when he'd gone to check on the intruders the night before. Quickly he pulled it out, and switched it on, playing the beam down into the pothole. To his relief, he saw that it wasn't very far down to the floor of the cave.

Neil patted Jake reassuringly on the head, and then slid into the pothole feet first. It was a tight squeeze, but he shrugged off his jacket and managed it. He scrabbled against the rock face below him, feeling for a foothold.

"I'll be back as soon as I can, Jake," he promised, and climbed down under the ridgeway.

Jake barked in confusion.

His master had gone.

Neil made his way cautiously down the side of the hole. The torch wasn't much help to him on his way down, because he needed both hands to cling on to the rock face, so he slipped it into his trouser pocket. But as soon as his feet touched the ground, he switched the torch on again, with a sigh of relief. The whole atmosphere felt damp, and he could feel a wetness lapping around his ankles. It would have been very scary indeed if he hadn't had the torch with him.

Neil saw straight away that there was only one way Molly could have gone, and that was down a small tunnel on his right. Too worried about the dog to let his fears get the better of him, he began to crawl after her on his hands and knees, trying to aim the torch ahead of him at the same time. The tunnel sloped downwards, making Neil feel as if he was crawling right into the centre of the earth, and the roof was so low in places that he had to lie on his stomach and wriggle his way through.

Neil came out into a much bigger cave, one in which he could just about stand upright. Quickly he shone the torch around, noting that there were three tunnels of different sizes leading off it. His heart sank. How would he know which way Molly had gone?

"Molly!" he yelled, his voice echoing round the cave. "Molly!"

Then Neil heard it – a bark, which seemed to be coming from the tunnel closest to him. Hoping he hadn't been deceived by an echo, Neil headed towards it, praying that he would find Molly soon, before she went any deeper underground.

"What's the matter with you?" Emily said to Chris, as he stumbled into the kennels office, clutching the side of his face. "You look as if you've had to have ten teeth out!"

"I *feel* like I've had ten teeth out!" Chris

complained. "I've had two fillings, and my mouth's still half-frozen! Where's Neil?"

Before Emily could reply, the phone rang. Emily answered it, and her eyes lit up. "Dad! You haven't phoned for ages!"

"Sorry, sweetheart," said Bob. "We've had a lot to talk about. How's things? How're Neil and Sarah?"

"We're all fine," Emily said quickly. "Have you – have you decided anything yet?"

"We're getting there," Bob said, and Emily noted that her father did sound a lot more cheerful. "Going away like this was just what we needed."

"You *will* be home on Tuesday, won't you?" Emily demanded anxiously.

"Of course we will!" Bob assured her. "Now, is Jack around? I'd like to have a quick chat with him."

Just at that moment Uncle Jack turned up at the office door to see who was calling, and Emily handed the phone over.

"Hello, Bob!" Jack said cheerfully. "Yes, everything's fine."

"Where's Neil?" Chris asked Emily in a low voice.

"He's taken Jake and Molly up onto the ridgeway for a walk," Emily said. "Kate's back, so she told us both to go and relax! She said we'd been working too hard!"

"Neil won't be relaxing much if he's walking that daft dog!" Chris chuckled. Then he stopped laughing suddenly, and squinted up the drive. "Hey, Em, did you say Neil had taken Jake with him?"

"Yes, why?" Emily said, then her eyes widened.

Jake was scurrying up the drive towards the office, yapping anxiously, his lead trailing along behind him. Emily ran over to the door, and Jake made a beeline for her, leaping into her arms as if he was really glad to see a friendly face.

"What's he doing here?" Chris said with a frown.

"Yes, and where's Neil?" Emily added, looking worried.

"Maybe Jake just got away from him!" Chris smiled. "We'll probably see him come charging after him in a minute with Molly right behind him!"

Emily grinned. "You're probably right. Those two animals are quite a handful!" She and Chris waited in the office doorway for a moment or two, expecting to see Neil and Molly any second. But neither of them appeared.

"I don't like this." Emily stared anxiously at Chris. "Neil would never let Jake run away from him like this unless—"

"Unless something was wrong." Chris finished the sentence for her. "Why don't we go up to the ridgeway and see if we can find him?"

"Uncle Jack!" Emily said urgently, as he said his goodbyes to Bob, and put the phone down. "Jake's come back without Neil and Molly – we think something might be wrong!"

Uncle Jack pulled a face. "And there's me telling your dad that we're all fine! I'm sure Neil's all right, but maybe we'd better go and take a look. We'll leave Sarah with Kate."

"We'll take Jake with us too," Emily said, hugging the puppy to her chest. "He might be able to lead us to Neil and Molly."

*

Neil was wet, cold and tired. And he was beginning to panic. For the past hour, he had been through so many caves and so many tunnels, he had completely lost his way, and he still hadn't found Molly. All the walls looked the same. Every so often he thought he heard a bark, and he kept going in that direction, but by now he was wondering if he was imagining things. There was simply no sign of Molly anywhere.

Then, suddenly, he heard a louder bark. Neil crawled down the tunnel he was in, as fast as he could, and came out into a really tall and spacious cave. To his utter relief, Molly was sitting on a rocky ledge, wagging her tail and giving little barks of joy.

"Molly!" Neil rushed over, picked the dog up, and buried his face in her damp fur. She was as wet and dirty as he was, but he didn't care. He'd found her, and she was safe!

"Come on, girl," Neil murmured, shaking all over with relief. "Let's go back." He just hoped he would be able to remember his way. Some of the caves he'd passed through had had lots of tunnels leading in and out of them. He wasn't at all sure he could find the way back – but he had to try.

Molly, however, had other ideas. She wriggled out of Neil's arms, and headed over to another tunnel.

"No, Molly!" Neil said, alarmed. "That'll just take us deeper underground! *This* way!" And he pointed to the tunnel he'd just crawled out of.

Molly wouldn't move, and started barking. Neil grabbed her and took her back across the cave, but Molly refused to go down the tunnel that he wanted her to. Neil couldn't carry her,

because he had to get down on his hands and knees, so short of pushing the little dog down the opening ahead of him, he didn't know what he could do. As soon as he put Molly down, though, she headed straight back over to the other tunnel.

Neil hesitated. Molly seemed to know where she was going, and he wasn't sure he could find his way back anyway, so what did he have to lose?

"All right," he told Molly. "You win! I'll follow you."

Molly wagged her tail, then turned, and plunged down the tunnel. Neil went after her. The way ahead was narrow, barely big enough for Neil to squeeze through in some places. Although Molly was leading the way, she never went very far without stopping and turning round to check that Neil was still there.

"Here I am, Molly!" Neil assured her, as, weary and wet, he struggled along on his hands and knees. "Keep going, girl!"

Molly seemed to understand what Neil was saying, and carried on sniffing her way down the tunnel. Neil dragged himself after her, hoping desperately that he was doing the right thing.

He was putting his faith in Molly to lead them both to safety, and he hoped she wouldn't let him down.

Suddenly Neil noticed the beam of his torch beginning to flicker faintly, and his heart plummeted. He stopped, and gave the torch a shake, hoping that it had just got damp, but he could tell that the battery was running out fast. It certainly wouldn't last much longer. Neil swallowed hard at the thought of being plunged into darkness, far underground, unable to see where he was going.

More than ever now, Molly was his only hope.

9

"There's no sign of them!" Emily looked around the ridgeway anxiously. "Where *can* they be?"

"Maybe they never came up here," Chris suggested, but Emily shook her head.

"No, Neil told Kate he was going up onto the ridgeway." She looked at her uncle with wide, scared eyes. "You don't think – you don't think they've been *kidnapped,* do you, Uncle Jack?"

"I'm sure they haven't," Uncle Jack said reassuringly, but he couldn't help sounding worried.

"What's the matter with Jake?" Chris asked, as he noticed the puppy scrabbling wildly at the ground next to a narrow pothole. "Come on, Jake! You're supposed to be helping us find Neil and Molly!"

Emily's eyes lit up. "Maybe he is! Maybe this is the last place he saw them!"

"But where would they have gone?" Chris asked with a frown.

They all glanced round the ridgeway, but there was still no sign of the missing pair. Then Emily looked down at the pothole, and gasped.

"Look!" cried Emily. "It's Neil's jacket! Uncle Jack!" she said, her eyes wide. "Do you think Neil and Molly could be down *there*?" And she pointed at the pothole.

"What on earth would they be doing down there?" Uncle Jack asked, puzzled. "Neil wouldn't be so silly – he knows how dangerous it is!"

"Maybe he didn't have any choice," Emily suggested. "Not if Molly went down there first!"

"What, you mean that daft dog Molly went down this pothole, and Neil's gone after her!" Uncle Jack exclaimed, his face white with anxiety.

The discarded garment lay scrunched up in a bundle beside the hole. Uncle Jack knelt down and picked it up. His face clouded over. Handing the jacket to Emily, Jack examined the ground round the pothole more closely. "There's definitely been something going on here," he said grimly. "The grass is all flattened, and look at these footprints."

"They look like they were made by a pair of trainers," Chris said, also squatting down to take a look.

"Neil was wearing his trainers this morning!" Emily pointed out in a shaky voice.

"But even if Neil went after Molly, he wouldn't leave Jake to go home on his own, would he?" Chris asked.

"Maybe he thought he'd tied him up safely, but Jake managed to get away," Emily suggested.

"That must be it, then." Uncle Jack stood up, looking sombre. "We'd better get back and ring Sergeant Moorhead to organize a search. If they've got lost in those caves . . ." He didn't finish the sentence, but Emily and Chris knew what he had been going to say. If Neil and Molly were lost underground, they might never see them again.

The torch battery had now failed completely, and Neil was crawling through the pitch-black tunnel. He was very scared, but Molly seemed to know how he was feeling, and had slowed her pace, so that she was trotting along just in front of him all the time. If Neil reached out, he could touch her damp fur, which he found very reassuring.

"Good girl, Molly," he whispered, stretching his hand into the darkness to stroke her. "You're doing fine."

Molly licked Neil's hand, and carried on slowly down the tunnel. She still seemed full of beans, but Neil was so tired, he could hardly move. Every bone in his body was aching, and his hands and knees were sore from crawling along the rocky floor. He was sure that he had made the right decision to follow Molly, but still he couldn't help feeling extremely frightened, as well as worried about Jake. What if they couldn't find a way out?

"Where did all these reporters come from?" Emily gasped, as she looked around the ridgeway. There were ten photographers, and as many reporters, being kept at bay about fifty metres away by a couple of policemen. Jake Fielding of the *Compton News* was one of them.

"News travels fast," Sergeant Moorhead

replied. He was a middle-aged, grey-haired man, who knew Bob Parker well. "Especially when a pop star's dog is involved."

"Where's that rescue team?" Uncle Jack demanded, looking pale with anxiety. "It's been nearly an hour since we called them."

Everyone was desperate with worry and it showed on their faces. They stood around the hole, as if hoping Neil's head might miraculously pop back up out of it and surprise them all.

"Here they come now," Sergeant Moorhead said quickly. A team of five men was hurrying across the ridgeway towards them, dressed in warm, waterproof clothes, and carrying coils of rope over their shoulders.

Emily clenched her fists, her face pale. "They've got to find Neil and Molly," she muttered. "Anything might have happened to them."

"They will," Chris assured her, wishing he felt as confident as he sounded.

"We think they went down this way," Sergeant Moorhead said to Colin Grahame, the leader of the rescue team, pointing at the pothole. "We tried shouting but haven't heard any reply yet."

Colin, a big, burly man with red hair, frowned. "That's too small for us to get through. We'll have to go in another way, but as near to this as we can."

Emily bit her lip. Everything was taking so *long*.

The tunnel began to widen out into a small cave. Molly barked loudly, as Neil got to his feet, thankfully. As he did so, it suddenly struck him that he could *see* – the cave wasn't as dark as the tunnel they'd just crawled out of. It was then that Neil glanced upwards, and noticed a small patch of daylight overhead, in the roof of the cave. He stared at it, dazed, for a few minutes, blinking in the sunshine that slanted through the hole, hardly able to believe his eyes. Molly had led him to safety! Neil gasped with relief. He had been right to put his trust in her.

"Good girl, Molly!" he said, rumpling her damp, furry coat. "Good girl!"

They still had one problem, though.

Neil couldn't see how he and Molly were going to get up to the hole, and back onto the ridgeway.

Although it wasn't very high, the rock face looked smooth, with few footholds, and it was also very steep. Neil wasn't at all sure that he could climb up there, especially as he would have to carry Molly too. He and Molly would have to make a noise and maybe attract someone's attention, but that could take hours.

He began to think that he would never get out.

Molly was barking and scrabbling about frantically at the foot of the rock face. Neil's eyes were slowly adjusting to the daylight, and as he looked over at Molly, he saw a shape running up the wall. He squinted slightly, and could now see clearly a very narrow, potholers' wire ladder resting against the rock face, which looked like it led right up to the hole in the roof.

"You're a genius, Molly!" Neil knelt down, and gave the dog a hug. "I *knew* you'd get us out!"

Neil could climb up the ladder, but Molly couldn't, so he would have to carry her. The only alternative was to leave Molly behind and go for help, but Neil knew that if he did, Molly might wander off back into the cave system, and be lost forever. Quickly he made a decision.

"Come on, Molly." He picked the dog up and placed her inside his warm baggy jumper, tucking it into his trousers so that she wouldn't fall out. Her face peered up at him from the stretched V-neck, and he gently stroked her forehead. "We're going up that ladder, so, please, Molly, keep as still as you can."

The ladder felt incredibly flimsy as Neil climbed higher, his every movement slow and deliberate. It swayed gently as he placed his foot on each thin rung, sending his stomach churning every few seconds. He didn't dare look down. The ceiling of the cave was higher than he'd thought, and the small patch of daylight above him didn't seem to be getting much closer, even though he felt as if he'd been climbing for ages.

So far, Molly had been as good as gold. She was keeping perfectly still, but Neil could feel her heart beating quickly against his chest. He could sense that she was as nervous as he was, but if they could both kept their heads, they could make it to safety. Molly had done all the hard work so far – now it was his turn.

The patch of daylight came nearer and nearer, the strong light making Neil's eyes water after being underground for so long. Molly raised her head slightly, and sniffed the fresh air streaming through the hole. Then she started to bark happily.

"Yeah, we're nearly there!" Neil told her triumphantly. "Just a little bit further!"

"What's that noise?" Emily said suddenly.

"What noise?" Uncle Jack and Chris said together.

"I thought I heard a dog barking!" Emily gasped, standing as still as a statue, and listening hard. Everyone else who was standing round listened too.

"You must be imagining things," Uncle Jack said.

Colin Grahame raised his hand. "Ssh! I think I heard something too!"

Everyone fell silent then, even the reporters and the photographers. For a few seconds, no one could hear anything. Then suddenly there was the sound of a ghostly bark, echoing across the ridgeway. This time everyone heard it.

"It's Molly! I know it is!" Emily shouted. "It's coming from over there!"

She pointed a little way up the ridgeway.

And ran.

Neil and Molly had to squeeze through the hole together, but it was narrow, and manoeuvring with Molly tucked inside his jumper was difficult. For one horrible moment Neil thought he was going to get stuck halfway, but then, with one

final wriggle, he was through. As he tumbled out into the daylight, Neil almost fainted with shock.

There was an explosion of flashbulbs as what sounded like hundreds of cameras all went off at once. The ridgeway seemed to be full of people racing towards him and Molly, all yelling and screaming, and taking photo after photo. Bewildered, Neil pulled himself shakily to his feet, uncovered Molly, and looked around. Emily, Uncle Jack and Chris were running towards him, beaming all over their faces.

"Neil!" Emily shouted, running up to him and throwing her arms round him. "Thank goodness you and Molly are safe!"

10

"Look at this one – you and Molly are on the front page!" Emily passed the newspaper to Neil, who pulled a face.

"I look terrible!" he complained. "I couldn't see a thing with all those flashbulbs going off!"

Molly, who was sitting on Neil's knee, barked loudly, as if she was agreeing with him.

"You daft dog!" Neil said affectionately, rumpling her ears. "I think it's about time you were properly trained, so that you stop getting into trouble all the time!"

It was the day after Neil and Molly's great escape. Despite being cold, tired, and wet through, neither of them had suffered any lasting ill effects. Newspaper reporters from all over the country had been ringing throughout the morning, to ask Neil questions about his ordeal, and Mrs Wilson had popped over to cook a special celebratory lunch for everyone, including Kate and Hasheem. Chris and Mrs Wilson had also brought a stack of newspapers with them, and Neil could hardly believe how many pictures and news reports there were about himself and Molly.

"This is a good one!" Chris showed Neil a large picture of himself, looking dazed, with Molly in his arms.

"I wonder if Mum and Dad will see these?" Neil said anxiously, as Molly jumped off his knee to join Jake under the table. He didn't want his parents rushing back, now all the drama was over.

"I don't think they can be bothering with newspapers," Emily replied. "There were quite a few pictures of you and Molly when she arrived at the kennels, and Dad never mentioned seeing them when he phoned."

"What's the matter?" Hasheem asked, as Neil continued to look anxious.

"I'm a bit worried about what Kerry Kirby's going to say," Neil confessed. Uncle Jack had phoned the contact number left by Kerry, as soon as Neil and Molly were safe, but he hadn't been able to speak to Kerry herself, and had left a message for her. Neil hoped Kerry wasn't going to blame him for losing Molly.

"It wasn't your fault, Neil," said Kate. "I'm sure Kerry won't be angry." She stood up. "I think I'd better get back to work. Thanks for that fantastic lunch, Mrs Wilson!"

Just then Jack popped his head round the door, beaming all over his face.

"A visitor for you, Neil!" he said, and in came Mike Turner with Sam.

"Sam!"

Neil tried his best not to excite the collie too much, but he was bursting with happiness as he knelt down and put his arm around Sam's neck. Sam nuzzled against Neil's face, and licked his cheek, his tail wagging furiously. He was obviously delighted to be home.

"He's doing OK," Mike Turner said with a grin. "But remember what I told you. He mustn't tire himself out."

"I know." Neil gently stroked Sam's silky flanks, as Molly and Jake also bounced over to greet the collie. "Careful, you two! Sam's got to be treated gently!"

"And that means no underground walks!" Uncle Jack wagged a teasing finger at Neil, then rolled his eyes as there was a ring at the doorbell. "This place is like Compton Station this morning!"

"Maybe it's another reporter or photographer!" Chris grinned. "Neil's really famous now!"

"Not as famous as Molly!" Neil raised his eyebrows as Molly suddenly pricked up her ears, then shot out of the room and streaked down the hall after Uncle Jack. "What's up with *her*?"

He soon found out. A moment later, Uncle Jack ushered Kerry Kirby into the room, carrying Molly in her arms. Molly was going mad with joy, and tugging vigorously at her mistress's dreadlocks with her teeth.

"Oh – hello, Kerry!" Neil said uncertainly. He was nervous about what the pop star might say to him, but Kerry was smiling reassuringly at him.

"I know I'm not meant to be picking Molly up till Tuesday, but I had to come and see you both after what happened," she explained. "So I sneaked out of the hotel this morning, and got Jeff to drive me down here. Rachel must be having a fit by now!"

"I'm sorry about what happened," Neil began guiltily, but Kerry shook her head at him.

"It's OK, Neil. I admit I was a bit concerned when I got your uncle's message, but when I read all that stuff in the papers, I realized I should have told you not to let Molly off her lead." Kerry gave Neil a rather shamefaced grin. "She goes bananas if she spots another animal like a cat or a rabbit – she won't come back even for me!"

Neil felt better when he heard that.

"Maybe you could think about having her trained," Neil suggested politely. "Then she'd learn to come when you call her."

"Do you think so?" Kerry looked doubtful. "Molly's so high-spirited, I'm not sure it would work."

"But Molly's a clever dog," Neil said quickly. "She'd be dead easy to train. She learned to sit really quickly—" He stopped abruptly, hoping Kerry wouldn't mind that he'd already started training Molly.

"Can she?" Kerry looked interested, and put Molly down on the floor. "Why don't you show me?"

Hoping Molly wouldn't let him down, Neil attracted the dog's attention, and raised his hand. Molly immediately sat.

"That's fantastic!" Kerry said, impressed. "I didn't realize she was so fond of other dogs too," she added as Molly and Jake began to roll about under the kitchen table together.

"Yes, it might be a good idea to get another dog to keep her company," Neil suggested eagerly.

Kerry nodded thoughtfully, then glanced at

her watch. "I've got to go – Rachel will be tearing her hair out by now!" She bent down, and picked Molly up again. The dog snuggled down into her arms, and Kerry kissed the top of her shaggy head. "Anyway, Neil, what I really came to say was how grateful I am that you risked your life to get Molly back. Thank you so much."

"It was Molly who helped *me*, really," Neil muttered, feeling embarrassed. "I'd never have found my way out again if it wasn't for her."

"But I might never have seen Molly again if it wasn't for *you*." Kerry smiled at him. "There's one more thing before I go – you have a rescue centre here, don't you?"

Neil nodded.

"Well, I've been talking to the other girls in the band, and we'd like to donate something from our gig in Manchester next week to your rescue centre!" Kerry announced. "To say a big thank you!"

Everyone gasped.

"Oh, and there'll be tickets to the concert for all of you, of course!" Kerry added, and everyone gasped again.

"Brilliant!" Emily found her voice in front of Kerry Kirby for the first time. "And please can I have your autograph?"

"With pleasure!" Kerry handed Molly to Neil. Then she pulled a publicity picture out of her bag, signed it and handed it to Emily.

"Bye, Molly – see you Tuesday!" She kissed Molly again, and grinned round at everyone else. "And I'll see you at the concert!"

"Isn't she *brilliant*?" Emily said adoringly, as Kerry hurried out, escorted by Uncle Jack. "I can't wait to go to the concert!"

"Looks like the Puppy Patrol's going to have even more money now!" Hasheem said with a grin.

"Yeah." But a sudden shadow crossed Neil's face. It was fantastic of All Spice to donate money to the rescue centre, but who would be running it in the future? It might not be the Parkers, if his parents decided to leave.

"Neil?" Uncle Jack put his head round the door again. "You're very popular this afternoon – you've got some more visitors!"

He pulled the door open wider, and Bob

and Carole Parker hurried in, looking dazed but smiling, and carrying a bundle of newspapers.

"Mum! Dad!" Neil gasped in disbelief, as Sarah hurled herself into her mother's arms. "What're *you* doing here?"

"What do you expect when I pop down to the village shop this morning for a pint of milk, and see my son plastered all over the front page?" Bob tossed the newspapers he was carrying onto the table, as he swept Sarah into a bear-hug. Then he looked round at everyone. "Now would someone like to tell us *exactly* what's been going on?"

"A lot, by the look of it." Carole kissed Neil, and then glanced anxiously at Uncle Jack's plaster cast.

Everyone started talking at once, so it took a few minutes before Bob and Carole could piece together the whole story.

"So this is Molly." Bob squatted down, and stroked her. "Hello, girl!" Molly barked and stood on her hind legs, front paws on Bob's knees, wagging her tail.

"I don't know!" Carole was shaking her head

in disbelief. "We go away for a little while, and everything starts happening round here!"

"You didn't have to come back early," Neil said anxiously. "We were managing OK." Although he was glad to see his parents, they'd obviously only come back because of the stories in the newspaper. He could hardly bear to ask them if they'd reached a decision about the future, but he needed to know.

"Dad," he began, "Did you—?"

"We did." Bob smiled at him.

Neil's heart leapt. He could tell from the look on his father's face that it was good news, but he wanted to be sure before he started celebrating.

"Are we staying at King Street, Dad?" he asked in a shaky voice.

"We certainly are!" said Bob firmly.

"*Yes!*" Neil, Emily, Chris and Hasheem all shouted out together, as they slapped each other on the back, beaming all over their faces. Mike, Mrs Wilson, Uncle Jack and Kate all looked thrilled too. Only Sarah was puzzled.

"Are we going somewhere?" she asked.

"No, sweetheart, we're staying right here!" Bob said firmly.

"I'm so pleased!" Kate gave Carole a hug. "This place wouldn't be the same without you!"

"We'd almost made up our minds the other way," Carole said in a shaky voice. "And then . . . well, we saw the newspapers this morning. How *could* we give all this up? The Parkers belong at King Street!"

Neil hugged her too, almost too choked with emotion to speak. "Thanks, Mum!"

Carole smiled. "And now we've got even more money to worry about spending, thanks to All Spice! Wasn't that generous of them, Bob?"

Bob nodded. "Absolutely."

"What are we going to do with it all?" Neil asked eagerly. "Are we going to expand King Street?"

Bob glanced at Carole. "We've been discussing this on the drive home, although we didn't know about the All Spice money then, of course. Your mother and I have decided to go ahead and build a bigger rescue centre!"

"So we can help lots more dogs!" Neil exclaimed, delighted. "Excellent!"

"We might even register it as a charity," Carole explained. "Then we can be independent of the local council, because we won't need to rely on them to fund it."

"What will happen to the old rescue centre?" Emily asked.

"We were thinking about turning it into a walk-in dog clinic." Bob grinned at Mike Turner. "Of course, we'd need a resident consultant there a few afternoons a week!"

"Sounds good!" Mike said eagerly. "We'll have to discuss it in detail."

"We'll be taking on another assistant too," Carole added. "Poor old Kate's overworked as it is!"

"And we've got something very special lined up for you three," laughed Bob. "We think it's only right that we go and visit Great-Aunt Victoria's grave to say thank you. So your father and I have decided that we're all going on holiday to Australia later this year!"

"Brilliant!" gasped Emily and Sarah, and

everyone began talking at once, except Neil. Instead he knelt down and picked Molly up in his arms.

"Thanks, Molly!" he said happily, hugging the little dog close. "Thanks to you, we're staying at King Street! You might be the poshest pup we've ever had staying here, but you're one of the best!"

Look out for

Out now!